F

The First Bc

Retirement Can Be Murder

"Susan Santangelo uses great characters, humor, and sort of a 'Desperate Housewives' backdrop to create a hilarious mystery.... An entertaining and light-hearted read from a real pro. The Baby Boomer mysteries promise to be as germane as *Murder She Wrote.* It would make a great television series."
–Midwest Book Review (five-star review)

"Santangelo has come up with an intriguing premise, drawing on the much-publicized fact that the baby boomer generation will soon be facing retirement, and she develops it cleverly....Especially enjoyable features of this debut are the little humorous headings that begin each chapter. We'll look forward to more Boomer mysteries in the years to come....Pure fun—and don't be surprised if retired sleuths become the next big trend."
–www.Booklist.com

"Susan Santangelo captures the everyday lives of Baby Boomers in ***Retirement Can Be Murder***....Be prepared to feel at home."
–Dotsie Bregel, founder, National Association of Baby Boomer Women

"This is a fun chick lit investigative tale starring Carol Andrews super sleuth supported by an eccentric bunch of BBs (baby boomers), the cop and the daughter. Carol tells the tale in an amusing frantic way that adds to the enjoyment of a fine lighthearted whodunit that affirms that "every wife has a story" and Carol's first is entertaining."
–Harriet Klausner, national book critic

"The over-50 crowd will love this....I love this lighthearted mystery. Susan Santangelo combines humor and mystery to create a great read. I am so glad to see a female lead character over 50....This is a must read!"

–Readers' Favorite

"Not since picking up one of Janet Evanovich's Stephanie Plum books have I ever laughed or enjoyed a book so much as Susan Santangelo's ***Retirement Can Be Murder***."

–Suspense Magazine

"Santangelo ... captures well the anxiety of a wife who must face the reality of her life turning upside down. Good thing she has her friends to help."

–Blog Critics

"Finally a cozy mystery with a heroine who's middle-aged, married, and a mother....What really makes ***Retirement Can be Murder*** special is the author's uncanny knack for finding humor in everyday situations....One of the funniest cozies I've ever read, and yet all of the humor flows naturally from the characters, the plot, and the dialogue."

–Patricia Rockwell, author, Sounds of Murder

"Susan Santangelo may be the next Jessica Fletcher, the mystery writer and amateur detective portrayed by Angela Lansbury in the award-winning television series *Murder She Wrote*.... Susan's found a niche in the mystery-writing genre that just might find its way to the television screen, judging by the popularity of her first book, ***Retirement Can Be Murder***."

–Shoreline Times

For Mary Lou –
Enjoy!

Moving *Can Be* Murder

Every Wife Has A Story

A Carol and Jim Andrews Baby Boomer Mystery

Second in the Series

Susan Santangelo

Moving Can Be Murder

A Baby Boomer Mysteries Press Book

PUBLISHING HISTORY

Baby Boomer Mysteries trade paperback edition/First Printing, May 2011

PUBLISHED BY

Baby Boomer Mysteries Press

P.O. Box 1491, West Dennis, MA

www.babyboomermysteries.com

Cover and Book Design by Grouper Design, Yarmouthport, MA.

Cover Art: Elizabeth Moisan

ISBN 978-0-615-45806-9

I'd like to thank the following...

My Personal Beloveds: Joe, Dave, Mark, Sandy, Jacob and Rebecca. You are all blessings in my life.

Mazie Bloom, my godmother, aunt, and avid mystery reader, who gave me my first Nancy Drew book many years ago.

Jan Fable, classmate, friend, and therapist extraordinaire, for answering all my questions about domestic violence. Any errors are mine.

The mailing team at the West Dennis, MA post office – Dave, Doug, Sue, and Tom, for taking such tender loving care of all my books. And for teaching me the importance of Delivery Confirmation.

Molly McKeown, friend and fellow Lilly Pulitzer enthusiast, for sharing her show house expertise.

Sister Beth Fischer, who helped me bring Sister Rose to life.

Lynn Pray, Pineridge English Cockers, for adding our baby, Boomer, to the pack.

Elizabeth Moisan, author of *Master of the Sweet Trade*, and talented artist, for the wonderful book cover artwork. And Joyce and Ron Elliot, whose beautiful porch and white rockers continue to be the cover's inspiration.

The Paperback Café really exists, in the Connecticut shoreline town of Old Saybrook. I've taken the liberty of moving the Café to Fairport. Hope Russell and the staff don't mind.

Everybody at the Cape Cod Hospital Thrift Shop, past and present. All my pals at the Barnstable Branch of the Cape Cod Hospital Auxiliary. And especially everyone from the Breast Cancer Survival Center.

The First Readers Club, especially Marti Baker, Nina Marino, Sandy Pendergast, Rhea Marrison, and Marie Sherman.

Marlene Stern, whose courage and faith inspires me every day.

Gwenn Friss, *Cape Cod Times* Food Editor, who came up with the brilliant idea of a recipe contest for this book. And to everyone who entered – the recipes are all yummy and you're all winners.

Special thanks to the thousands of readers who were so positive about the first book in the Baby Boomer mystery series, ***Retirement Can Be Murder***, and who shared their stories with me at countless book events and via the Internet.

And to everyone who e-mailed me with terrific chapter headings. Keep them coming!

Moving Day for Carol (and Jim): A.K.A. Seller's Remorse

I had to say goodbye one more time. But how does anyone say goodbye to 34 years of memories?

"It's just a house, Carol. It's not a person." I could hear My Beloved Husband Jim's voice telling me that over and over again. "It's much too big for just the two of us. We should cash out and move now, before the real estate market gets worse."

He'd finally worn me down. I'd agreed to sell our beautiful antique home in the historic district of Fairport, Connecticut, and downsize to a nearby active adult community. Surprisingly, the house sold quickly. Part of that was no doubt due to Fairport's proximity to New York City – it's a great commuter town – and also to the super marketing skills of our listing broker, my very best friend, Nancy Green, from Dream Homes Realty ("We make your dreams a reality.").

I wish she hadn't done such a good job.

She'd convinced me to take a video of my house, intact, before I started to pack up all our things. OK, my things. Jim was much more willing than I was to let so many things go.

The moving truck had come today, and all of our cherished possessions had gone into storage. Our new home wouldn't be ready to move into for two more months. I wanted to postpone the closing, but Jim, not wanting to lose the buyer – God forbid – opted to move us and our two English cocker spaniels, Lucy and Ethel, into a furnished one-bedroom apartment temporarily. It was quite a come-down – trading a five-bedroom home for a space smaller than our old master bedroom suite.

When My Beloved had taken early retirement from his high-pressure job at Gibson Gillespie Public Relations in New York City, I'd dreaded the thought of him being home all the time. But within a month after his retirement, Jim had signed on as a columnist for our weekly newspaper, the Fairport News, *which kept him busy and out of my hair most of the time.*

That is, he was out of my hair in a five-bedroom house. How that would translate to our temporary cramped digs remained to be seen.

I'd tried to put on a brave face when we walked out the kitchen door and locked it for the last time. But I felt like something I truly loved had died.

I know, I know. I was being ridiculous.

Later that night, after hours of tossing and turning in a strange bed and listening to My Beloved's snoring, I decided to go back to my house one more time. I wanted to be in each room and let the memories wash over me. And once I had done that, I would let the house go. Once and for all.

That was my plan.

Until I stumbled over the dead body in my living room.

Chapter 1

If a husband speaks in the wilderness, and his wife is not there to hear him, is he still wrong?

"Turn the thermostat down to sixty-three," My Beloved barked at me. "That's plenty warm enough for this time of year."

Sixty-three was warm enough for this time of year? In New England? It was January, in case Jim hadn't noticed. There was snow on the ground and a cold wind was blowing through our drafty front door.

I decided not to argue with him, pushed the thermostat down, and went to add another sweatshirt to my layers of clothing. I hoped I'd still be able to bend my arms.

The furnace protested. It clanked, shuddered, sighed, and finally shut off. Maybe the furnace was cold, too.

"The way this old house bleeds money, it should be owned by a millionaire," said Jim, who'd followed me into our bedroom to continue his tirade. "You know that since I retired we need to be careful with our finances, Carol. I shouldn't have to keep reminding you."

Yeah, yeah. I'd heard it all before. Often. In fact, I heard the same complaints before My Beloved had retired. I knew we weren't millionaires, and we sure didn't live like we were.

"I think we should seriously consider putting the house on the market in the spring. It's getting to be too much to take care of."

I'd heard that one before, too. But I knew he wasn't serious. Moving meant Jim would have to organize and clean up all his clutter, now piled high in two unused bedrooms. This was a task he'd been successfully avoiding for years. And besides, except for his weekly newspaper column for the *Fairport News*, what else did he have to do with himself besides putter around the house doing necessary – and sometimes unnecessary – repairs?

He'd never move out of here.

We'd owned our antique house in Fairport, Connecticut – a hop, skip and quick commuter train ride from New York City – for the past 34 years. While Fairport didn't have the "cachet" of other Fairfield County, Connecticut towns like, say, Greenwich or New Canaan, it was still considered a desirable bedroom community for those who traveled daily to jobs in Manhattan. I absolutely loved the town, and had no intentions of selling my wonderful house.

Still, I had noticed Jim reading the real estate section of the paper more often these days. And once or twice, when I logged onto the computer after him, I realized the last web site he'd looked at was Realtor.com.

Hmm. This could be more serious than I thought.

Rummaging around in the back of my walk-in closet, I grabbed the first thing I could find, which turned out to be a hooded sweatshirt that proclaimed, "I decided to bake some anatomically correct men. Didn't give them any brains."

"Very funny, Carol," said Jim as I struggled to put my head through the opening.

"Did you wash this in hot water and deliberately shrink it?" I tried not to sound like I was accusing him of a crime, but since Jim recently assumed the family laundry duties, several articles of my clothing have registered complaints. "It wasn't this tight the last time I wore it."

"Maybe you've just gained a few pounds," said My Beloved.

Ouch. That really hurt. I swiveled around to face him and give him a smartass answer, but he'd already stomped out of the room and headed to the kitchen.

Being me, hardheaded to a fault, I couldn't let his remark pass so I stomped right after him. I found him with his head stuck in the refrigerator, rummaging around for a snack.

"It seems to me, dear, that you're the one who always has his head in the refrigerator." Among other places. "I'll have you know that I weighed myself this morning and I haven't gained an ounce. What do you think about that?"

"Ha," said Jim, unwilling to let it go. "Scales aren't always accurate. I just know what I see when I look at you. Let's just say there's a little more to love than there used to be."

Jeez. He was the one who, since his retirement, hadn't been able to fasten the top button on his favorite jeans.

"Play nice, kids," said our daughter Jenny, home from teaching at Fairport Community College a little earlier than expected. "I can't leave you two alone for a minute." She hugged us both, then said, "Now, kiss and make up. Or I'll have to send you to your room without supper."

"How the worm has turned," I said, laughing just a little to let our daughter know that her dad and I weren't really mad at each other.

I gave Jim a quick peck on the cheek, and he gave my arm a squeeze. Probably checking to see if there was any extra fat on it, but thanks to all the layers I was wearing, he couldn't tell.

"Here's the mail," said Jenny. "Since when do you subscribe to *Retirement Relocation* magazine, Dad?"

Huh? My Beloved had paid actual money for a magazine subscription on places to retire? When he could have read it at our library – for free?

This was beyond serious. This was a crisis-in-the-making.

Chapter 2

I can only please one person a day. Today is not your day. Tomorrow's not looking good either.

Dinner that night was strained. Not the food, the atmosphere. (We may be older, but we can still chew.) I wanted to confront My Beloved about his real estate musings – I had a right to know, after all. But I didn't want to have an argument in front of Jenny. And somehow, I knew Jim and I would have an argument.

I chewed thoughtfully, oblivious to the conversation Jim and Jenny were having about the courses she was involved in this semester. Jenny had returned home last summer after spending a few years in L.A. pursuing a graduate degree in English, and being pursued – and sometimes caught – by a variety of highly unsuitable young men, in my humble opinion. Especially the last one, Jeff, whose controlling attitude had finally driven Jenny back to the East Coast.

Not that I would have ever voiced that to my daughter, of course. I do have a big mouth, but I'm not that stupid. Both Jim and I were delighted that she now was pursuing a graduate degree and supporting herself (with a little help from good old Mom and Dad) with a part-time teaching assistant's job at the local college.

And I was over the moon about Jenny's new relationship. Her boyfriend du jour, whom I hoped would be The One, was Mark Anderson, who had been a classmate of Jenny's way back in grade school. He was also a local police detective, and he and Jenny had become reacquainted last summer when My Beloved had been (falsely, of course!)

suspected of committing a homicide. I was the one who had finally figured out who the real culprit was, but modestly, I let the police department take all the credit.

"Carol, are you ever going to swallow that food? We're not having a blackout meal tonight, are we?" Jim interrupted my daydreaming with a feeble attempt at humor.

Blackout meals used to be my specialty. Our part of the country was subject to power failure after power failure in the mid-80s. The family used to tease me that I'd take advantage of the situation by cleaning all the leftovers out of the refrigerator and slapping them together into some sort of makeshift meal before everything spoiled. Frequently, no one could identify what they were eating. Jenny and our son Mike called them blackout meals, and always eyed them with great suspicion.

I admit that I did come up with some pretty unusual combinations – leftover hamburger with a side order of pineapple Jello was one of them. I never claimed to be a gourmet cook; I just hate to waste food.

"No, Jim," I replied, washing down my food with a dainty sip of chardonnay, "I can assure you that a blackout meal is not the menu tonight. Nor is all-day meat, in case you were wondering."

If you don't understand that phrase, think of chewing a tough piece of meat forever and ever – all day, in fact. Hey, in those days Jim had me on a pretty strict grocery budget. No filet mignon for us.

Come to think of it, not much had changed on that score.

Sensing a tad of tension in the air once again, Jenny tried to lighten the mood by going down memory lane a little more. "Mom, one of my all-time favorite meals is your meatloaf. We haven't had that in ages. Maybe now that I'm a grown-up, you'll finally share the secret ingredient with me so mine will come out as good as yours does."

I laughed. "The secret ingredient is pretty simple, Jenny. It's adding a pinch of allspice to the meat mixture. You know," I went on, getting into the spirit of things a little more, "I remember the night we did the meatloaf poll."

"The what?" asked Jim, clearly confused by this reference.

"It was one of those nights that you were out of town on business," I said, thinking that those were the good old days. "Mike never liked meatloaf, and he used to grab his throat and roll all over the kitchen floor whenever I served it. Just getting him to eat one forkful was a major event.

"This one night – I guess you were about twelve, Jenny, so Mike must have been ten – I got sick and tired of his antics and I challenged him to call his friends to see how many of them liked meatloaf. We made a deal that he could call eight of his friends, and if five or more of them liked meatloaf, he had to clean his plate."

"Pretty clever, Carol. Did it work?"

"It sure did, Dad," Jenny chimed in. "Mike was really mad when he found out so many of his buddies liked meatloaf. In fact, I think a lot of them wanted to know the next time Mom was making it so they could come for dinner. I wonder if Mike remembers that. Maybe I'll e-mail him a little later and ask him."

"But he did take two hours to clean his plate," I reminded Jenny. "And there was a lot of eye-rolling and coughing, too. I always wondered how much he actually ate, and how much he snuck under the table to feed Tuppence. She was such a great dog."

By now I was in a much better mood. I guess living in the past makes me feel better.

I briefly wondered if I could use the same technique on My Beloved. What if I phoned some of our friends and took a poll about the merits of moving into an active adult community? Nah. This time, I was afraid to take the chance, unless I knew I could stack the deck and win.

"Need any help cleaning up?" Jim asked.

"Not tonight, Dad. I can do it. Mom and I need to catch up. I could tell she wasn't listening to me at supper. And you know how she hates to miss anything," said our daughter.

"Guilty as charged," I admitted. "On both counts. I promise I'll hang on your every word, sweetie. I'll scrape and rinse and you load the dishwasher."

Jim grabbed the evening paper and shambled off toward the family room, Lucy and Ethel at his heels.

This is nice, I thought to myself, as Jenny and I worked companionably for a few minutes.

But Jenny wasn't saying anything.

I was immediately apprehensive. Call it mother's intuition, but I had a feeling that what she wanted to talk to me about was more important than just catching me up on school stuff.

"Um, Mom," she finally said. "I wanted to tell you this first, before I told Dad. I found a condo to rent today. It's in the same complex as Mark's. I'm moving out of the house at the end of the month."

Chapter 3

If we can put a man on the moon,
why can't we teach him to pick up his socks?

Whoa. Talk about surprises. I wondered if there was going to be a full moon tonight. What was it with my family and moving all of a sudden?

Fortunately, I was facing the sink when Jenny made her big announcement, so I had a chance to compose myself before I responded. I was never any good at hiding my feelings when I was a child, and since I've gotten older, that's one of the few things about me that hasn't changed. I knew she was hoping for a positive response from me. I channeled the fantasy that what Jenny had really said was, "Mom, Mark and I are getting married," and reacted accordingly by putting a big grin on my face and hugging her. I hoped she didn't see that my eyes were brimming with tears.

"Oh, honey, that's wonderful," I lied. "I can't wait to see it. Is it a studio, or a one-bedroom? You know, when Dad and I were first married, we had a studio apartment in New York that was so small that Dad could literally stand in the middle of the room and reach out with his arms and touch both walls. No kidding."

Jenny eyed me critically. She knew me too well and didn't believe my enthusiasm for a single minute.

"I know this is a shock for you, Mom. And it will take you some time to get used to the idea. That's why I wanted to tell you first, before I told Dad."

"Don't be silly, honey. You know how much we like Mark. And I've tried very hard not to interfere in your relationship." Well, I had. If I hadn't succeeded, I'd done my best.

Honest.

"But having you home for a while has been great. I confess I got used to having you here. I don't mean to be selfish, but I am. I can't help it. At heart, I'm just a selfish only child."

Jenny laughed. "No need to be so hard on yourself, Mom." She gave me a kiss on the cheek. "I know you and Dad like Mark, despite the rocky way our relationship began. But this doesn't mean we're moving in together. I made that mistake with Jeff, and look how badly that turned out.

"Mark and I don't want to rush into anything. He's been burned, too, remember? Worse than I've been, actually. His fiancée practically left him standing at the altar. We decided that if we live close to each other, we'll have a chance to get to know each other better. You know what I'm talking about, right? More privacy? But we'll each have our own place to go back to if we want to." She flushed a little as she explained this to me.

Heck, I knew what she was talking about. My Beloved and I had been young once, too. I'd heard this arrangement referred to on one of the talk shows recently as "neighbors with benefits."

"When can I see it, honey?" I asked, recovering my composure and showing the hoped-for enthusiasm. "When did you say you're moving in? Do you have to paint first? How does that work with a condo?"

Oh, stupid me. "I just realized. Mark will be the one to help you with all this."

"Don't be silly, Mom. Of course I want you to see it, as soon as we can get in. It's rented now, but the tenant is moving out at the end of next week. And you know I'll depend on you for decorating advice. Men aren't so good at that kind of stuff. Even Mark.

"We'll make a date and go over as soon as we can. Now, I'm going to break the news to Dad."

I sure hoped Jim took it well. Jenny was the apple of his eye. Not that he didn't love Mike. But there's something about men and their daughters. Their little girls. It was hard for My Beloved to see Jenny grow up.

I had to hand it to my sensible daughter, though. This idea of living "together but separately" made a lot of sense. I briefly wondered if our marriage would perk up, recapture some of that old zing, if each of us had our own private space. Despite the fact that our house was large, now that Jim was retired and home more, we often seemed to be occupying the exact same place at the exact same time.

All of a sudden, I had a brilliant thought. Wouldn't it be fabulous if My Beloved and I each had our own master bedroom suite? Hmm. I wondered if those active adult communities Jim was researching had two master suites.

Maybe this was worth pursuing. We could each have our own space – mine extremely neat, My Beloved's extremely messy – and neither of us would intrude on the other's. Wow! Just think of the arguments we wouldn't be having – "Carol, I put my car keys on the dresser. Did you touch them? Damn it, I hate it when you move my things."

"Jim, can you puleeze pick up your dirty socks and throw them in the hamper? Is that too much to ask? A little common courtesy? If your poor dead mother could see what a slob you are, she'd be shocked." And be fed up, as I was, with picking up after him.

Wait a minute. What was the matter with me? Was I actually considering the "M" word too? Well, what could it hurt if I were to take a quick peek at Jim's retirement magazine?

Just to improve my knowledge.

In case anyone asked my opinion.

While Jenny was talking to Jim, I finished cleaning up in the kitchen. My Beloved had left his new magazine on the hall table, so I scooped it up and put it away in the cutlery drawer for a private read after he went to bed. I didn't want to answer any questions about my sudden interest in it. Especially in case what I saw really turned me off.

I heard low voices in the family room, then laughter. It sounded like all was going well for Jenny. At least Jim wasn't raising his voice and telling her he thought her plan made no sense. I knew he liked Mark, and if he had to give up his little girl, which was inevitable, at least it would be to someone we both knew and trusted.

Not that that mattered, of course. I was smart enough to know that parents can object to a grown child's decision, but keeping mum is the best tack to take most of the time. We were lucky our kids let us know what was going on in their lives most of the time. So many kids these days didn't.

Since the coast seemed to be clear, I carefully eased the cutlery drawer open and retrieved the magazine. I scanned the table of contents, and realized most of the stories and ads seemed to be about communities in the South and West. Florida, of course. Texas. Arizona. North Carolina. There was one article on eight terrific low-tax towns for retirees. I was sure that Jim would read every word of that one. Jeez, didn't anyone want to retire in the northeastern United States?

There was a classified section in the back of the magazine, and I was interested to see that there was a handful of active adult communities listed in Fairfield County. And there were many more on the Connecticut shoreline north of New Haven.

But I sure didn't want to live at the shore. Hordes of tourists in the summer and sidewalks rolled up in the winter. No thanks.

Some of the southern communities looked pretty enticing, with their swimming pools and golf courses and tennis courts. Not that we played golf or tennis. Nor did I intend to learn either sport at this stage of my life, and I doubted whether Jim did. He always made fun of men who spent every waking moment on the golf course. We did enjoy swimming, but the beach in Fairport during the summer months and the YMCA community pool in the winter answered all our needs in that department just fine.

I sighed deeply, lost in thought. Could Jim and I ever be happy in one of these places? I was not ready to discuss any of this with My Beloved. Not yet. Maybe, not ever.

"So which ones do you want to check out, Carol?"

I jumped guiltily. "Jim, you snuck up on me. I thought you were talking to Jenny."

"I was talking to Jenny, and even though I'm not thrilled with the arrangement she and Mark have worked out, at least they're not moving in together right away. And don't try and weasel out of this. I saw you flipping through the retirement magazine. You can't deny it."

I was flustered, yes indeedy. Way to go, Carol, I congratulated myself. The one conversation you did not want to have seems to have started, thanks entirely to your stupidity.

Jim chuckled. "I knew that if I got that magazine you wouldn't be able to resist looking at it. You just love seeing how other people live. You fell right into my little trap."

Huh? Had My Beloved set me up?

Jim reached out and took the magazine from my hand. "Come on, what do you say? We haven't looked at real estate together in over thirty-five years. We're not too old to have a new adventure or two.

"Besides, I made appointments for us to see two of them tomorrow. It'll be fun just to look. For the hell of it."

And he walked out of the kitchen whistling, leaving me standing there with my mouth hanging open.

Chapter 4

In my next life, I'm gonna get organized!

The next morning brought gray skies and drizzle, what the Irish would call "a soft day." The color of the sky perfectly matched my mood. I'd had a restless night in our big four-poster bed, my sleep punctuated with dreams of strangers knocking on our front door, moving vans, and my purse being stolen.

The purse dream is one I have quite often. I read a book on interpreting dreams a while back, and apparently, the purse is the symbol of a woman's identity. It makes sense when you think about it, because of all the stuff we cart around in them. Anyway, dreaming about losing one's purse is supposed to mean a woman is subconsciously worried about losing her identity. Food for thought.

My friends disagree with this interpretation, however. They claim that dreaming about losing your purse means you're afraid of losing your memory, not your identity. Which also makes some sense. How many times recently have I walked from one room into another, and then have completely forgotten why I walked in there in the first place?

And I've also noticed my communication skills have lessened since I've gotten older. Nouns, for instance, seem to gallop right out of my head much too often. Fortunately, my friends are mostly the same age, so we have the same memories and we can fill in each others' blank spots.

Jim's side of the bed was still warm, so he hadn't been up very long. I hoped he'd put the coffee on. One of the perks – forgive the pun – of having My Beloved retired was that he made the coffee every morning. I hated to admit it, but he did make better coffee than I did.

I stared at the window overlooking our front yard and contemplated my options, none of which were appealing. I'd been so mad at Jim last night that I deliberately stayed up and watched a late movie, so we didn't have to talk about his plan to kidnap me and whisk me away to see some active adult communities today. By the time I came upstairs to bed, he was sawing wood like a chainsaw.

I didn't want to start the day with a fight with My Beloved, but damn it, I wasn't going with him to check out those places. I wasn't old, and I wasn't moving. That was all there was to it.

I heard the furnace groan and then kick in. I knew exactly how it felt. I was groaning too, because it was time to face Jim and get an unpleasant conversation over with.

I was splashing cold water on my face and counting my new wrinkles in the bathroom mirror when I hear Jim come back into our bedroom.

"Hi honey," he said. "You should have stayed in bed a little longer. I brought you breakfast."

Huh? Was my hearing failing me too? My Beloved had brought me breakfast? I hadn't had that treat since Mother's Day 20 years ago. Boy, was he buttering me up. Well, he wasn't going to get on my good side that easily.

I tried to ignore that niggling little voice inside my head reminding me that Jim was using the same underhanded method on me that I'd used on him for years. It sure felt different to be on the receiving end.

I decided I could eat and make my position crystal clear at the same time. I knew how to play this game.

"This coffee's delicious," I said to Jim, taking a sip and trying hard not to spill it. "Thanks for bringing it up to me, and for the cereal, too. But don't think this is going to make me change my mind and go with you today. I'm really mad at you for making these appointments without talking to me first. I thought we made decisions like this as a couple."

I slammed the coffee cup down into the saucer – fortunately, it wasn't my good china – and gave him a withering look.

Jim threw up his hands in a motion of defeat. "Carol, you've got this all wrong. I did it as a surprise for you. I thought you'd love the idea. It'll be an adventure. We're not going to buy anything, for God's sake. We're just going to look at a few places. Get some ideas. Maybe we'll even go out to lunch."

Out to lunch? Jim's idea of going out to lunch was my packing sandwiches for the car and eating them while we were driving.

Then I remembered those beautiful places I'd seen in Jim's glossy magazine. Was it possible that communities like that existed around here? With – gasp – two master bedroom suites?

What the heck. I'd go along with him, just this one time. I'd just keep repeating my mantra – two master suites, two master suites, two master suites.

My Beloved reached over and squeezed my hand. "This is a good idea, Carol. You'll see. It'll be fun. We haven't gone house-hunting in such a long time, not since we were first married."

Yeah, I thought. Only this time, we can afford something that's not a fixer-upper. I immediately felt disloyal to my beautiful antique house, but when we first bought it, it was no beauty. I remembered the leaky roof and the peeling paint and the sagging floors. It was a money pit for a few years, that's for sure. But that was the only reason we could afford such a big house. It needed so much work, and we were young and naïve, and Jim was convinced he could do most of the work himself.

Naturally, he couldn't, and we ended up making a lot of local contractors rich over the years.

Jim was yakking away about how much fun we were bound to have on our new adventure, and I guess I must have dozed off. The next thing

I knew, he'd pulled the car into what looked like a rest stop overlooking the highway.

"This can't be right," I said, squinting a little at a sign which read, "Welcome To Eagles' Nest. Find Your Perfect Home With Us."

"Even eagles would have a tough time building a nest here, unless they were hard of hearing," I said. To prove my point, two eighteen-wheeler trucks whizzed by on the road below. "This place is right on the highway. I don't even want to bother going in."

"Come on, Carol, don't be silly. We're here now, and we have an appointment with the real estate agent. If nothing else, it'll give us a basis of comparison with anything else we may see today." He pulled me out of the car.

At least the homes, which were in various stages of construction, were separate from each other. Of course, all the lots were postage-stamp size compared to our current acreage.

One house was finished and appeared to be both the model home and sales office. We didn't even have time to knock before the door flew open and a Botoxed blonde beauty greeted us with a phony smile plastered on her face.

"You must be Jim and Carol Andrews. Welcome. Come right in. I'm Jessie Johnson. We spoke on the phone. I hope you didn't have any trouble finding us."

We went through the usual preliminary small talk, and then Jessie let us meander around the model house alone. I was sure, though, that she was hearing every word we whispered to each other. The entire place was probably bugged.

As we checked out each room, I grimaced at Jim to let him know I wasn't impressed with what I was seeing. The kitchen was tiny, there was only one full bath (although, to be fair, there were two half baths), and only one master bedroom, which was on the second floor. Jeez, if this was supposed to be something to see us into our twilight years, I sure didn't want to climb stairs every night to go to bed. Although we used a bedroom on the second floor in our current home, there was a room on the first floor with its own full bath that could easily be converted to a master suite if and when the need presented itself.

"Do you have any questions?" Jessie asked brightly, stretching her face so much with her smile that I feared it would crack.

What the heck. I piped up. Boy, was Jim surprised.

"I have a question, Jessie. Jim and I are just starting to look at active adult communities," so don't get your hopes up that you're going to make a sale, sweetie, "and I've seen so many in magazines that advertise tennis courts, swimming pools, that kind of thing. Are there plans for amenities like that here?"

Jessie laughed, a little self-consciously. "This is a cozy community that will have twenty-five houses when it's completed," she said. "The builders want to keep that sense of community, not cheapen it in any way with things like tennis courts and pools. But they have come up with a wonderful amenity which will be available for all the owners. Perhaps you noticed it on the way in to the complex?"

At our puzzled looks, she hastened to explain. "It's our darling little gazebo, which will serve as the centerpiece attraction for Eagles' Nest. We plan to decorate it to go along with each of the holidays – you know, hearts for Valentine's Day, wreaths for Christmas, bunnies for Easter. It's going to be great."

She waited for us to gush out our enthusiasm.

"What a lovely idea, Jessie," I replied, when Jim didn't say anything. I guess the gazebo had overwhelmed him with decorating possibilities.

I reached out to shake her hand. "Thank you so much for showing us Eagles' Nest. We'll take the packet with us. You've given us a lot to think about."

"Let's get out of here," I telegraphed to My Beloved.

For once, we were both on the same wave length, and bid as quick a farewell to Eagles' Nest and Jessie as we could without being rude.

She looked so sad to see us go that I was afraid she was going to kiss us goodbye.

"At least that place was easy to get to," My Beloved said in defense of his first active adult community choice.

I didn't respond. I just gave him a look.

"OK, Carol. You're right. It's much too close to the highway."

"Well, it did have that lovely gazebo," I said with just the right touch (I thought) of sarcasm. "Think of the fun we'll have decorating it with red, white and blue streamers for the Fourth of July. We could even organize a fireworks display."

"Very funny," Jim snapped, never one to take criticism well. "Let's just cross it off the list. The next one is supposed to be 'nestled in the bucolic countryside.' So it can't be close to a major interstate."

Forty minutes later, when we were bouncing along one unpaved road after another, I asked, "Where is this place, anyway? Is it in the middle of a pasture?"

Jim replied by tossing me the information he'd printed off of MapQuest. "We're supposed to be looking for a split rail fence on the left, and then a sign to lead us into the development. It's called Bertram's Hollow."

"More like Sleepy Hollow," I snorted, trying to make some sense out of the directions. We passed by some houses with abandoned cars rusting on the front lawn. "Nice decorating touch."

Then I screamed, "Stop, Jim. There it is."

Jim screeched to a halt, then backed up and turned into another rutted road. I thought I heard him mutter, "This one better be good," but I didn't comment. I do know when to keep my mouth shut. Sometimes.

Suffice it to say that Bertram's Hollow, which was a small community of semi-detached homes, didn't pass muster with us, either. Despite their cute slogan: "It's not about counting the years. It's about making the years count."

The model house/sales office was small and packed with way too much furniture. The kitchen was postage-stamp size. There was only one master bedroom suite, and it was on the second floor.

We were back in the car in less than ten minutes. We made a quick escape because the salesman, who looked younger than both of our kids, had another couple enthralled with his sales pitch and he'd left us to our own devices. "This one didn't even have a gazebo, Jim," I pointed out as we made our way back to a paved road and civilization.

Two master suites was beginning to look like a fantasy. An unattainable one.

Chapter 5

No outfit is complete without dog hair.

I was tired, I was cranky, and I was hungry. Not necessarily in that order. And also, a little bit smug. I'd done what My Beloved wanted. I'd looked at two active adult communities. And we had both – both! – agreed that they weren't for us.

As far as I was concerned, the discussion was over. I wanted to go home, let my dogs out for a run, have a late lunch in my beautiful kitchen with its granite counter tops, and chill out.

Imagine my surprise when Jim drove into neighboring Westfield and pulled into a parking spot in front of Chita, the trendy tapas restaurant everyone was talking about.

Huh? You mean we were going out to lunch, as in "out at a real restaurant"? I was immediately suspicious. Maybe the day wasn't over yet. This was certainly untypical behavior for My Beloved.

Then I thought, Jim must have a coupon. Although I doubted that a restaurant this new, and this popular, had to stoop to offering coupons to get customers.

The maitre d' waved us to a table, and in no time Jim had placed our order – in Spanish, yet.

I was duly impressed. But still suspicious.

"What's this all about, Jim? Since when are you a foodie? And how in the world did you manage to get us in here today, much less find a parking spot right in front of the restaurant? This is the hottest new place in town."

Before My Beloved could answer, a young man, obviously the owner from the mantle of authority he wore over his crisp navy blazer with "Chita" emblazoned on the breast pocket, arrived at our table with two margaritas. "On the house, Señor and Señora Andrews. Welcome to Chita. We are honored to have Mike's parents as guests here." He bowed slightly, then left to attend to another table.

I had to laugh. "So that's how you did it, Jim. It's not who you know that counts. It's who your kids know."

"Let's face it, Carol," Jim said. "Our parents called these the golden years. I don't know if that's true, but we're still here and we might as well make the best of it, right? Cheers." He raised his glass and toasted me.

What the heck. I could be a sport. I mimicked his toast and took a sip of my drink. And choked.

I am not a serious drinker. Unless you count wine, of course. Which I don't.

"So how did this happen, Jim?" I asked once I'd stopped coughing. "I want details. Who is this guy, how does Mike know him, and how did you find out about the connection?"

With the ability Jim had perfected over the years as a public relations agent in New York, he neatly deflected my questions and changed the subject. Oh, well, I could e-mail Mike later and get the details, so I let him get away with it.

Until I realized that he'd placed a glossy folder in front of me with the legend "Eden's Grove – One of the Top 100 Active Adult Communities in America" stamped on the front. My head was a little buzzy from the margarita, but not that much.

"I thought we were through looking at these places," I said, and took another sip of my drink. "I went along with you, we saw two, and we both decided they weren't for us."

I turned my palms up. "End of story."

"I just wanted you to see those two first for a basis of comparison," My Beloved said. He slapped his hand on the folder and nudged it closer to me. "This is the one I really want us to look at. It sounds fabulous. Just look at all these amenities. It has an indoor and an outdoor pool, exercise rooms, tennis courts, and a golf course. If we moved there, we'd feel like we were on vacation all the time. Look at these photos, honey."

Right then and there, I should have stopped him. But he was so excited, I just couldn't throw cold water on his enthusiasm. At least, that's what I told my best friends Nancy and Mary Alice later when I brought them up to date on our foray into active adulthood.

I hadn't seen Jim this energized since his first meeting with his retirement coach, Davis Rhodes. And look how that worked out, Carol, my little voice reminded me. Jim ended up being suspected of murdering him.

"But Jim," I countered weakly, trying to inject some reality into the situation, "neither one of us plays golf or tennis."

"We're not too old to learn," he snapped back. "Come on, Carol. Let's finish our lunch and go check it out. What have we got to lose?"

My beautiful home for one thing, I thought.

But it meant so much to him. The last time I saw such a pleading look was when Lucy and Ethel wanted to go outside and romp around the yard. And when I ignored that look, I was always sorry.

What the heck. I raised my margarita glass and said, "Eden's Grove, here we come."

And I repeated my mantra silently: Two master suites. Two master suites.

"The Eden's Grove entrance is pretty impressive," Jim said.

"Hmm," I said. "It's different."

With its stone fence, guard house, and gate, I thought the community looked more like a prison than my idea of an active adult community.

"I wonder if they're keeping the bad guys out, or keeping the residents in."

"Very funny, Carol," My Beloved said. "Try to keep an open mind. I think you'll really like this place." He took my hand and eased me from the car.

I took a closer look around the grounds. I had to admit that they looked beautifully cared for. Despite the fact that it was January, all the sidewalks were completely free of snow and ice. And the steps leading into the sales office were pristine.

I thought guiltily of our icy front walk and rutted driveway. I was always nervous someone was going to fall when we had company this time of year.

Of course, the Eden's Grove management paid big bucks to keep the property looking this great, I reminded myself. And poor Jim did the best he could with our snow blower. When it was working.

Sighing, I followed Jim into the sales office. At least it would be warm inside.

"Welcome to Eden's Grove," said a pleasant-looking woman who was the point-of-entry at the reception desk. "You must be Jim and Carol Andrews. I'll get Eve for you. I know she's been expecting you."

I resisted the urge to giggle. Eve? At Eden's Grove? Would Adam be joining us too?

Jim shot me a look. I've heard that when you've been married as long as we have, couples often read each other's thoughts. Not when it really counts, of course, such as, "Honey, will you please take out the garbage?" But this time, he could tell I was about to whisper a wise-ass comment. I got the message, and kept my mouth shut.

We were joined by a well-groomed woman who looked like she was in her early fifties but was probably older. "Hello, I'm Eve Hamill, the sales manager here. So glad to meet you both. And before you ask, no, my husband's name isn't Adam." She laughed. "Everyone asks me that. It's just coincidence that I ended up working at Eden's Grove. But my name is always a good icebreaker.

"Why don't we start by having me give you both a tour? Then I'll sit down and run some numbers with you, and turn you over to one of our Ambassador Couples for a nice cup of tea. Sound good?"

Not giving us a chance to respond, she continued, "Follow me."

I hated to admit it, but I was impressed. I could tell that Jim was, too, but of course, he had expected to be.

There was a lot to like about Eden's Grove. Two pools, the 600-seat ballroom with its own stage (what we'd use that for, I had no clue), the beauty salon, the woodworking room, the nail salon, the barber shop, the computer center, the exercise room, the other exercise room, the arts and crafts room, the library, the darts and billiards room – well, I think you get the picture. This place was like a small city. The only thing it lacked was a food store, and even that was convenient, less than a mile away.

"This place has everything," Jim said, clearly amazed at all we'd seen on our tour.

"I'm glad you think so," Eve replied. "I'm sure you two would love living at Eden's Grove. I'm even thinking of buying here myself.

"I know it's cold outside," she continued, not giving us a chance to respond, "but I want you to see two of the models we currently have available. It's just a quick walk from here. Both styles are what we called semi-detached housing, meaning they are attached to another unit on one side."

"Do either of these styles have two master suites?" I piped up.

"We get a lot of requests for that," Eve said. "I guess a desire for some breathing room is common to a lot of couples when they've been married for a long time. One style has two master suites, but unfortunately, there are none of those available at the present time."

Bummer, I thought. But Eve was one smart salesperson. She could tell how important that feature was to me. "There are units under construction, ready for early summer occupancy, that will have two master suites. They're very popular, so if that's a real priority for you two, you'd be wise to put down a deposit now so you won't be disappointed."

She whisked us into first one, then the other, model home, and I was dazzled by the stainless steel appliances and hardwood floors. And how bright and open everything was. Skylights, lots of windows. The units were gorgeous. Smaller than what I was used to, but gorgeous.

I hated to admit it to myself, much less to My Beloved, but Eden's Grove might actually be a place I could live in. If I decided to move. Which I had definitely not decided to do. Yet.

I didn't dare look at Jim. He could read my face too well, and I didn't want any pressure from him on the ride home.

"How about a nice cup of tea and some cookies?" asked Eve as she ushered us back into the sales center. She reached for her cell phone. "I want you to meet one of our Ambassador Couples, the Bakers, who can tell you first-hand how great it is to live here."

I looked at my watch. Yikes! It was almost 4:00. We'd been gone almost all day.

"Jim, we really can't stay any longer," I said. "Lucy and Ethel have been alone since ten this morning."

Eve gave me a startled look. "Lucy and Ethel? Who are they? Your grandchildren?"

I laughed. "No, but they do think they're human. They're our two dogs."

Eve recoiled. "Dogs? As in more than one? I'm sorry, but residents are only allowed to have one pet here."

Forget the stainless steel appliances and the gleaming hardwood floors. Goodbye two master bedroom suites.

I shot a quick look at Jim and telegraphed, "No way we're moving without the girls."

This was a deal breaker for me.

Chapter 6

When a girl marries, she exchanges the attentions of many men for the inattention of one.

"We are not going to discuss it," I said to My Beloved. "There is no way I'm giving up one of our dogs to move into that place! In fact…" Fortunately, I caught myself before I said something really hurtful, like I'd sooner give him up than either of the dogs.

Jim kept his eyes focused on the road ahead of him and his mouth shut. Smart man. Forget about that drivel from the old movie *Love Story*. Remember that famous line: "Love means never having to say you're sorry"? Not true. Love means knowing when to keep your mouth shut.

"This was a wasted day," I continued. "I should have stayed home and cleaned the bathrooms instead." I hoped I made my point crystal clear to My Beloved. He knows how much I hate to clean the bathrooms.

"The lunch was nice," Jim countered. "And you have to admit that Eden's Grove has everything."

"Everything except dogs," I said, stating the obvious. "And we have two dogs. Whom we love dearly. So Eden's Grove does not, and never will have, us. End of discussion. Now, let's go home. And I don't want to hear the words 'moving' and 'active adult community' again. Deal?"

Jim sighed. He knew when he was licked.

"Deal, Carol."

A week had passed since our Geezer Tour, as I called it when I filled in Nancy and Mary Alice about our adventure in house-hunting. Predictably, Nancy was angry at me because Jim and I had looked at houses without her. Being a real estate agent in such a down market had made her a little paranoid, so I forgave her.

"Nancy, for heaven's sake, they didn't buy anything," Mary Alice said in my defense. We were sitting in our favorite coffee shop, The Paperback Café, in the center of Fairport. No Starbucks for us, thank you very much. We'd been coming to this place since we were in high school. It served two kinds of coffee – regular and decaf. No lattes, chais, or any of those other fancy drinks. The Paperback Café was one of the few holdouts in town against the plague of upscale chain stores and yuppie boutiques that were taking over our fair community. Plus, their shelves were filled with books of every description, all available to the clientele to peruse while sipping their coffee. They even had a special shelf featuring local authors, and frequently hosted book signings to promote them. Sort of like a library with caffeine. And all their baked goods were made fresh daily, on the premises. What's not to like about a place like that?

I sipped my coffee, burned my tongue, and grimaced. It was piping hot, as usual.

"God punished me for my sins, Nancy," I said. "I burned my tongue and I'm suffering. I hope you're satisfied. See." I stuck my tongue out at her.

"Take a drink of this cold water and hold it in your mouth, Carol," said Mary Alice. "Roll it around on your tongue a little and it should feel better."

"Once a nurse, always a nurse," said Nancy. She reached over and patted my hand. "I forgive you. I was just so shocked I got a little carried away. You're not really going to move, are you?"

"Not if I have anything to say about it," I said. "I plan to be carried out of my house feet first. In a body bag."

Mary Alice recoiled at that. "God, what an image, Carol."

"When we got home from the Geezer Tour, I sat down and made a list of the pros and cons of moving to an active adult community."

I put my glasses on, then continued. "I made a list of what needs to happen to keep our house running, and assigned each task to either Jim or me. Feel free to jump in if I've left anything out. Here's Jim's list: lawn and landscaping, house painting and outdoor upkeep, snow removal, garbage and recycling. If we moved to an active adult community, Jim wouldn't have to do any of this. They'd all be included in the monthly common charge, which isn't cheap."

I took a quick bite of the special muffin of the day – chocolate chip. Yum.

"Here's my list: cooking, food service and cleanup, house cleaning, laundry – although Jim's taken over some of that, much to my dismay – changing beds, pet care. These are the ones I thought of very quickly. Notice anything about my list?"

"That's all the things a woman does around the house every day," Nancy said. "But I see where you're going with this. If you moved into an active adult community, you'd still have to do all your jobs, right?"

"That's right," I said. "I even asked if there was a maid service at Eden's Grove, and the sales agent looked at me like I was crazy. And I'm not giving up my dogs. I told Jim that I am not moving to Eden's Grove – no way, José."

"Good for you, Carol," said Mary Alice. "But Jenny's going to be moving out this month, right?"

"I can't be selfish about that," I said. "Jim and I have loved having her home since last summer. She was wonderful last year when Jim was in that awful mess about his retirement coach. I don't know what I would have done without her. But it's time for her to be out on her own again. And I have to admit, I'm thrilled that she and Mark Anderson are getting so close. Although I've tried not to push the relationship. I doubt Jenny even knows how much I'd love to see them become a permanent couple."

"Yeah, Carol," said Nancy with the wisdom of someone who's known me since grammar school, "we all know how subtle you can be when you want something.

"Not!"

"Hey," I protested. "I can be subtle."

"Humph," retorted Nancy. "Manipulative, yes. Subtle, no."

"Anyway," I went on, determined not to let Nancy's needling get to me, "we haven't seen much of Mark the last few days. He's up to his ears in that hit and run accident case. The one that happened at Fairport Community College last Friday night."

"That was so awful," Mary Alice said. "I'd gotten called to work at the emergency room that night, and by the time the paramedics got that poor girl to the hospital, she was gone. I can't imagine what her parents must be going through, losing a child so tragically."

Nancy and I didn't respond right away. We were both remembering the premature death of Mary Alice's husband, Brian, killed in an auto accident some twenty years ago. It must have been extra tough for our friend to deal with the young accident casualty and her grieving family.

"What I can't imagine is how anyone could be so cowardly as to hit someone in the dark and then just drive away and leave her to die," Nancy said in disgust. "I hope the police find who did it and put him away for life."

At that moment, my cell phone rang. It was Jenny. She didn't waste time with pleasantries.

"Dad's had a heart attack. You've got to get to the hospital right away."

Chapter 7

There's so little difference between husbands that you might as well keep your first one. Just look at all the time you've spent breaking him in. Do you really want to go through that again?

Thank God I was with Mary Alice and Nancy when I got Jenny's call. I was so upset I know I would've had an accident driving to the hospital myself.

By the time we got there, breaking who-knows-how-many traffic laws, I was relieved to see Jim was already sitting in the out-patient area, ready to be released. Typical man, he assumed an ornery persona when he saw that Nancy and Mary Alice were with me. I think he was embarrassed at causing all this excitement.

"God, Carol, you didn't have to bring reinforcements with you. I'm not dying."

I started to blubber and Jim stood up – a little unsteadily, I thought – and gave me a hug. "I'm really all right. It was just a scare. A mild angina attack, the doctor said. He's referred me to a cardiologist, as a precaution. And then he released me." Jim fished in his jacket pocket and held up a card. "See? I'll call and make an appointment right away when we get home. Promise."

"But, Jim, why did this happen? What were you doing?"

I knew My Beloved was hardly a couch potato, but he wasn't an exercise nut either, like some men I know.

"All I was doing was clearing more of the ice off the front sidewalk," he said defensively. "You know how worried you always are that someone's going to fall and sue us."

Humph. Seemed to me that he was the one who worried about getting sued. Not a good time to argue about that point, however.

"Sorry I gave you such a scare," he said. "Fortunately, Jenny was home and she called nine-one-one and here I am." At my questioning look, Jim continued, "she stayed with me until the doctor saw me, but then she had to leave to go teach a class."

"As long as you're all right, Jim, Mary Alice and I'll get out of here," said Nancy, who had remained uncharacteristically quiet.

"Wait a minute, Nancy," said Mary Alice. "We have to give them a lift home. I'm sure they don't want to travel in an ambulance. You can pick up your own car later, Carol. It's safe in the Paperback Café parking lot."

"I'm just glad to be going home," Jim said. "I was afraid the doctors were going to keep me overnight for observation."

"Are you sure it's safe for you to leave the hospital, Jim?" I couldn't help it. I was scared, and if I sounded overprotective, I didn't care.

"I'm fine, Carol," Jim snapped back. "For God's sake, don't make this into a crisis."

I couldn't help myself. This was first sign that one of us was showing signs of our mortality. I know we all have an expiration date. I just didn't want Jim's to come too soon.

For the next few days, I hovered over My Beloved like a hawk stalking its prey. I drove him so crazy that he even started going to the newspaper office even when he didn't need to, just to get away from me.

I also spent a lot of time wrestling with my conscience. What right did I have to insist on staying in our house if Jim's health was at stake?

I forced myself to take another look at my home-maintenance jobs list, and realized that Jim's were all labor-intensive, requiring physical energy that could seriously damage his heart. Of course, in my own melodramatic way, I could easily imagine My Beloved keeling over, clutching his chest, just from taking out a bag of garbage, and saying with his last breath, "Honey, I'm sorry. I was only doing it for you."

You can't take that chance, Carol.

I made the only decision I could, under the circumstances. I called Nancy and told her I wanted to list our house for sale.

"You're absolutely sure you want to do this?" asked Nancy. "You don't want to talk it over with Jim first before you sign the listing agreement?"

It was a few days before Valentine's Day, and Nancy was helping me set the tables for our monthly Bunco game, which is a game of dice requiring no brain power whatsoever. My Beloved claims that Bunco is just an excuse for a group of women to get together for eating, drinking, and gossiping. And laughing – there's always a lot of that.

Bunco night is the one night of the month when Jim can't get out of the house fast enough. He's even has been known to walk on the wild side and pay full price for a movie instead of a twilight bargain show, something he'd never consider doing under any other circumstances.

Nancy had arrived long before the other players. Come to think of it, she was spending much more time in my house these days than in her own. Her husband, Bob – or The Bobster, as we called him when we were kids – was a financial guru and always seemed to be on the road solving one crisis after another for clients. I knew Nancy would never admit it, but I think she was lonely. Which is probably why she was such a successful real estate agent – she put all her energy into her job rather than her own home.

Not that I'm one to criticize anyone else's priorities.

Nancy pulled the listing agreement out of her Gucci briefcase and carefully put it down in front of me. She then took the next ten minutes to try and talk me out of what I was determined to do.

"I want you to be absolutely sure about this, Carol," she said. "I've known you too long, and I know you too well. You love this house. Once you and Jim sign the agreement, you're in a contract relationship. Not that you have to take any offer that's made. But I don't want this to spoil our friendship, and it could, if you haven't really thought this through and try to back out."

"I don't want to sell my house," I said. "But if I have to choose between keeping our house and Jim's health...." My eyes spilled over as the enormity of what I was signing hit me. And the equal enormity of what could happen if I didn't. Talk about being between a rock and a hard place.

So I switched gears, an avoidance technique that's worked well for me over the years. "Are you cold, Nancy? Now that Jim's gone out, I can push up the thermostat."

"Don't worry about it, Carol," Nancy said. "Once everybody gets here, all the gabbing and laughing will keep us warm. And no trying to change the subject. Are you positive you want me to list the house?"

I immediately became defensive. "I'm entitled to change the subject in my own home." I gestured around my dining room with its beautiful fireplace, built-in corner china cabinet, and gorgeous wainscoting. "And this is still my home. Until you sell it. Besides, Jim has to sign the listing agreement, too. You know the house is in both of our names. It won't be final until he does. I want to give him the listing agreement as his Valentine's Day present. The way you're trying to talk me out of this, it sounds like you don't want the listing."

"Of course I want the listing, you doofus," said my friend. "I just want to be sure you really know what you're doing. I know how impulsive you can be."

She held out a pen and several sheets of paper. "I only wrote the contract for a three-month listing, and I cut my usual percentage from six percent to four. That wasn't easy with our new boss, but I managed to persuade him. And I left the listing price out for now. We'll deal with that after you talk to Jim. Let's get this show on the road. Go ahead and sign. In two places. I've highlighted them to make it easier for you."

I grabbed the pen and did the deed. "Now, zip your lip. I'm not telling anyone about this until I spring it on Jim."

I took the listing agreement and shoved it in the pocket of my jeans, then gave Nancy some silverware and napkins. "There are three other tables to set besides the one in the dining room. Remember, I invited some of the younger neighbors as well as the usual players, so I've set up card tables in the family room and my office. We'll have to use the kitchen counter and island for the bar and buffet. There should be sixteen of us, if everyone comes. Get going. They'll be here any minute. All I need is for a neighbor to hear us talking about moving. It'll be all over the block in a millisecond."

"Hey," protested Nancy, "I'm a Realtor. It's natural for me to talk about moving. Why don't you put me with some of the older neighbors, so I can see if anyone else is thinking of putting their house on the market? It's always good to know about possible competition, especially when we set the price. If I should happen to pick up any neighborhood gossip, I'll let you know."

"Who has neighborhood gossip?" asked Mary Alice, coming into the kitchen loaded down with three shopping bags. "You guys were yakking away and didn't even hear me knock. Good thing you left the door unlocked, Carol, or I would have frozen to death out there."

"First of all, you don't live in this neighborhood," kidded Nancy. "And second, you don't listen to gossip. At least, that's what you always tell us."

"Ha!" I said, grabbing two of the bags. "Don't kid me. Everybody listens to gossip.

"Let's set these on the island. You've got enough food here for an army, Mary Alice. Why'd you bring so much? Did you forget that everyone is supposed to bring only one thing to share?"

"You know me," Mary Alice said. "I worry there won't be enough healthy stuff, and all that we'll have to snack on are nachos and chips. And cheap wine."

"What's wrong with that?" called Nancy from the family room. I swear, that woman has the ears of an elephant. And an appetite to match. Incredibly, she can still eat just about anything, including junk food, and not have it travel immediately to her hips and thighs.

Although she is my best friend, I sincerely hate her for that.

"I miss Claire," Mary Alice said, dumping the contents of one of her cartons onto a plate and stirring it around to try and make it look presentable. "She was the one who always set out all the food and made it look so appetizing. Why did she and Larry have to buy that condo in Florida anyway?"

"Remember that question the next time you're shoveling out your car," said Nancy. "I think the answer will become pretty clear."

"And she does e-mail us at least once a week," I added.

"Yeah," said Nancy. "In between visits to the beach and the condo swimming pool. What a life."

The good news for me about Claire and Larry's move southward was that their condo was only a few miles away from Mike, our second-born child, who had deserted the rigors of New England winters a few years ago to sample the high life of South Beach, Florida. He was now part owner of a successful club called Cosmo's, frequented by all the so-called beautiful people. Claire made an effort, surreptitiously of course, to keep on eye on Mike and report back to Jim and me.

"I miss her, too," I said, "but she won't be back until late May, so we'll just have to do the best we can. Nobody comes to Bunco to critique the food presentation anyway. All people care about is that there's plenty of it. Especially the desserts."

"Did you put out the nametags with everyone's first names and addresses on them like I suggested?" Nancy asked as she returned to the kitchen with leftover plates and cutlery. "It's a great icebreaker."

Rats. I'd completely forgotten.

"Sorry, Nance. I had other things on my mind."

The doorbell rang, and Nancy raced to answer it before Lucy and Ethel started to bark. Fat chance of that. I'd confined both dogs to the master bedroom and they were complaining bitterly, even though I'd explained that this was a special treat and just this once they could snooze on the king-size bed without being reprimanded.

The doorbell continued to ring as more guests arrived. I could hear Nancy chatting away, taking coats and stuffing them in our already packed front hall closet. That was another thing I didn't do – empty out the coat closet. You'd think I had never entertained before.

One of my neighbors, Sara Miller, was the next to appear in the kitchen, carrying a sterling silver chafing dish containing "Great Aunt Sharon's Marvelous Meatballs," a secret family recipe she claimed her aunt had given only to her, "since I'm the gourmet cook in the family." Sara worshipped at the shrine of Martha Stewart, and never met a fancy recipe she wouldn't try. Some of her experiments were successful, and others were not. One thing she was absolutely adamant about, though, was using only the freshest organic ingredients known to womankind. No frozen or canned for her. I had to hide the electric can opener when she was around.

I wondered what culinary delight we were in store for tonight. I hoped it was a recipe that had already been tested on some other lucky neighborhood guinea pigs.

Sara was dressed with her customary touch of purple – this time a tunic over black leggings. She looked like an eggplant with legs.

My counters and island began to look like the takeout area of a local restaurant. Mary Alice took over, and organized desserts on one side and appetizers on the other.

"OK, everybody, we have four Bunco tables tonight," I said in my most take-charge voice. As usual, everyone was crowded in the kitchen, mixing in and having a great time. And not listening to a word I was saying.

I had to move things along. "One Bunco table's in the dining room, two are in the family room, and the other one's in the office, so pick out where you want to sit. And help yourselves to some wine and an hors d'oeuvre or two."

"Or three," piped up Phyllis Stevens, the head of the Old Fairport Turnpike Homeowners' Association. Phyllis and her husband Bill were part of the "Old Guard" of the area. Their home had been in Phyllis's family for three generations. She and Bill were one of only a handful of couples left in the neighborhood who were older than Jim and me.

That was something I liked about our neighborhood, though – the influx of younger families. I knew I would have trouble adjusting to living in a place where everyone was about the same age – older than dirt, as Mike would say. I liked seeing the young mothers wheeling their babies around the block. It reminded me of when Jenny and Mike were little.

Of course, in my day, I walked behind the carriage. These mommies jogged. They always appeared in a group and managed to both jog and talk at the same time, without losing either a single step or their breath. Amazing.

It amused me to see My Beloved suck in his stomach if he happened to be outside when any of these young lovelies jogged by.

Three of the jogging mommies were here tonight: Deb Myers, Liz Stone, and Stacy O'Keefe. Their color was already rosy. I couldn't tell if it was because they'd jogged to my house or had hit the wine bottle a few times when they got here.

"This is so cool, Carol," said Liz. At least, I think it was Liz. They all had blonde ponytails and sometimes I had trouble telling them apart. "Thanks for inviting us. I've never played Bunco before, and I'm dying to learn. I hope it's easy."

"Yeah," added Stacy. "After a day with the twins, my mind is mush."

"I remember those days," I said. "I used to long for adult conversation. The highlight of my day used to be a visit from the mailman, especially if he had a package that had to be signed for. That meant he had to ring the doorbell."

"Things haven't changed that much, Carol," Stacy assured me. "I still look forward to the mailman. Or any adult at my door these days. Even someone selling magazine subscriptions."

"By the way, did you hear that the police arrested someone for the hit and run accident at the college?" Liz asked.

"Thank God," Mary Alice said. "I hope they put him in prison and throw away the key without bothering with a trial."

"That's a little strong, Mary Alice," said Phyllis. "Everyone deserves his day in court, and is innocent until proven guilty."

Mary Alice snorted. "Listen, anyone who would hit a defenseless person and then drive away and leave her to die deserves to be locked up for life, as far as I'm concerned. Or, better yet, executed." She took a hearty gulp of her red wine.

The kitchen suddenly was very quiet. Everyone, it seemed, was listening to this exchange.

"I don't agree," said Phyllis, her cheeks getting a little pink. "Everyone is entitled to a fair trial. That's one of the principles this country was founded on."

"My husband Brian was killed in a car accident by a kid who was driving with only a learner's permit," said Mary Alice. She was so upset now that she was shaking. "The judge let him off with only two years in jail and five years' probation. How's that for justice?

"That kid ruined my life and my boys' lives. I swear, if I ever see him again, I'll kill him.

"I mean it."

Then she slammed her wine glass down on my granite counter, grabbed her coat, and left without saying another word.

Chapter 8

An archeologist is the best husband any woman could want. The older she gets, the more interesting she is to him.

"I've never seen Mary Alice so upset," I said to My Beloved. It was Valentine's Day and we were finally going to have some time to ourselves. I was filling Jim in on the Bunco party while we enjoyed a pre-dinner glass of merlot in front of a cozy fire in the living room.

"It's nice that Mark's not working tonight so he and Jenny can be together," I continued. "The last few days have been non-stop, packing her up and helping her move into her new condo."

I reached over and grabbed Jim's hand. "I know this has been hard for you, but when she came home last year, we knew she wouldn't be here forever. And Mark is such a good guy."

"When he's not suspecting me of bumping somebody off," Jim groused. He winked at me to show he wasn't serious.

"I don't want to talk about Mary Alice, or even Jenny and Mark, right now," he said. "I know we usually don't make a big deal about Valentine's Day, but this year, after everything we've been through together, I wanted to get you something extra special."

He handed me a small box. I opened it and found a strand of cultured pearls and matching bracelet inside.

"Oh, Jim, I love them," I said. "I can't believe you did this for me. Thank you, so much." I threw my arms round My Beloved and gave him the smooch he deserved for such a romantic gesture.

"I have something special for you too," I said, pulling out the envelope that contained a funny valentine and the agreement I'd already signed to list our house for sale.

"Here. Open it," I said. "I guarantee you're going to love it." I was wriggling with excitement. I love surprises. As long as they're happy ones.

"I hope you didn't spend too much money," Jim said.

"You are so predictable," I said. "For your information, I didn't spend any money on your gift. But I'm sure we're going to make some."

Jim looked at me quizzically, then pushed his glasses up onto his forehead so he could read the card. Honestly, the man will not admit that he needs bifocals. And women are supposed to be the vainer sex.

The valentine featured good old Charlie Brown saying, "I knew I'd have to look through a million valentines before I found the right card for you..... Because you're one in a million." We've never been into giving each other mushy greeting cards. This was as close as it got.

"Good one, Carol. What's this inside?"

"Happy Valentine's Day," I said, raising my wine glass. "Here's to the rest of our lives. May they be long, healthy, and full of new adventures."

"Are you sure about this?" asked Jim, holding the listing agreement and good old Charlie Brown in a death grip. "I'm not forcing you to move. I know how much you love this house."

"I'm sure I want to start having new adventures with you as soon as possible," I said, neatly sidestepping his question. "It'll be fun to fill in the details as we go along. Now, sign." I held out a pen. "I already did."

After a romantic dinner and a delightful interlude in our Jacuzzi – I don't have to tell you everything! – I called Nancy to tell her it was official. We were listing the house for sale.

And that's when our troubles really started.

Chapter 9

The first time a man got into trouble,
he put the blame on a woman.

"I thought you loved our house," I said to Nancy. "All you're doing now is finding things to criticize about it."

"You've got to stop thinking about this as your house, Carol," said my crackerjack real estate agent and former best friend. "I was afraid you'd be like this. That's why I was hesitant to take this listing. You've got to let go and let me do my job. Which, in case you've forgotten, is selling your house."

It was a few days after Valentine's Day. Nancy and Marcia Fischer, the "staging expert" from Superior Interiors ("Your Home, Only Better"), a local upscale furniture and design studio, were going through my house from top to bottom, scrutinizing every room, opening every closet door, and taking copious notes. Marcia was also photographing each room with her digital camera.

I felt like I had been invaded.

Lucy and Ethel followed us from room to room, probably checking to be sure Marcia – whom I disliked on sight for no reason other than the fact that she rolled her eyes at Nancy every time we went into another room – wasn't swiping anything.

"You need to remove all these personal photographs," said Marcia, surveying my beautiful living room and its built-in bookcases with obvious disdain. "Buyers have to be able to imagine themselves in a house. No one wants to look at pictures of someone else's family." She looked at Nancy, who nodded in agreement.

"The dogs will definitely have to leave when we have the open house on St. Patrick's Day," Marcia continued. "As a matter of fact, they should be out of the house for at least a week before the open house to get rid of that awful doggy odor." She wrinkled up her nose in distaste. "No agent's going to show a house to a potential buyer with this stench."

Stench! What? No way. I was a meticulous housekeeper. Now I was really angry.

Before I hauled off and slugged her, Nancy intervened. "Marcia's right, I'm afraid. You're just so used to living with dogs that you don't notice it. But believe me, a potential buyer will.

"It never bothered me, though," she added, trying to soothe me. "You know how much I love the girls." To prove it, Nancy reached down and gave each of them a scratch on their silky heads.

I was momentarily pacified. I guess I knew in my heart that Marcia and Nancy were right. But I also knew I couldn't stand hearing my beautiful house criticized so ruthlessly.

"Nancy, you're my best friend. I trust you to do your job," I said, trying to convince myself that I really meant what I was saying. I didn't say a word about Marcia, though. I'm not a complete hypocrite.

"The dogs and I are going to get out of your way. You figure out what needs to be done, make your list, and Jim and I'll do what you say."

I held up my right hand and said, "Girl Scout's honor." I hope she didn't notice that my left hand was behind my back. Those fingers were crossed.

"You want to price the house much too low," My Beloved sputtered at Nancy the next evening. The three of us were seated around our kitchen table, where we'd all sat together hundreds of times before. This time, though, we weren't friends getting together for a friendly cup of coffee or a glass of wine. We were there to hammer out the final details of the house listing. This was a business meeting, and Jim meant business.

He leaned forward in his chair, breathing hard, like he usually does when money is involved. "There is no way I'm letting this property be listed for such a low price."

Keep your mouth shut, I told myself. Let the two of them hammer it out.

Unless they came to blows, of course. Then I'd have to break it up.

I had a momentary, cheery thought. Maybe if Jim couldn't agree with Nancy about a listing price, he wouldn't want to sell the house.

Yeah, and then he'd keel over from a heart attack when he was shoveling the sidewalk or mowing the lawn.

So much for that fantasy. No way that was going to happen, if I could prevent it.

Nancy reached into her designer briefcase, pulled out a sheaf of papers, and slapped them on the table in front of Jim. I had the sneaky feeling she wanted to slap him with the papers, and was working hard to restrain herself. Maybe listing the house with a close friend hadn't been such a good idea after all. Too late now. And I knew she would've killed me if Jim and I had listed the house with any other real estate agent.

"These are comps from houses that have sold in this neighborhood in the past two years," Nancy said to Jim. "I want you to study them carefully, and see if you notice a trend."

My Beloved pushed his glasses on top of his head and squinted to read the information. "You see," he said after just a few seconds, "these comps prove my point. Most of these houses sold for over a million dollars."

"Look again, Jim," said Nancy. "You're missing the point. All the ones that sold for over a million dollars were newer homes." She pointed out three houses she had highlighted in yellow. "The antiques all sold for considerably less. The highest one, four months ago, sold for eight hundred twenty-five thousand dollars. It was on the market for over a year, and the sellers had to come way down on their asking price to finally get it sold. Buyers today want open floor plans and skylights, not cozy rooms with low ceilings and uneven floors. This isn't going to be an easy sell. You've got to price a house right in this competitive market. This property should be listed in the sevens."

I could see the calculator in Jim's brain figure out the bottom line. He looked at me for guidance, but no way was I going to get in the middle of this one. He'd always been the financial genius in the family.

I raised my eyebrows, then sent him a look which said, "Whatever you do is fine with me."

My Beloved sighed in defeat. "Seven hundred seventy-five thousand dollars," he said. "And not a penny less."

"Exactly the figure I was thinking of," said Nancy. She winked at me, and handed him a pen "You'll see that I'm right, Jim. Leave everything to me."

For the next few weeks, Jim and I worked like, forgive the expression, dogs. We rented a storage unit in town, and I was assigned the job of packing away all our personal items. Since we'd been in the house over thirty years, we were drowning in stuff, much of it saved for reasons that neither of us could remember. I wanted to throw a lot away, and Jim wanted to save all the things that I didn't. Funny that women are accused of being packrats, and it's the men who can't part with that tattered college sweatshirt or magazines that are years out of date.

I finally convinced My Beloved to hire a dumpster. I was well on my way to filling it, too – and having myself a great time with my purging – until I accidentally threw out Jim's favorite L.L. Bean jacket, which he had carelessly left on the garage floor. After that debacle, I reined myself in. Reluctantly.

We hadn't made any decision on where we were moving to, but since Nancy expected the sale of our house to take a while, neither of us was concerned.

"Wherever we go, I promise that we'll take both dogs with us," Jim said. What a softie. I knew he loved the girls as much as I did, especially now that he was retired and able to spend more "quality" time with them.

Jenny was a big help in the purging and packing. Probably because she had moved out of the house and was starting her own adventure with Mark. I was dying of curiosity about the progress of that relationship, but I restrained myself from cross-examining her. Like asking whether there were any wedding plans.

Our dear son, however, was not taking our move out of the family homestead as well. In fact, if e-mails could ignite a computer, his constant flood of them would have burned our house down. They basically all had the same tone, but varied in intensity as we got closer to the open house. Such as:

The Big Move

Mom, don't touch my stuff! I'll come home and go through it all myself. Just give me a little time to get things wrapped up in Florida. Do not – I repeat, DO NOT! – under any circumstances, go into my closet and start to pack things up. Especially my comic book collection. Your anxious son.

His comic book collection? Since when was that so precious? I remembered that Mike had been into comics when he was in junior high. He even had a box or two stored away, but nothing that could possibly stir up this kind of long-distance panic.

I decided Mike must have years' worth of *Playboy* magazines stashed under his comics and he didn't want me to know that. That made much more sense.

I had an easy solution. I would delegate packing up Mike's room to My Beloved. It would give him a nice break from re-grouting the master bathroom tile, touching up the baseboard paint and trim in the kitchen, and helping me wash the windows until they sparkled. Etc. etc.

It sure looked easier to prep a house for sale on Home and Garden Television. Where was the *Designed-To-Sell* team when we needed them?

A week before the open house, I moved Lucy and Ethel, along with their food, bowls, toys, blankets, crates, and doggy snacks, over to Mary Alice's house. We hadn't talked much since her Bunco party outburst, and this gave me a convenient excuse to catch up with her. Plus, she loves Lucy and Ethel almost as much as I do. And truth be told, they love her, too. Not as much as they love me, of course.

The dogs were puzzled by their change of digs, but once Mary Alice helped me unload all their gear, they settled right in like it was home. I tried to suppress a pang of jealousy when Lucy, ignoring me completely, nudged Mary Alice's arm as hard as she could, demanding attention. Ethel had already curled up in her crate for a snooze.

Mary Alice laughed at my reaction. "Don't worry, I know I'm just the dog sitter. I won't steal them from you."

"I didn't realize I was being that obvious," I confessed. "I want them to like being here, but…"

"But not as much as being with you," Mary Alice finished.

"I'm glad you asked me to take care of the dogs," she went on. "I hope it means you forgive me for my behavior the night of the Bunco party. I don't know what got into me, carrying on like that."

"Since you brought it up, I have been worried about you," I answered. "It's been so crazy trying to get the house ready to sell that I haven't called you for a while. But are you sure you're OK? Really?"

"You're one of the few people who know that Brian and I had a huge fight right before he had his car accident," Mary Alice said. "It took a lot for me to admit that to you. I've felt guilty for years that I never had the chance to tell him I was sorry." Tears glistened in her eyes.

I covered her hand with mine and gave it a little squeeze. "You don't owe me any explanation," I said.

"I guess I'm trying to explain my behavior at the Bunco party to myself as much as to you," Mary Alice said.

"I've been doing pretty well for years, but being in the emergency room the night that poor hit and run victim was brought in triggered all sorts of bad memories. And when Phyllis started carrying on about the hit and run driver being innocent until proven guilty, I snapped, even though I knew she was right. She was just so self-righteous about it. I wonder how she'd feel if someone in her own family died like that."

She stopped herself just in time. "I'm doing it again, aren't I? I'm sorry. It's just that I can be honest with you, because you know the whole story. Sometimes I feel that I killed Brian, because he wasn't concentrating on his driving after the awful fight we had."

Lucy licked Mary Alice's hand, sensing her misery.

I didn't know what to say. I hadn't realized how much this was eating away at her.

"That's enough of my self-pity," she said abruptly. "Time to change the subject. Are you all set for the open house? If Nancy wouldn't freak out, could I stop by and check out the changes you've made? I don't mean to be nosy."

"You're not being nosy," I said. "That's a great idea. You can be my personal set of eyes and ears, since Jim and I have been banished for the day. And you can be sure that no one has too much to drink and falls asleep on my bed."

Mary Alice raised her eyebrows quizzically.

"You didn't know? The open house is on St. Patrick's Day, and Nancy's making it into an Irish festival. I think she's even serving Irish coffee and Guinness.

"Thank God I talked her out of the step dancers."

St. Patrick's Day dawned with gray skies and a light drizzle. The house had never looked better. All the clutter was gone. No photographs of family events decorated the bookshelves. It looked like a move-in-ready model home. I had to admit that Marcia the Super Stager knew what she was doing.

Nancy insisted that Jim and I be out of the house before 9 a.m. "And no parking across the street to keep tabs on who comes. I'll give you a complete report later."

Nancy had done a Realtors' open house on Friday, March 16th. According to her, several Realtors had come and claimed they had clients "who'd be just perfect for this darling antique house." She was expecting a big crowd at the public open house, especially since the advertising had highlighted the fact that Guinness and Irish coffee would be served. I hoped that no one got too inebriated that they forgot this was a real estate event and not a wild party.

I needn't have worried. At least, not about that. When My Beloved and I arrived home at 4 p.m., having run out of places to go to kill time and anxious for a report, Nancy announced that the open house was a fantastic success.

"People came in droves," she said. "Of course, a lot of them were lookie-loos from the neighborhood. They may give a song and dance story that they're checking out the listing for a friend, but Realtors can always tell they just want to check out someone else's house.

"I've never done an open house that was this popular. I suppose it could have been the liquor I served. Good thing Mary Alice showed up to help show people around. Everyone raved about the house. Marcia did a great job staging it. I know you don't like her, but she knows her job."

Nancy paused for maximum effect.

"So, do you want to know the big news?"

Without giving either Jim or me a chance to respond, she blurted out, “We had a full-price offer on the house. Closing in thirty days, subject to standard inspections.

“And the buyer is pre-approved for a mortgage, so this is the real deal,” she crowed. “I hope you’re both pleased.”

Pleased? We were in shock.

Worse than that, we were homeless.

Chapter 10

Before marriage, a man will lie awake all night thinking about something you said. After marriage, he'll fall asleep before you finish saying it.

My Beloved insisted that we accept the offer that very day. He didn't want to take the chance that the buyer would change his mind.

"This is a corporate transfer, so we don't have to worry about this buyer having to sell a home so he can buy yours," said Nancy, switching from her best friend persona to her hard-core real estate one. She could tell I was having major doubts about being rushed into such a huge decision, so she went in for the kill.

"The Cartwrights are a nice family, Carol. They love the house. I know you'd never want to sell to anyone who wouldn't care for it as much as you have. Imagine how wonderful it'll be to have young children in the house again. They have two, a boy and a girl, just like you. Can't you imagine their kids playing in the back yard, just like Jenny and Mike did?

"But here's the best part. You won't believe this." Nancy waited a beat for us to respond.

I snuck a look at Jim. I was sure he was mentally calculating what the net proceeds from the house sale would be after we paid Nancy's commission.

"Alyssa Cartwright's parents are Sara and Chuck Miller. Can you believe it? That's one of the prime reasons why they wanted to live in this neighborhood, to be close to her family. She and Jack are absolutely thrilled with this opportunity. You can't break their hearts, Carol. You've gotta say yes."

Nancy knew that appealing to my emotions suckered me in every time. Funny that, after all these years of marriage, my husband still didn't understand that.

In my heart, I knew she was right. I just didn't want to be strong-armed into anything.

"It sounds like a great offer," I said, stalling for time. "But I'm not sure I'm quite ready to do this. It's all happening so fast."

Jim and Nancy both stared at me like I was nuts.

"Carol, you can't be serious," Nancy said. "Do you know how lucky you are to get a full price offer at the first open house? That never happens."

"Honey, I know this is hard for you," My Beloved said. "But you know this is for the best."

I just sat there like an idiot. Then, mercifully, the front doorbell rang. Saved by the bell, I thought, as I scurried to answer it, leaving Nancy and Jim in the kitchen. Thank God for a distraction so I'd have time to sort out my feelings.

I opened the door to a good-looking young man in his late thirties.

"Can I help you?" I asked, figuring he was lost and needed directions. My mother raised me to be polite.

The man was neatly dressed for an early spring Connecticut weekend in a tan leather bomber jacket and pressed chinos. His light brown hair was slightly mussed from the wind. Not particularly tall or short. Just...um...ordinary in height. I did notice a slim body under the bomber jacket that looked like it got a gym workout every day.

He gave me a huge smile, showing off straight, even teeth that must have cost his parents a fortune.

Believe me, I know all about that.

"I know this is irregular," my unexpected visitor said, "but I just wanted to look at your beautiful front staircase one more time. I hope you don't mind if I come inside."

Huh?

He moved his body around me, and the next thing I knew I had this perfect stranger standing in my foyer.

Who the heck was this guy? An open-house leftover? I wasn't frightened, though. Just irritated.

"I'm sorry," I said, letting my annoyance show, "but the open house is over." So go away, you pushy person.

"I'm the one who should apologize," the young man said. "I should have introduced myself when you answered the door."

He took my right hand and crushed it in his. I noticed his palms were wet, which always grosses me out.

"I'm Jack Cartwright." He continued to pump my hand. "My family and I saw your house this afternoon, and we just love it. We want to buy it. It's exactly what we've been looking for.

"Oh, hello, Mrs. Green." This last was directed at Nancy who, hearing voices, had come to the front of the house along with My Beloved. She hates to miss anything.

"Why, Jack," Nancy said. "This is a surprise. Why are you back here so soon? Are you alone? Where's your Realtor?"

"I was anxious to see how our offer was received," Jack confessed, flashing his perfect teeth again in a boyish grin. "I guess I shouldn't have showed up this way, but Alyssa is in love with this house. She thinks it's perfect for us. And the fact that it's in this neighborhood, right near her family, is great. I love seeing her so happy, and I hope you'll accept our offer.

"Mr. Andrews," Jack said, turning the full force of his considerable charm on My Beloved and shaking his hand, "it's such a pleasure to meet you, sir. The job you've done landscaping the house is spectacular. I can tell you've taken years to get the yard looking as good as it does. What curb appeal. I want to hear all about how you did it. I know I have a lot to learn, and you're obviously a master gardener."

Huh? Give me a break. Our yard is nice, but Jim had a long way to go to qualify as a master gardener. Jack Cartwright reminded me a little of

Eddie Haskell on *Leave It To Beaver.* Remember him? "That's a lovely dress you're wearing, Mrs. Cleaver." What a suck-up.

Of course, My Beloved reacted to this shameless flattery like a typical guy. The next thing I knew, he and Jack were settled at the dining room table chatting away like old buddies.

I rolled my eyes at Nancy. She, however, pulled up a chair to join them. And had the nerve to pour each of them an Irish coffee.

Jeez.

Was I the only one who thought Jack Cartwright was pushy? And noticed that, when he talked, he never made eye contact with the person he was talking to? He also was adept at bending the truth, if his remark about Jim being a master gardener was any indication of his character.

I ignored that little voice in my head that announced, Takes one to know one.

I was nitpicking. Trying to find fault with the poor guy so I wouldn't have to sell his family our house. Truth to tell, I was also not happy that, if the house sale went through, my persnickety neighbor Sara Miller would have free rein here. I could already hear her, going from room to room with her daughter, criticizing my decorating choices.

Oh, Carol, get a grip.

Jack and Alyssa Cartwright loved our house. And it would be wonderful to have this place filled with a young family again.

So what if his palms were sweaty? He was probably nervous.

Well, what else could I do? I gave in, reluctantly, and accepted the offer. And then I had a large Irish coffee myself.

Sláinte!

The closer we came to moving day, the grumpier I became. And we still hadn't found a permanent place to live. We had a temporary rental, a one-bedroom furnished apartment the size of a shoe box. It was the only place we could find that allowed dogs. As a bonus, we could rent week-to-week, so when we found a property to buy, which I prayed would be soon, there wouldn't be a problem getting out of a lease.

I was making slow-to-no progress with the packing. Jim, cynic that he was, accused me of dragging my feet to delay the closing, which was totally untrue. Since our rental was furnished, we only needed personal items and some clothes to go with us. The rest, including Mike's precious comics, was going into the storage unit since, according to our son, it was impossible for him to come home and do his own packing on such short notice.

At the rate I was going, I'd probably still be packing when the moving truck pulled up to the door.

I needed help – in more ways than one – so I enlisted Jenny. I could always count on my daughter to be sympathetic to my feelings. She even let me whine to my heart's content without criticism. Most of the time.

"I hate the feeling of being unsettled," I said for probably the hundredth time as we worked side by side in the dining room, packing up the good china and crystal. "I wish Dad and I had found a new home before being forced out of our old one."

"You and Dad are more than welcome to move in with me," said my darling daughter as she helped me wrap some Waterford crystal goblets in bubble paper. "Of course, you'd have to sleep on the sofa bed in the living room. Unless I moved in with Mark." She smiled at me mischievously.

I considered my reply carefully, for once. Jenny was a grown-up woman and I had already assumed that her relationship with Mark had progressed beyond the platonic. Was she hinting that a wedding could be in the near future? Nah, that was probably just wishful thinking on my part, coupled with my bad habit of jumping to conclusions.

"That's so nice of you to offer, sweetie," I said, ignoring the chance to ask a few personal questions, which just about killed me. "But I'm afraid that if we moved into a small condo like yours, it might point your father in that direction as a permanent solution. You know his new mantra for a place to live – something we can lock and leave. I'm sure he learned that phrase on HGTV. And what about the dogs? Are they allowed in your complex?"

"The offer's good if you get desperate, Mom. Don't worry about Lucy and Ethel. I've seen other tenants walking dogs, so I'm sure they're allowed.

"Where's Dad this morning? I thought he'd be here helping you pack."

"I wish I knew," I said in frustration. "He was reading the paper this morning as usual. Scissors in hand, just in case he found something to clip. You know how he is."

Jenny laughed and rolled her eyes.

"I was talking about how miserable I felt. Well, I was complaining, really." I sighed. "Poor man, he must be sick of listening to me by now. Anyway, the next thing I knew, he shot out of his chair and said he had to go out for a little while. No explanation. And he's been gone for more than two hours. With all this to do." I gestured around at the growing mass of boxes that seemed to be taking over every part of the house.

The more I thought about Jim's behavior, the madder I got. Here we were, with less than two weeks to go before we moved out, and My Beloved, whose health was the main reason I'd agreed to move in the first place, was nowhere to be found.

"Which would you rather have, Mom?" asked Jenny. "Your husband second-guessing every packing decision you make and driving you crazy, or one who's temporarily a.w.o.l.?"

No contest there.

"When you put it like that, I guess I'm lucky he's out of the house," I agreed. "Let's see how much more we can get done before he shows up to re-organize us."

I heard the kitchen door slam, and the dogs began to bark.

"Too late," said Jenny. "I'll go get the lay of the land. You keep packing. No dilly-dallying."

"Yes, ma'am," I said. "I'll get right back to it, ma'am." Jeez. When did my daughter become so bossy?

I was standing on the step stool, reaching for my good serving platter, which remained maddeningly beyond my grasp, when My Beloved materialized to help.

"Carol, you might fall. I'll get the platter down for you."

I bit back a sarcastic reply, like, "Better late than never," and when Jim handed me the platter, I took a good look at him. He was quivering with excitement, like Lucy and Ethel are when they're anticipating a treat.

Something was definitely up.

"Sit down, honey. I have some great news. You're going to be so happy."

Jim was bouncing up and down on the balls of his feet now.

I swept some bubble wrap off a dining room chair and gave him my complete attention. Lower your expectations, I warned myself, having learned over the years that Jim's idea of great news (a five-cent drop in gas at the pump) and mine (I tried on a Size 6 dress and actually zipped it up) were usually miles apart.

"Eden's Grove had a full-page ad in this morning's paper. You remember that place, right?"

Remember it? How could I forget it? The active adult community that was so "active" I'd need pep pills to keep up with the pace there. To say nothing of their single-pet policy, which had completely turned me off.

I felt a prickle of foreboding.

"They've re-thought their marketing strategy to be more competitive in the current real estate market," My Beloved continued. "The owners have figured out that multi-pet families like ours could expand their potential buyer pool. Especially since all the other active adult communities have a single-pet policy. So they're building a section of free-standing homes that's pet-friendly. It's even going to have a fenced-in dog park. Isn't that a great idea?"

I briefly wondered if the dogs would have scheduled activities as frantic as the humans'.

"Lucy and Ethel will love it there as much as we will. I put down a deposit on a house this morning. All you have to do is sign and we'll be the first home owners in the new section. They may even use us in their advertising to attract other buyers.

"So you don't have to worry anymore about where we're going after we close on this house. It's all set. Isn't that terrific?"

Obviously Jim thought he'd pulled off a huge coup. I wasn't so sure. And I was plenty aggravated that he hadn't consulted me first before making such a major decision.

Of course, I hadn't consulted him when I signed the listing agreement to sell our house, either. But I knew he'd go along with it.

Oh, what the heck. We were moving to a brand new place with top-of-the-line everything and I could keep both dogs.

My Beloved would learn to play golf. We would swim leisurely laps in the pool.

And I could always lock the door and take a long nap if the frantic pace of activities overwhelmed me.

I hoped I'd at least be able to pick the color scheme for our new digs.

Chapter 11

Some people sweat. I'm so glam, I ooze glitter.

The last box had been packed and labeled. The last closet had been emptied. Even the garage looked clean, for the first time in twenty years.

My Beloved and I walked through each room hand in hand, our footsteps echoing in the now-empty house. I was having trouble holding my emotions in check. Even Jim, who is rarely emotional, had tears in his eyes, though he'd never admit it.

"Well, I guess it's time to go," he said.

"Goodbye house. We've loved every minute here."

Hand-in-hand, we walked out the kitchen door and locked it for the last time.

And didn't look back.

I couldn't sleep.

It was a strange bed, with lots of lumps and bumps. Or maybe the lumps and bumps were my aging body. Anyway, this new apartment was going to take some getting used to. Thank God it was only for a few months, until our Eden's Woods house was ready. Assuming it was completed on time, which, according to Nancy was rare in the construction world.

As if sleeping in a lumpy bed wasn't bad enough, I also was having hot flashes for the first time in years. I figured the stress of moving must have activated my power surge mechanism. Rats. Who needed this?

My Beloved, of course, was having no trouble sleeping. His rhythmic snores were a pleasant, familiar sound. Even my tossing and turning didn't disturb him. Lucy and Ethel had adjusted pretty quickly to the new digs, too, each finding a comfortable spot on the bedroom carpeting and zonking out. Ah, a dog's life is one to be envied. Maybe in my next life, I'd come back as one.

I yanked the blanket off and threw my right leg on top of it. I forced myself to think of snow and sleet and polar ice caps.

It was no use. I was still hot and sleep was out of the question. I had to get out of the apartment and get some fresh air.

When my bare feet hit the icy floor, I winced. Now, I was cold. But definitely wide awake. I grabbed my sweats, socks and sneakers and dressed quietly. I was out the door, car keys in hand, in a New York minute.

I sat in my car, motor running, and pondered my options. What would be open at this time of night? A Dunkin' Donuts? The Fairport Diner?

What you don't need, Carol, is a shot of caffeine.

Nah. Who was I kidding? I knew where I was going.

I turned in the direction of my soon-to-be-former home. I was going to give myself a private pity party and walk through it one more time all by myself.

As I drove into our driveway, I wondered fleetingly if I could be charged with breaking and entering. I squelched that thought. It was still our house until we signed the papers at tomorrow morning's closing.

The house looked unloved already. Jim had made arrangements to turn off the electricity – God forbid we would pay an extra dollar to the utility company – so there was no cheery front porch light on to greet me. Luckily for me, I kept a flashlight in my car.

The kitchen door stuck, then squeaked as it swung open.

"Hello, beautiful kitchen," I said as I walked into the dark room. My eyes immediately filled up. "I mean, goodbye, beautiful kitchen," I said. "I'm sure going to miss you."

I straightened my shoulders and ordered myself not to wallow in memories. Easier ordered than done.

I ran my hands over the granite countertops. I remembered so well the day they were installed. And how thrilled I'd been to finally replace all that worn-out Formica.

Sob.

Another memory came, completely out of the blue. Or black, since it was so dark in here, even with the flashlight. This memory was less pleasant. The workmen had measured for the countertops incorrectly. So the first time they tried to install the darn things, the granite was too long. And the second time, when the measurements were correct, one of the installers dropped the piece of granite in the driveway and it shattered into a million pieces. Man, was I angry about that.

OK, so not everything that happened here was fairy-tale perfect.

I allowed myself the luxury of sobbing as I went from room to room. Stupid, I know, but there was no one around to hear me. "Goodbye beautiful fireplaces," I said aloud. So the chimneys weren't lined and we were never able to use most of them. They looked great decorated for the holidays.

Whimper.

Goodbye pine floors, well-scuffed from years of walking by the people I loved.

Sniff.

I touched the doorway which still had faint pencil marks measuring Jenny and Mike's heights. I closed my eyes, and I could almost hear the kids squabbling about who was taller. How I wished I'd taken Nancy's advice and replaced that door molding, so I could take the old piece to our new home

Sob.

On to the dining room, scene of so many wonderful celebrations. Kids' birthday parties. Our wedding anniversaries. Holidays. I bid farewell to my beautiful corner cupboard, the fabulous wainscoting, and the fireplace with its magnificent mantle.

Every year, we put a Christmas tree in the dining room as well as ones in the living room and family room. If I squeezed my eyes just right, I could imagine the lights twinkling in front of the window.

God, now I was crying so hard I needed to sit down on the floor. Maybe this wasn't such a good idea after all.

Come on, Carol, get up. You can do this.

At this rate, by the time I got through all the rooms, the sun would be coming up. I needed to hurry myself along, in order to get back to the apartment and get a little sleep before Closing Day. And, even more important, before My Beloved woke up and figured out I was missing.

I headed across the front hall to the living room. The moon was shining through the sidelights of the front door, so I could see just fine.

Not. I immediately tripped over something on the floor and twisted my ankle.

"Damn it," I said, allowing myself a rare curse word as I massaged my poor foot.

I aimed the flashlight at the offending object and had to laugh. It was a man's shoe. How appropriate, I thought. Jim had a habit of leaving his shoes right in front of every door in the house. He claimed he didn't want to track debris in from the yard. I was always after him to move them out of the way, put them in the closet – anything. Futile. The man simply didn't pick up after himself, anywhere, anytime.

"One of Jim's shoes must have fallen out of a suitcase this afternoon," I told myself, my voice echoing in the empty house. I hated to admit it, but now my house felt kind of spooky.

I continued into the living room. There was a pile of clothing bunched in a corner. Strange. I didn't remember that being there when Jim and I had walked through earlier.

"Those movers really were careless. Jim'll have a fit about this."

The next thing I noticed was Jim's other shoe, peeking out from under the pile of clothes. I smiled. Well, I'd just have to pick up after My Beloved one more time. A fitting way to say goodbye to my house.

Then, I took a closer look.

Oops. This wasn't Jim's shoe after all. Unfortunately, this one had a foot in it. The foot was attached to a man who was quite dead. In my living room.

I didn't know whether to cry or throw up. But my insatiable curiosity won out over my churning stomach, and I shined my flashlight onto the man's face.

The house closing was definitely off.

The dead man was our buyer, Jack Cartwright.

Chapter 12

All men may be different, but all husbands are the same.

The next thing I remember, I was outside on Old Fairport Turnpike, screaming my lungs out. It never occurred to me to use my cell phone to summon help. Nor did I care that it was now probably after midnight.

I guess I'm blessed with a good set of lungs, because within seconds Phyllis and Bill Stevens appeared at their front door, matching plaid bathrobes wrapped tightly around them.

"Who the hell is carrying on like that?" bellowed Bill from his stoop. He switched on his porch light to see what was going on. "Don't you know what time it is? People are trying to sleep."

"Bill, thank God," I cried, happy to see a familiar face even though it was also an angry one. "It's Carol Andrews. I need help. " I ran across the street as fast as my chubby little legs could carry me and threw myself into his arms, sobbing.

"Carol," said Phyllis. "What's wrong?" She looked at me critically, as if a woman babbling in the arms of her husband was something she didn't allow. "What are you doing here at this time of night? Aren't you closing on your house later today? Lord, you look like you've seen a ghost."

"Please," I said, "you've got to call the police right now. There's a dead body in my living room."

"What?" Bill and Phyllis said at exactly the same time. Phyllis leaned close to my face, ever so slightly. Probably checking for a telltale liquor odor on my breath.

"I know this sounds nuts, but you've got to help me," I said. "I came back to the house to do one more walk-through and say goodbye." I blinked back tears, which were falling faster than I could keep up with them. My nose was running too. Jeez. How attractive I must look.

"When I got to the living room, I found a dead body." I paused and a tremor went through my body as I remembered the horrible sight. "Oh, God, it's our buyer, Jack Cartwright."

I started to cry even harder, then – how embarrassing – I started to hiccup. I couldn't stop. I was sure Phyllis thought I'd been drinking.

They led me inside their house and had me sit down on the sofa in the family room. Phyllis gave me a paper bag to breathe into, which she claimed would cure my hiccups. Bill, meanwhile, phoned the police.

The paper bag trick didn't work. I was hiccupping, crying, and sniffling all at the same time. A true mess.

"Does Jim know you came back to the house?" asked Phyllis.

"Jim!" I cried. "I have to let him know what's happened."

There was no way to predict My Beloved's reaction. He could be angry at me for sneaking out and going to the house, scared on my behalf, angry that the closing was off – anything was possible. Especially if he was awakened from a sound sleep. Although, I reminded myself, he'd had more experience with finding dead bodies than I had, since he'd discovered his retirement coach's last summer.

"Bill," I pleaded, hiccupping for added emphasis, "can you please call Jim for me? I'm too upset to make any sense." I held out a scrap of paper. "Here's his cell number."

Good old Bill. He was happy to be given still another prominent role in the melodrama playing out in his family room. He made eye contact with Phyllis, probably asking permission to use the phone again, patted me on the shoulder, and took the cordless phone into the kitchen to make the call.

A few seconds later, the doorbell rang and my nemesis, Paul Wheeler, the shortest and nastiest detective on our town's police force, strode in. Oh, joy. He and I had crossed swords last year. I prayed he wouldn't remember me.

No such luck.

"Don't I know you?" Paul asked me, scowling. "Aren't you Carol Andrews, from across the street?" At least he didn't say, "Aren't you that busybody Carol Andrews?"

"What's this all about?"

Paul gestured for me to sit on the sofa while he remained standing. I immediately realized he was doing that to intimidate me. And that my sitting while he continued to stand was the only way he would ever be taller than I was.

As succinctly as I could, I described the sale of our house, our temporary move into an apartment, my coming back to check the house (I didn't call it a "pity party"), and finding the dead body in my living room. I was proud that my voice was calm, and I just gave the bare facts. No embellishments or opinions.

And, miracle of miracles, my hiccups had disappeared. Paul had accomplished what a paper bag couldn't.

When I came to the part about the identity of the dead man, however, Paul stopped me. "How did you know it was your buyer?" he asked, raising himself up to his full (short) height and attempting to loom over me.

I recognized him, stupid.

I didn't really say that, of course.

At this point, I became aware of flashing lights and activity across the street. More police, no doubt. And the emergency squad, though it was too late to do anything for poor Jack.

"I left my front door open when I ran outside," I explained. I didn't want Paul to think the house had been broken into. In fact, the house had showed no signs of forced entry. I filed that fact away to think about later.

Paul sat down opposite me and made himself comfortable, legs spread apart. He took out his notebook and glared at me. "One more time, and don't leave anything out."

I started to reply, then stopped myself. I wondered if I needed a lawyer. Poor Jim had tried to help the police out last year and ended up being suspected of a crime.

I couldn't help bristling at Paul's tone. It sounded like he was accusing me of misleading him.

OK, I had been guilty of doing that during our previous encounters.

I guess he remembered that, too.

"My husband and I decided to put our house on the market and move to an active adult community." Too much information, Carol. He doesn't care about that.

"The house sold immediately. Perhaps you remember what a beautiful house it is."

I paused to give him a chance to respond, but Paul just looked impatient. I do have a tendency to drag stories out, especially when I'm nervous. Which I certainly was at that moment.

"The house was purchased by a nice young family, the Cartwrights. Jim and I moved out today. I mean, yesterday. The closing was supposed to be tomorrow. I mean today." I knew I wasn't making any sense.

"Anyway, I came back to the house by myself to take a final walk-through. And I found the dead body of our buyer, Jack Cartwright, in our living room. That's all."

"Were you and your husband in agreement about selling the house?" Paul asked me.

"Well, no, actually in the beginning, I didn't want to sell it," I admitted. "In fact, I was really opposed to it."

Paul pounced on my reply.

"So, Mrs. Andrews, perhaps you had a motive to stop the sale of the house. By eliminating the buyer. Permanently."

"Don't answer him, Carol," said My Beloved, racing into the room like Sir Galahad to the rescue. I flung myself into his familiar arms and began to bawl.

"My wife has had a terrible shock," said Jim. "You have no right to make such an outrageous accusation."

The combination of Jim's tone of voice – who knew My Beloved could be so forceful? – and my continued crying stopped the questioning for a brief moment.

And then, Paul's cell phone rang. Not just any ring, mind you, but the song "Bad Boys," the theme from the television show *Cops.* Words as well as music. And I quote, "Whatcha going to do when they come for you? Bad boys, bad boys." It made me laugh. I couldn't stop myself. OK, by that time I was probably verging on hysteria, but it was so ridiculous. Fairport Detective Paul Wheeler, television-reality-show-star-wanna-be.

He listened to whomever was on the other end of the phone, then snapped it shut. "I was only thinking out loud," he said to us. "I wasn't accusing anyone of a crime. Yet. It's much too early for that."

Was it my imagination, or had Paul emphasized the word "yet"?

"You'll have to come down to the station in the morning and sign a formal statement, Mrs. Andrews. I need to get over to the crime scene now."

The crime scene, a.k.a. my beautiful living room. Oh, God.

Jim glared at Paul. "I resent that implication. There's no way of knowing that this is a crime. It could be just an unfortunate accident."

As we were leaving, I remembered my manners and thanked Bill and Phyllis profusely for their help. I knew they were glad to see us go. But I suspected the thrill of being involved in a possible crime, however vicariously, would make them the center of a neighborhood drama for a long time to come.

Jim put his arm around my shoulder and guided me out of the room. "Come on, Carol, let's go home."

I looked at him blankly. "Go home, Jim? Where the heck is that?"

Chapter 13

Some days are a complete waste of makeup.

"Oh my God, Carol. This is terrible." Nancy's voice was even shriller than usual. "Why didn't you call me? I couldn't believe it when I heard the news this morning. This has never happened to me before."

"Gee, what a coincidence," I answered. "It's never happened to me before either."

Nancy was instantly contrite. "Sweetie, I'm sorry. I'm not thinking clearly. It must have been horrible for you, finding Jack Cartwright like that. But what in the world were you thinking, to go back to the house all alone at that time of night?"

I started to cry. If there was one thing I didn't need right now, it was someone else interrogating me about my actions the previous night.

"I shouldn't have to defend myself to you, of all people," I said. "First the police, then Jim, and now you, all asking me the same question. I wanted to say goodbye to my house. Alone. You know how hard it's been for me to let go of it."

I reached across the Formica kitchen counter and grabbed a napkin to mop my leaking eyes.

"And besides," I continued, "even if I hadn't gone back to the house, Jack would still be dead. I just wouldn't have had the bad luck to find him. That's what I've been trying to explain to Jim. Over and over and over. It was an unfortunate coincidence. But he doesn't get it."

I started to cry all over again. Lucy and Ethel nuzzled my legs, showing that they, at least, were on my side.

"I'm sure Jim gets it, Carol," Nancy said. "He's just scared for you, and probably feels terrible about what you went through last night. And he can't do anything to fix it. You know how men are. They have a lot of trouble giving emotional support to the people they love. But that doesn't mean they don't care."

"You may be right," I conceded. "He was terrific last night when that twerpy detective, Paul Wheeler, was putting the thumb screws to me. Just my luck that he was on duty and heard the nine-one-one call.

"Neither one of us got much sleep," I continued. "Between the shock of finding Jack Cartwright, and sleeping in a strange bed, I feel like I didn't close my eyes for more than ten minutes. We let Lucy and Ethel climb into bed with us, and I guess we must have finally fallen asleep."

"Where's Jim now?" Nancy asked. "Is he still in bed?"

"You must be kidding," I said. "Don't you remember how small this place is? If he was still here, I wouldn't be able to talk without him interrupting me."

I felt better already. Sharing the trauma of last night with my best friend had put things into perspective for me. The authorities were dealing with Jack Cartwright's tragic death. I had other things on my mind.

"I know Jim's going to ask about this when he comes back," I said. "What happens now about the house sale? Is it off? Is the closing just postponed? How do we find out what's happening? God, I feel so selfish asking about this under the circumstances."

"I think we can safely assume that the closing is off, at least for today," Nancy said, with more than a touch of sarcasm in her voice. "But buyers can be very funny. It's possible that Alyssa Cartwright may decide to go ahead with the purchase after all, once the shock of Jack's death wears off. We can't assume anything."

I bit my lip. She was right. But I hated the idea of just sitting around doing nothing.

"How about this?" Nancy suggested. "I'll contact the Cartwrights' Realtor and see what she knows. I'll also check with Tim Casey, the Dream Homes attorney. He may have some idea about how and when to proceed. He was going to handle your house closing anyway, so he's familiar with the deal."

"Just not this part of it," I retorted. "I doubt if he's ever had to deal with anything like this before."

"You never know. I'll be back in touch as soon as I know something." She clicked off.

I was starting to get a headache. Whether it was from lack of sleep, finding Jack Cartwright, or caffeine deprivation didn't matter. I wasn't about to go back to bed and risk dreaming about my late night adventure.

Maybe My Beloved had gone out for coffee and (hopefully) was going to bring back a gallon or two of high test to share with me. But I couldn't wait that long.

"All right, girls," I said to Lucy and Ethel, who were still snoozing on the bed. "We have to unpack a box and hope our coffee pot is in it. Keep your paws crossed."

They telegraphed me a look which clearly said, *Forget the coffee pot. Find the dog food and feed us breakfast.*

"Sorry, kids, but humans come first this morning. And don't get too used to sleeping on the bed. Last night was an exception."

I squinted at the pile of boxes. I thought I'd been so organized, but I couldn't find the one that was marked "Kitchen."

Rats.

I did see the one marked "Dogs," however. "I guess that proves who are more important around here," I said. As if there was ever any doubt.

I rummaged around for a water bowl and paper plates. The dogs came tearing into the kitchen and danced around my legs. *See,* they said. *We knew we'd get fed first.*

"Not so fast, chums" I said. "You have to go out first. And on leashes. We're not home any more."

I opened the door with my two canines in tow and found two thermoses of coffee on the front steps, one labeled "regular" and the other "decaf." Ah, heaven! There was a note from My Beloved taped to a bag of muffins.

"I thought you needed to start the day with an extra bonus, so I made an early morning drive to The Paperback Café and picked up some goodies for you. I'm going to drive around for a while and try to sort out what's happened. Be back soon. Love, J."

"Well, isn't this the nicest thing?" I asked Lucy and Ethel as they sniffed around the small patch of grass in front of the apartment trying to find an appropriate spot to do their doggy business. "What a great guy. I feel better already.

"Let's go inside and get breakfast for all of us. You get served first, as soon as I pour myself a full cup of regular. No diluting it with decaf this morning. I need all the caffeine I can get."

I tossed each dog a Milk Bone, then rummaged in a drawer looking for a can opener. It seemed so strange not to know where everything was. "You're going to have to be patient with me," I said. "We're not home any more, and I have to hunt for things."

"How about if we turn on the television while we eat, girls? If I can find the remote control, that is."

The furnished apartment came equipped with only the bare essentials, and cable television was not one of them. My Beloved hadn't wanted to spring for the extra connection cost – no surprise. "It makes no sense, Carol," he'd said. "We're only going to be here a short time. We'll have to settle for over-the-air channels for a little while."

I wondered how he'd like it when he figured out that he wasn't going to be able to get his beloved Red Sox games on NESN. I smiled at the thought.

After fruitlessly surfing through all the channels, I settled for the local station from Fairport Community College. No choice. It was the only one

I could get without snow. Not that I cared. I just wanted to hear another human voice.

I was only half concentrating until I heard the reporter say, "I'm standing in front of where local police are saying a body was discovered last night. The empty house is for sale, and it looks like people are dying to buy it." He paused to give his unseen audience a chance to appreciate his comedic genius.

"This is the home's owner," the reporter went on, turning to the person beside him. "Do you have any comment, Mr. Andrews?'

I only had a millisecond to react before the reporter stuck a microphone in the face of My Beloved. And Jenny was standing right beside him.

Chapter 14

I may not be a housewife, but I sure am desperate.

"Mom, you should have called me!"

Immediately after the television interview, Jenny had driven to our temporary digs and was now letting me have it with both barrels.

I don't think I've ever seen Jenny so angry at me. Except for the time when I accidentally threw out her treasured U2 hoodie. How was I to know it'd been tossed to her by Bono himself during a once-in-a-lifetime concert? She did forgive me, but it took two weeks before our relationship was back to normal.

This situation could take longer to heal.

Don't say what you were really thinking, Carol –that you weren't sure where she was at that time of night. Jenny had made it clear that part of her life was not something she intended to share with her parents, and Jim and I made every effort to respect her privacy.

"It was so late, sweetie," I said in my defense. "And I didn't want to upset you." Remembering the horrible scene in my beautiful house made me start to tremble. "It was awful, finding Jack Cartwright dead.

"Your father has been on my case about it, too. What I really need from everyone is a little sympathy and support. He keeps asking me over and over why I went back to the house in the middle of the night. He can't get it through his thick skull that I just wanted to say goodbye to our house. Alone. You understand, don't you honey?"

I started to cry. Again. I hate myself when I act that way, but I couldn't stand to have Jenny mad at me, too.

Lucy and Ethel, always in tune with the Andrews family's emotional temperature, came over and gave my hand wet kisses. Then they looked at Jenny with what was – I swear – a reproachful expression. It was crystal clear to me what they were communicating: *How can you be so angry at your mother, who is the most wonderful human being on earth? Especially when she's had such a major shock?*

Jenny reached out her hands. Both dogs came to her side and gave her a tentative sniff. And waited.

"OK, you guys," Jenny said, laughing. "I can tell whose side you're on. And that you want Mom and me to make up. Our own personal mediators."

"The hand that wields the can opener rules the house," I said. "Barack Obama could probably use Lucy and Ethel to settle the Middle-East conflict."

"He has Bo now, remember?" said Jenny. "I've heard that Portuguese water dogs are better at negotiating than English cockers."

She gave me a quick hug. "Sorry I got a little carried away, Mom. I was just so upset when I found out what happened last night. It must have been awful for you. Do you feel up to talking about it? I promise not to interrupt. Much. I am your daughter, after all, and you know neither one of us can keep quiet for very long."

I had to laugh. "Sad, but true. I've also been told that I take twenty minutes to tell a story when it could be done in less than five. Oh, well."

As I repeated my story for what seemed like the umpteenth time, I realized how unbelievable it sounded. Middle-aged (OK, late middle-aged) housewife returns to visit her about-to-be-sold home alone, late at night, and discovers the dead body of her home's buyer in her living room. I didn't think Home and Garden Television had a program that covered those circumstances.

"Were there any signs of a fight?" Jenny asked. "Mark is always talking about how important it is to notice every detail at the scene of a suspicious death, no matter how small it may seem."

"I didn't notice anything except Jack," I said. "Of course, at first I didn't know it was a person. I thought one of the movers had accidentally dropped some clothing."

I shuddered. "I can't talk about this any more. Let me make us both a cup of green tea." I jumped up and headed in the direction of the kitchen. After opening and closing the three small cupboards, I gave up. "I can't find a tea kettle. How's that for stupidity. I'm going to have to use a pot to boil the water. I don't think I can find any tea either."

"Forget the tea, Mom," Jenny said. "I promise I won't ask you any more questions about last night. Girl Scout's honor. I have to leave for campus in about fifteen minutes."

"I hate green tea, anyway," I said. "It tastes like medicine. Yuck." I wrinkled my nose for emphasis.

"Do you think Mark would know anything about the investigation?" I asked hopefully. "I have to go to the police station today and give a formal statement about what happened last night. It'd sure help me if he was there." It'd be even better if he came here and with a fill-in-the-blanks statement for me to sign. Or, better yet, tell me that a formal statement wasn't necessary at all. He'd certainly been helpful to My Beloved in the past.

Not that I was pushing my luck.

"Even though Mark and Paul both joined the Fairport police, they don't always work on the same cases," Jenny reminded me.

"But he couldn't be involved in this, no matter what. Because Mark and I are, well, because he and I *are*. You know what I mean. So you won't be able to pump him for information."

Humph. The implication that I would take advantage of Mark's and Jenny's relationship was totally out of line. And exactly what did Jenny mean by the phrase, "Mark and I *are*." Are what? Good friends? A couple?

Neighbors with benefits? Engaged? If nothing else, Jenny had successfully distracted my thought process.

"What do you know about Alyssa Cartwright?" I asked. "Was she in your class? Or Mike's? Of course, she would have been Alyssa Miller then. I don't seem to remember much about her."

"Alyssa didn't go to school with either Mike or me," Jenny said. "She was home-schooled until eighth grade, and then went away to some boarding school in Massachusetts. I always thought that was odd."

"Now I remember," I said. "She's an only child, and Sara and Chuck were very protective of her.

"God, I can't imagine what that family must be going through today. Do you think I should call and see how everyone is?"

"It might be better to wait a while, Mom," advised Jenny. "You can't predict what kind of a reception you'll get."

"Why, sweetie, that's just plain crazy," I said, conveniently disregarding the very opinion I had asked my daughter for. "Sara and I are friends. We've been neighbors for over twenty years. She's even part of our regular Bunco group. We may not be as close as Nancy and I are, but we're friends. I'm sure she'll be glad to hear from me. Maybe I can even arrange for some food to be delivered."

I felt better. I had a plan of action. Plus, I was doing a good deed.

"Yes, that's what I'll do. I'll call Sara first and express our condolences. Then I'll call Maria's Trattoria and have food delivered to the family. I know Sara's a gourmet cook, but everyone loves the food at Maria's."

"I'm not sure calling the Millers is a good idea, Mom," said Jenny. "But I know you when your mind's made up." She gave me a quick peck on the cheek. "I have to go. For God's sake, don't get into any more trouble today."

She threw her arms around me and gave me a crushing hug.

"Mom, I love you so much. I'm sorry if I yelled at you before. But I can't imagine my life without you in it." Then, she was gone.

"How about that?" I said to Lucy and Ethel. "I don't think she's ever said that to me before. At least, not for a long time." We are not an overly demonstrative family.

I hesitated, mulling over Jenny's words of caution. To call, or not to call. That was the question. Heck, I knew Sara. She probably thought it was odd that I hadn't called already.

Three rings. Four rings. Five rings. Six rings. Then, the Millers' voice mail kicked in. I realized it was possible they were screening calls, and perhaps they hadn't recognized my number, because I was using a cell phone.

"Sara, it's Carol. I'm calling because I wanted you all to know how terribly sorry Jim and I are about this tragedy. You must all be beside yourselves."

I hear a click, then a high-pitched female voice which I identified as Sara's.

"Sorry, Carol? You called to say you and Jim are *sorry* about this tragedy," she said, mimicking me and throwing my words back at me.

"Because of you and Jim, and that awful, rundown house of yours, my beautiful daughter…" her voice cracked. "My beautiful daughter is now a widow. And my two precious grandchildren will grow up without a father.

"Sorry? You bet you and Jim are going to be sorry. Chuck and I are going to see to it personally. That old wreck of a house was full of accidents just waiting to happen. We're going to sue you for criminal negligence. And if I can convince the police, you'll be charged with manslaughter, too.

"You'll be hearing from our attorney. And don't call here again."

Then she banged the phone down in my ear.

Chapter 15

I can do anything with the right shoes.

I'm not going to lie to you. My first reaction to an outburst like this has always been to burst into tears. I bet you're sick of hearing me admit this by now. But I just hate it when someone is mad at me. Sometimes I think my tear ducts are on automatic pilot, like a sprinkler system set to water the lawn at a certain time of day.

This time was different, though, because I finally realized I'd shed too many tears in the last twelve hours. And I wasn't going to be a cry baby any more.

So, I got angry.

Damn it, I sold my beautiful house out of selfless love for My Beloved. To protect him and his health. To ensure that "Till death do us part" didn't come earlier than absolutely necessary. And what did I get for thanks? A dead body.

Wasn't it bad enough that I had discovered Jack's body in my house? Didn't anyone care how traumatic that was for me? And then to be cross-examined by that little pipsqueak of a detective, like Jack's death was my fault.

And finally, having my good friend – well, that was stretching it just a bit – having my neighbor Sara Miller accuse Jim and me of criminal negligence, which resulted in her son-in-law's death. How dare she?

The more I thought about it, the madder I got.

Well, after that phone call, I certainly wasn't going to send any food over to comfort the family. In her current frame of mind, Sara would probably think I was trying to poison them.

But then, I realized this wasn't really Sara talking. Who could blame her for lashing out at me under the circumstances?

I needed to talk to Mary Alice. She was the only one of my friends who could give me advice on dealing with Sara, since she'd had so much experience as a nurse counseling grieving families. Plus dealing with her own personal heartbreak.

When her voice mail came on, I hesitated. I wasn't sure what to say that wouldn't upset her. Probably telling her that I had discovered a dead body in my living room wasn't the best message to leave.

I forced myself to sound normal. "Hi Mary Alice. It's Carol. A little problem has come up that I really need to talk to you about. Could you call me back as soon as you get this message? Thanks."

I hoped that would do the trick. But I knew Mary Alice wasn't nearly as anal as I was about checking either voice mail or e-mail messages.

"Let's give her an hour," I said to the dogs. "If we haven't heard from her, we'll call her again. Meanwhile, we've got some unpacking to do." I knew I also had to go to the police station sometime today and give a formal statement. But I was in no rush to do that, and certainly wouldn't go without My Beloved as moral support.

I was on my hands and knees searching through a box labeled "Emergency Supplies" when the phone rang. I scrambled to my feet and, as I did, felt a searing pain shoot through my lower back. Rats. It would probably take at least two weeks before I was back to "normal."

I dropped back onto my knees and willed myself to ignore the pain as I grabbed for the phone.

"Hello, hello. Mary Alice? Thank God you called me back so quickly."

"This is Detective Paul Wheeler of the Fairport Police," said the voice at the other end of the phone. "What time this morning will you be at the police station to answer more questions about last night's incident at your home? I expected to see you by now."

I started to speak, but he interrupted me.

"I'm sure you want to cooperate with the police. Unless you have something to hide, of course."

Give me a break.

A variety of responses flashed across my mind in a millisecond, ranging from smartass to sniveling and pathetic. He's just trying to goad you, Carol. Don't let him get to you.

"Why, Paul, I'm so glad you called," I said in what My Beloved refers to as my saccharine voice. "I'm looking forward to answering your questions and getting any confusion straightened out as soon as possible." Yes, sirree. I can't wait until you shine a bright light in my eyes and put the thumbscrews to me.

"I'll be there by eleven-thirty, if that's convenient."

"Be on time," he said. And then I heard the dial tone.

"He is unbelievably rude," I said to the dogs. "And to think that Jim and I are taxpayers and pay his salary." Hmm, that was an interesting thought. Maybe I could get the little twerp fired. A pleasant fantasy, but there was no time to dwell on that now.

"If I can find bath towels and soap, I'm going to take a shower and get down to police headquarters," I announced to the dogs. "And if Jim doesn't show up by the time I leave, I'm going alone."

Lucy and Ethel gave me doggy stares. They know me too well.

"You're right," I said. "I can't go alone. I need support. I'm dreading this.

"You can both come with me." I swear, Lucy's tail began to wag. "But you can't come into the police station. The way my luck is going, one of you might accidentally nip a policeman and I'll be thrown in jail."

As things turned out, My Beloved arrived back at our temporary digs just as I was loading the dogs into the car.

"Nice television appearance, Jim," I said. "How did you get trapped into it? I didn't know you were going back to the house this morning."

Jim became defensive. "I didn't think it would do any harm to go back to the house and see if the police were still there. When that college kid came with his camera crew, I didn't think it was a big deal to answer his questions. After all, I've prepped lots of clients for television appearances over the years. How did I know the kid would turn out to be so aggressive? He must have taken interview lessons from Jerry Springer, for God's sake.

"Where are you and the dogs off to?" he asked, neatly changing the subject.

"No where fun," I replied. "I have to go to police headquarters and sign a statement, remember? That obnoxious Paul Wheeler has already called to remind me to get over there pronto. Oh, and wait till I tell you what happened with Sara Miller."

Rats. Don't tell him about that now, Carol. Are you crazy?

Luckily, by that time Jim had turned away so I was talking to his back. "Wait a few minutes and I'll go with you," he said. "I don't want you facing the police alone.

"It's not like we have any other place to go this morning, like to the lawyer's office to close on the house."

I'd driven by the Fairport Police Station hundreds of times over the years. Slowly, of course. Didn't want my lead foot to get me arrested for speeding.

The building looked like it had been designed by someone with no architectural knowledge except what he got playing with Tinker Toys as a child. The money it cost the town to build our police station was a sticking point in the craw of many a resident, including My Beloved – a fiscal conservative to the core.

"This monstrosity is a perfect example of why our taxes are so high," groused Jim.

I ignored him. The butterflies in my stomach were increasing and multiplying as we got closer to the front door of the station. The only experience I'd had with interrogation were from My Beloved. "Where did you get that ...? How much did you pay for it? Did you really need it?" Etc. etc. ad nauseum. Any wife worth her wedding ring knows that drill. I figured that, with all those years of practice dodging those questions, a police interrogation would be a piece of cake.

I willed myself to relax. Hah!

Go in and get it over with, I told myself. You have nothing to hide.

"Wow," I exclaimed as I caught sight of the spacious lobby for the first time. "This is a lot nicer than I expected. Check out the fancy furniture. It looks like it's real leather."

"Humph," said My Beloved. "Another exorbitant example of wasting the taxpayers' money." I could see the wheels turning in his head. It looked like Jim had a subject for his next "State of the Town" column. He loves pointing out examples of fiscal incompetence whenever he gets the chance.

Unfortunately, he does it with me too, but let's not get into that now.

The receptionist looked up from filing her nails and pushed back the glass window separating her from possible felons. I wondered if it was bulletproof glass.

"May I help you?" she asked in an overly perky tone. I guess we didn't look too threatening.

"I'm Mrs. Carol Andrews," I said. "I'm here to see Detective Paul Wheeler. He's expecting me."

"Oh, Carol, yes," she said. "Detective Wheeler will be with you shortly." She gestured toward chairs across the lobby. "Have a seat and I'll tell him you're here." She looked quizzically at Jim. "And you are?"

"He's *Mr.* Andrews," I said. "I'm *Mrs.* Andrews. And you are?"

The receptionist gave me a puzzled look, then said, "I'll buzz Detective Wheeler for you now."

"Honestly," I said to Jim as I attempted to get comfortable on the chair's slippery leather seat, "that's one thing that really bugs me. That receptionist is young enough to be our daughter, for Pete's sake. Who told her she could call me by my first name?"

"May I offer you some coffee while you wait?" asked our hostess, whose name badge read Tammy.

Even though it had been less than an hour since my last cup, I figured another shot of caffeine couldn't hurt. Besides, I wanted to find out for myself if all those tales of horrific police station coffee were true.

"Dunkin' Donuts or Starbucks?" Tammy continued. "Regular or decaf? Cappuccino, espresso, latte? Skim milk? Cream? Sugar?" She gave us a toothy smile. "We just got a new coffee machine. I've been dying to try it out."

Jim interrupted her. "No thanks. I thought this was a police station, not a damn coffee bar!"

"Suit yourself." Tammy slammed the window shut and resumed her manicure.

I don't know how long we sat there, but it seemed like an eternity. I found myself wishing I'd brought a book along to pass the time. At one point I whispered to Jim, "Where is everybody? I know we don't have a lot of crime in Fairport, but I never thought we'd be the only ones here."

"Maybe they bring the serious criminals in by the back door," My Beloved replied.

The waiting time continued with no end in sight, and Jim began to shift in his chair. If there's one thing My Beloved hates more than wasting money, it's wasting time.

Tammy slid open her window again. "The rest room is all the way down the hall on the right hand side," she announced.

Jim flushed scarlet. I couldn't tell if it was from anger or embarrassment. But either way, I knew we were getting into dangerous waters.

"Don't respond," I whispered, and squeezed his hand.

At least I wasn't nervous any more. Well, not as much.

The phone buzzed again.

"Yes, sir, I'll tell her. Right away."

Tammy had the grace to look embarrassed when she relayed the message. "Detective Wheeler is on his way back to the scene of the incident. He's asked that you meet him there."

"God, what a jerk," Jim said, grabbing my hand and pulling me out of my chair. "Come on, Carol. Let's go home."

"I never liked yellow and green together," I said to My Beloved as we pulled into our yard. The yellow "Police Line, Do Not Cross" tape was stretched across our green picket fence. A small group of curious neighbors walked by and pretended they didn't see us.

"Let's get this over with, Carol," said Jim. "At least we're on our own turf. That should make the questioning a little easier on you."

"You wouldn't say that if you'd been here last night," I shot back, then immediately regretted it.

Sometimes my mouth has a mind of its own. He's only trying to help, I reminded myself. Cut the guy some slack.

Lucy and Ethel began to bark and hop around in the back of our Jeep. They knew they were back in their own yard and were dying to run around.

"All right, you guys," I said, opening the tailgate so they could hop out. And buying myself a little more time before I went into the house. My stomach was doing flip flops again. I hadn't felt so queasy since I was pregnant with Mike. Which reminded me.

"I haven't heard from Mike all week," I said to Jim. "Have you? I worry when we don't hear from him."

"He's probably still sulking over his precious comic book collection," Jim replied. "He'll e-mail or call us soon.

"Come on, let's get this over with. You'll feel much better then," My Beloved said, taking my arm and propelling me toward our side door.

Once again I found myself in my empty kitchen, but I had no chance to wallow in self-pity this time. Detective Paul pounced on us as soon as we walked in the door.

"We don't need you here, Mr. Andrews," he said. "Please wait outside."

Jim immediately began to sputter, and I intervened. I don't read all those mystery books for nothing.

"If Jim can't stay, I'm going to call our lawyer," I said. "I'm not going through this interview without some support." And protection, I added silently.

"And, by the way, I think you owe us an apology for keeping us waiting at the police station all that time, and then ordering us to meet you here instead."

I fixed him with my official mommy stare, the one that used to strike fear into my kids when they'd done something wrong and I'd caught them.

"All right, he can stay," Paul said grudgingly, making it clear he was doing us a huge favor. "But no interfering with my questioning," he ordered Jim.

"Now," addressing me, "show me exactly what you did last night. And don't leave anything out." He brandished a tape recorder. "I'm going to tape what you tell me."

That frightened me. "Why are you taping me?" I asked. "Last year when I was interviewed, you and Mark took notes."

Oops, that was stupid, Carol. No need to remind him that you've been through a police interrogation before.

"The last time, you weren't directly involved in the situation. This time, you are."

I took a deep breath and began my story. Again. Truth to tell, I was getting a little sick of telling it, so I'm not going to bore you with all the details of my "interrogation." Suffice it to say that it took a lot longer than it should have, mainly due to the fact that My Beloved, who had been told to keep his mouth shut during the interview, kept interrupting Paul's questions with some of his own. At times, it was hard to figure out who was conducting the interview. Every time I started to explain what I did, when I did it, and where I did it, Jim would jump in and ask something like, "Why did you do that, Carol?" Or "I don't understand how you could have done that. It makes no sense to me."

By this time, they were both beginning to grate on my nerves. I mean, whose side was My Beloved on, anyway?

I was just about to tell both of them to knock it off when I heard the kitchen door open.

Mary Alice came running into the house and threw her arms around me. "Carol, what's going on? I waited here for you for half an hour last night. Where were you? Why is there police tape outside the house?"

Chapter 16

Let's all assume I know everything and get this over with.

I don't know which surprised me more – Mary Alice's sudden appearance or what she blurted out. And I didn't have a clue what she was talking about.

Detective Paul switched off the tape recorder. I could imagine what he was thinking. Not only did he get to grill me, but now another possible witness had dropped in. His lucky day.

"Why is everybody staring at me like that?" Mary Alice asked. "What did I say?"

To his credit, My Beloved stepped in to ease the situation before Paul could answer.

"There's been a little hitch in the house sale," Jim said in a masterstroke of understatement. "Our buyer had an accident here last night, and…"

"That's enough, Mr. Andrews," said Paul. Turning to Mary Alice, he said, "I'm Detective Paul Wheeler of the Fairport police. Who are you?"

"This is Mary Alice Costello," I said, putting my arm around her shoulder. "She's one of my best friends.

"Though I don't know why you thought we were meeting here last night," I continued. "Did I ask you to come?"

"I'll ask the questions," said Paul with obvious impatience.

"I have enough information to prepare a statement for you to sign, Mrs. Andrews. You two can leave now. I want to talk to Mrs. Costello alone.

"This is still our house," said Jim. "We're not going anywhere. Any questions you ask Mary Alice you'll do in front of us."

Whoa, Jim. Way to go. Although I feared that his sudden burst of bravado wouldn't sit too well with Paul. I didn't want to be hauled back to the police station again, even if there was fresh latte being brewed just for us.

Jim was right, though. This still was our house. So I switched into a familiar role – hostess.

"Why don't we all sit down?" I suggested. I looked around and realized that there wasn't a single stick of furniture left. The only thing I could come up with was the front staircase. Well, it would have to do.

"Come on," I patted the lowest step, "sit beside me, Mary Alice." And tell me what the heck you meant about meeting me here last night. Are you trying to get into trouble with the police, too?

I didn't really say that, of course.

"I'll stand," said Paul. Of course, he would stand. It was the only way he'd be taller than the rest of us. He switched on the tape recorder again. "I'm continuing to record this. Now, once again, give me your name and relationship to the Andrews family."

"I'm Mary Alice Costello, and I've been a close friend of Carol's and Jim's for over thirty-five years. But I don't understand why you're asking me these questions. Can someone please tell me what's going on?"

"All in good time," said Paul. "Now, you say you were here at the Andrews home last night? For what reason?"

"I came to meet Carol." She looked at me, questioning whether it was OK to go on. Since I had no clue what she was going to say, I nodded my head.

"Carol and Jim sold their house, and the closing is today. The idea of leaving the home where they had raised their kids was especially hard for her. So we came up with the idea of hiding something small in the house that would be meaningful, so that a part of the Andrews family would always be here.

"Don't you remember, Carol? You saw this suggestion on *New England Dream House.* It was about tips to conquer seller's remorse."

Say what? This was news to me. Of course, with all the stress of packing and moving, I could have forgotten.

I started to ask her a question, but Detective Paul stopped me.

"Don't interrupt, Mrs. Andrews," said Paul.

He then began to barrage her with questions himself, the little jerk.

"What time did you arrive? Did you see anything out of the ordinary when you got here? What time did you leave? Can you prove what time you left?"

To her credit, Mary Alice didn't lose her cool. I remember she told me once that, whenever someone gave her a hard time, she pictured him in a hospital Johnny gown that was way too small. I figured she was using that technique now. I pushed that image out of my mind. It was too ugly a picture for me!

"I got here at ten-thirty, which is the time Carol and I had agreed to meet," Mary Alice said. "I waited for half an hour, and she didn't come. I figured she'd changed her mind, so I went home. I didn't try to call her, because I know ten-thirty's past her usual bedtime and I didn't want to take a chance on waking her up."

She flashed me a quick smile, which I returned.

"Did you go into the house?" Paul asked, not giving Mary Alice a chance to catch her breath.

"Of course I didn't," she answered with obvious impatience. "Why would I? How could I? It was all locked up and nobody was around. I sat in my car and waited for Carol."

At that point, a canine chorus from Lucy and Ethel began from outside. I had completely forgotten about them.

"Jim, would you…?"

The side door opened again and the dogs raced into the house, followed by Nancy.

Bless their doggy hearts, they immediately ran to Paul and gave him a thorough sniff. *Friend or foe*, they wanted to know? *And what's he doing in our house?*

They accomplished in a matter of seconds what I'd been trying to do since I walked back into my house. Paul immediately brushed away the dogs and turned off his tape recorder.

"I'll type up these statements and get them to you to sign."

He couldn't get out of the house fast enough.

Never trust a man who doesn't like dogs.

There are two spots in Fairport, in addition to The Paperback Café, that my group of friends patronize on a regular basis: Crimpers, our local hair salon, and Maria's Trattoria, which specializes in the best Northern Italian food around and is run by one of our kids' former teachers, Maria Lesco.

Deciding that the situation would look brighter after we had a good meal – especially one that we didn't have to cook ourselves or clean up after – Nancy, Mary Alice and I were settled into a corner table at Maria's. Jim had elected to take the dogs back to our temporary digs. I think the idea of having lunch with three women was too much for him to handle on top of everything else that had happened. Not that I could blame him.

"This is unbelievable," Mary Alice said for the umpteenth time. "If only I'd looked in the living room window. It just never occurred to me."

"There was nothing you could have done," I reassured her. "Don't beat yourself up about it. It was just an unfortunate accident.

"Besides, I have more things to feel guilty about than you do. If I'd remembered I was supposed to meet you last night, maybe we would have found Jack in time to save him. But instead, I decided to go back to the house later for my own private pity party, and look at the mess Jim and I are in now. And I didn't tell you that Sara Miller's threatening to sue us for negligence."

I looked at Nancy, who had remained unusually quiet so far. "Can the family really do that?"

"I have good news and bad news," Nancy replied, toying with her coffee spoon. "Which do you want to hear first?"

I'm always one to take the bad news first. That way, the good news sounds even better.

"Our attorney called the Cartwrights' attorney this morning to get a preliminary read on the situation," Nancy said. "Poor guy. He hasn't had much experience with a situation like this."

Nancy reached over and squeezed my hand. "Not that I'm suggesting that you have, sweetie."

"Thanks. I think."

"Well, what's going to happen about the house sale?" asked Mary Alice.

"It looks like the sale is off," Nancy said. "At least, that's what the Cartwrights' attorney implied. He didn't say anything about a lawsuit, though."

"Small comfort," I said. "Is that supposed to make me feel better?"

"I think Sara's threat about a lawsuit was just grief talking," said Mary Alice. "She's very upset, and took it out on you."

"Mary Alice is right," said Nancy. "Remember that your house passed inspection with no trouble at all. If there had been any potential hazards there, the inspector would have found them. And you and Jim would have fixed them."

Jim! The man who's made penny-pinching his life's work.

"Jim's going to freak when he finds out the sale is definitely off, and we are now the proud owners of not one, but two houses. I don't know how we're going to afford this. How soon can the house go back on the market? Can it happen today?"

Nancy paused and took a deep breath. "Here's the other piece of the bad news. Your house is now what we call in the real estate business 'psychologically impacted.' That means something dire has happened in it – in this case, the potential buyer has died on the premises under somewhat suspicious circumstances – and that has to be disclosed to potential buyers. It often makes a property difficult, if not impossible to sell."

I gaped at Nancy. "Are you telling me that we can't sell our house? Ever? I thought what I went through last night was bad. But this…this is even worse. What are we going to do?"

At that moment, the cell phone in my purse began to play my favorite Four Seasons' song, "Big Girls Don't Cry," which had taken on a whole new meaning in the last 24 hours.

"Carol honey, it's Claire. I'll bet you and Nancy and Mary Alice are at Maria's celebrating the house sale. God, I wish I was there. I miss all of you."

I started to cry. Again. And handed my phone over to Mary Alice. "It's Claire. Can you talk to her and tell her what's happened? I just can't deal with it."

"Let me handle it," said Nancy, snatching the phone away from Mary Alice. "You'll take too long to get to the point. I'll go outside to talk to her. You deal with Carol. Try to calm her down, if you can."

Mary Alice glared at Nancy's retreating back. "Well!" she huffed. "It's a good thing we're friends or I'd follow her outside and give her a smack upside the head.

"Here, Carol," she said, handing me a fresh tissue. "Wipe your eyes. And look on the bright side."

"The bright side," I said, my response muffled by the tissue. "And what would that be?"

"Why, you were smart enough to wear waterproof eye makeup this morning, of course," said Mary Alice. "You always plan ahead."

"It's comforting to know that I don't have raccoon eyes," I said, massaging my right temple. "I have a splitting headache. Do you have any drugs with you?"

Mary Alice looked at me like I was crazy.

"Not hard drugs, Mary Alice. I didn't mean it that way. I just need some aspirin. You usually have something in your purse."

"What you need is some food," Mary Alice said. "When you get something in your stomach besides coffee, you're bound to feel better.

"Nancy's coming back. Don't worry. I'm not really going to smack her."

"Well, that's all taken care of," Nancy said, sliding into her chair and handing me back my phone. "Claire's very worried about you and Jim, sweetie. God, she asks a lot of questions! Probably because she's married to an attorney.

"She did have a suggestion, which I hope will be all right with you, Carol, because I told her to go ahead." She paused and took a sip of her now cold coffee.

"Ugh," she said, signaling the waitress for a fresh cup. "Did you two order already?" Mary Alice was looking daggers at her, but Nancy, as usual, was oblivious.

"We'll all have the risotto with a house salad," Nancy said to our server, who scurried away to place the order. "I hope that's OK with everyone?"

"Would it matter if it wasn't?" asked Mary Alice. "You really are something."

"This is a very stressful day for all of us," Nancy said, and squeezed Mary Alice's hand.

This was probably as close to an apology that Mary Alice was going to get under the circumstances, so she gave Nancy a tight smile.

"What was Claire's suggestion?" I asked, anxious to diffuse the tension between two of my closest friends. "Was it about selling the house?"

"No, not exactly," replied Nancy. "She was wondering about Mike. She was worried that he'd be upset if he saw anything about Jack Cartwright's death on one of those trash T.V. shows. She offered to go to

Cosmo's today and tell him what happened in person. I told her to go ahead. I hope that was OK."

"Of course that's OK," I said. "Thank God for friends like Claire. And you. I don't know what I'd do without you. Both of you." I squeezed their hands for emphasis. Equally.

"Well, I'm glad that's settled," said Nancy. "Now, do you want to hear the good news?"

"I'll bet the good news is that you're putting this lunch on your expense account," said Mary Alice, not missing another chance to get a little dig in at Nancy's expense.

"No, smarty pants," Nancy shot back. "It's a great idea about how to make Carol and Jim's house saleable again. If this works, and there's no reason why it won't, we'll have buyers in a bidding war within the next two months."

I brightened. A bidding war? Jim would love that.

"OK, I'll bite. What's this miracle idea of yours?"

"It's not my idea. It's Marcia Fischer's. The home stager from Superior Interiors. You remember her, Carol. She did such a terrific job with the house."

I remembered that Marcia was a royal pain in the patootie, but I wasn't going to say that.

"Marcia wants to make your house into a show house to benefit a local charity. Isn't that a terrific idea?"

Chapter 17

My favorite shade of nail polish is Starter Wife.

"A show house? Are you kidding?" I said in astonishment. "You mean turn our house into something that people would buy tickets to tour? I've heard about these things, but I've never been to one."

I sat back in my chair so our waitress could serve us our lunch. Yum. It smelled delicious. I was feeling better already. Mary Alice was right, as usual. Food always gets me in a better mood. Unfortunately, as my ever tightening waist band kept reminding me, I needed to find another stress buster soon or go up another size in my clothes.

"OK," I said, my mouth full of risotto, "how does a show house work? And how can I convince Jim that this is a good idea?"

Mary Alice interjected a comment before Nancy had a chance to answer. "I went to a show house a few years ago that benefitted the hospital. One of the volunteers told me that it took two years to pull the whole thing together. How do you expect to get it organized in such a short period of time, Nancy? Carol and Jim" – she looked at me apologetically – "well, forgive my bluntness, but you guys are desperate. You don't have time to fool around with this."

Nancy shot Mary Alice a look. "You ought to know that I wouldn't suggest anything this radical unless all the pieces were already in place to pull it off successfully. Give me a little credit, please."

Mary Alice rolled her eyes.

Nancy turned to me and continued. "Here's the deal. Dream Homes Realty and Superior Interiors have partnered with Sally's Place, the local domestic violence program, to do a show house as a fundraiser for them. A lot of people, especially Marcia, have been working on the project for quite a while. We've been keeping everything quiet until all the designers were chosen. Then we'd start a huge publicity blitz."

She paused and took a quick bite of her lunch.

"First, we had to find the perfect property – something large and jazzy, but which could use a major facelift. We had a house all set, and Marcia put out a call for interior designers to come, preview the property, and bid on a room to re-design. Things were moving along great, and then the home owner backed out of the deal. He decided to sell the property privately to a family member. We couldn't believe it! All that work down the drain. We've been on hold for the past week, and the office has been going crazy trying to find another property.

"Your house is perfect, Carol. It's an antique in Fairport's historic district. You know how people always want to see what the inside of those houses look like, especially during the annual Christmas stroll. And your house is completely empty now. Marcia says that one of the biggest hurdles in putting together a show house is moving out all the owner's furniture and putting it into storage. But we wouldn't have to do that with your house, because you and Jim have already moved out.

"Don't you see what a perfect fit this is? It's absolutely brilliant."

"It's really a good idea," Mary Alice admitted grudgingly. "I've heard about Sally's Place. They do terrific things to help families in crisis. I've seen some domestic abuse victims when they've come to the hospital for treatment. You wouldn't believe some of the things that go on behind closed doors in this town. Domestic violence is one of life's dirty little secrets."

"Sally's Place is a wonderful organization," Nancy said, warming to the subject even more. "It offers counseling and support services for families in crisis, and provides temporary safe housing for victims of domestic violence. And it runs a thrift shop in Fairport as another way to raise funds."

"A thrift shop?" This surprised me. I didn't think there was a shopping opportunity in all of Fairfield County, Connecticut, that I hadn't heard about. And patronized. Often.

Nancy nodded her head. "Yes, Sally's Closet. It's on Sanborn Street, right near the train station. Marcia took me there a few weeks ago and I was amazed at the great bargains."

I shook my head. "You both know how much I love to shop. But I can't imagine wearing something that someone else owned and then got rid of. Too icky for words."

"Boy, and I thought I was a snob," Nancy said. "First of all, when you're shopping in one of the local department stores, how do you know who's already tried on that gorgeous little black dress you simply must have? Or, even worse, actually put the tags inside, wore the dress, then returned it? Now, that, my friend, is icky."

She held up her Coach purse. "I got this at Sally's Place for only thirty-five bucks. With the original price ticket still on it. Which read 'one hundred and sixty-five dollars.' Have I convinced you yet?"

"Wow, that's incredible." My eyes glazed over at the thought of all those bargains waiting to be snapped up. "I'll have to go and check it out. Jim couldn't object to my spending a little money at a thrift shop, even though cash flow is tight right now."

"How do you think Jim will react to this show house idea?" Mary Alice asked, bringing me back to reality with a thud.

"He's going to jump at the chance," said Nancy. "To sweeten the deal, I convinced my boss at Dream Homes Realty to pay all of your furniture storage fees for the duration of the show house. And the rent for your temporary apartment. We need your house.

"Plus…" she paused dramatically. "Plus, we're going to try and get you an in-kind tax write-off for this. How could Jim refuse?

"Of course, the yellow 'scene of the crime' tape would have to be removed before the official opening."

I dawdled at Maria's for another half hour after Mary Alice and Nancy left. Nancy had left me with some printed information on show houses to peruse – including a contract – so I amused myself by reading some of the material.

"Wow! I never realized all there was to putting together a show house before," I said aloud. Then, I stopped myself. Under normal circumstances, I'd be sharing this with Lucy and Ethel. But I knew patrons of Maria's would look at me funny if I carried on a conversation with myself.

I had hoped to catch up with Maria while I was here, but since the restaurant had become such a hit in town, I knew she was spending more time doing off-premise special events catering than running the Trattoria.

Come to think of it, it was funny that I wanted to catch up with Maria. When she was teaching Mark or Jenny, I used to dread those back-to-school nights. She was a tough teacher, and even the parents – me included – were intimidated by her.

But now, Maria had become what I call an "unexpected friend." Someone whom I initially disliked – yes, even misjudged – but when I got to know her better, was a real sweetie. I'd like to think every person has people in their life like that, but maybe I'm the only one.

Anyway, I was in no hurry to go anywhere, particularly back to our tiny rental and have The Conversation with Jim. Nancy had promised to stop by later and give us more of the particulars. I dreaded telling My Beloved that the house sale was off. Although he'd probably figured that out for himself. He's no dummy, after all, and if the buyer is – well, dead – that tends to put a damper on the sale.

But a show house. Convincing him to go along with that idea would be an entirely different matter, despite the potential tax write-off and free storage. If I knew him – and after all these years of marriage, I certainly did – he'd just want to slap a little paint on the walls and put the house right back on the market.

In my brief and stressful visit home this morning for my "interrogation," I couldn't help but notice, now that all the pictures were off the walls and the furniture was gone, how many places there were in the house that needed a touch-up. Well, if I was honest, all the rooms needed to be completely painted.

Jim likes to take charge of those projects himself. He's pretty adamant about color choice – neutrals like "Autumn Wheat" are the only thing he'll consider unless I really kick up a fuss. God, when I remember the fight we had about painting the kitchen, it makes me cringe. (I won, though. We painted the walls light yellow and even My Beloved admitted – finally – that they looked good.)

Mark and Jenny used to kid their father all the time about painting the outside of the house, too. In his younger days, that was his personal warm weather project, and he only did one side a year. I always had my heart set on a white house. Thank God the house we bought was already white, and not some off-beat color like sage green or red.

Thinking about the kids made me decide to try and reach Mike myself and fill him in on what had happened. Not that I didn't trust Claire, of course. But sometimes a "child" needs to hear a parent's voice. Or, maybe, the other way around.

I punched his number in my cell phone address book – I hope you're all impressed with the fact that I've become such a techie – and listened to 4, 5, 6 rings. Then, voice mail came on, and the automated response said, "Mail box full. Please try again later."

That was odd. Like most members of the twenty-something generation, Mike lived by his phone, Blackberry, iPhone – you name it. He never failed to pick up messages immediately. Hmm.

I pushed that little tremor of worry out of my mind that mothers always get when they can't reach their offspring, no matter how old they are. He's absolutely fine, I told myself. Probably just extra busy with Cosmo's and hasn't had a chance to check his messages today. Claire will see him today and e-mail or call later. Or he will.

I couldn't sit at this table much longer. The restaurant staff was starting to set the tables for the dinner shift.

What you need, Carol, is a little retail therapy. Consider it helping a worthy cause.

I decided to check out Sally's Closet on my way back to the apartment.

I must have driven by the thrift shop hundreds of times on my way to and from the train station. Funny, I'd never noticed it before. On-street parking is always a challenge in Fairport, but luckily we still had our parking sticker for the railroad commuter lot. And, even luckier, there actually was a choice of spots today. I took that as a good sign that my luck was changing.

I stopped to check out the thrift shop windows. I'd already made up my mind that if I didn't find anything attractive in the window, I wouldn't go in. I mean, Nancy's Coach purse was an incredible bargain, but I was sure that kind of thing didn't happen very often.

I had to admit that the place looked inviting from the outside. Housed in a white colonial-type building so favored in Connecticut, Sally's Closet advertised "gently loved clothing for women and children." Most of the window displays featured up-to-date merchandise that…wait a minute! Did I see a Lilly Pulitzer dress in the window? Well. Sally's Closet just might be selling that beauty to me.

I knew finding that parking space was a good omen.

The bell on the front door tinkled discreetly as I entered. First, I gave the interior the "sniff test." You know what I mean. Some shops that feature "antique" or "gently used" goods have a distinctive musty odor that makes me gag. I'm outta those in a skinny second.

Sally's Closet had a lovely hint of lavender. One of my favorite scents. Score one point. Two women – probably volunteers – were unloading a cart full of merchandise. I noticed they were wearing lavender aprons. I liked that too. A uniform look, so customers would know to ask them for help if needed. Score another point, for professionalism.

Now, on to the important stuff – the merchandise itself.

I looked around the sales floor. Well, this was impressive. Everything was arranged by color, and then by size. Sweaters, short-sleeved and long-sleeved tops, blouses, pants, shorts, skirts, dresses, suits, evening wear. All neatly pressed and beautifully displayed.

There were shelves for purses, gloves, and scarves as well. Sally's Closet was certainly a lot neater than my own closet.

My eyes were drawn to one rack with the sign "Designer Duds." Hmm. This required closer inspection, so I whipped out my bifocals to check it out. Ralph Lauren, Jones NY, Liz Claiborne, and – joy of joys – a few of the distinctive multi-colored prints that Lilly Pulitzer is known for. All pretty current styles, too. I couldn't believe that some of the clothes had original tickets on them.

I was peering at a particularly adorable pink, green and yellow Lilly dress – it was sleeveless but I could always wear a sweater over it to camouflage my "bye-bye" upper arms – when someone tapped me on the shoulder. I squealed and jumped a foot. Well, not a foot, but a couple of inches.

"Hi, Carol," said one of my young neighbors. Fortunately, she was wearing a name tag on her lavender apron that identified her as Liz.

"Hi Liz," I said, giving her a little hug. "I didn't know you volunteered at Sally's Closet." I gestured around the store. "I've never been here before. What a great place."

"I'm here two afternoons a week while the kids are at their swim class," Liz said. "Volunteering keeps me sane. I get a little 'over-mommied' at times, if you know what I mean."

I nodded my head. I remembered those days well.

"I'm surprised to see you in here today, Carol," said Liz. "Didn't you close on your house this morning? You and Jim should be in some fancy restaurant, celebrating."

Evidently, Liz hadn't heard the house sale news yet, and I had no desire to enlighten her. She'd find out soon enough.

"Deb and Stacy and I are really excited about another young family moving into the neighborhood," Liz went on. "Not that we didn't all love you and Jim, of course. But Alyssa and Jack seem like such a great couple. We met them last week at the neighborhood cocktail party Sara gave for them."

A neighborhood cocktail party? That Jim and I hadn't been invited to?

At my surprised look, Liz hastened to cover her gaffe. "I guess I stuck my foot in my mouth there. It wasn't exactly a neighborhood cocktail party. I mean, not everyone in the whole neighborhood was there. Just the younger ones."

She clapped her hand over her mouth. "I can't seem to get out of this one. I think I'll just shut up now."

I laughed, showing that I was not offended. Even though I was.

"Nancy was showing off a great Coach purse she said she got here." I said. "I can't resist a bargain. Why don't you give me a tour of the place?"

I peered around the shop. "And what's with the decorating scheme? The walls are a light purple, aren't they? That's an interesting color choice."

Liz looked surprised at my question. "Don't you know that purple is the color for domestic violence abuse, the way red denotes AIDS or women's heart disease?"

I was properly chagrined. "You're right. I should have known that."

"All the proceeds from Sally's Closet go to support our parent organization," Liz went on. "You've heard of Sally's Place, right? It's a wonderful organization that supports and protects the victims of domestic violence here in Fairport. You'd be shocked at how many families the agency helps in a single year."

She sighed. "But it looks like we need to do a better job at marketing. There just doesn't seem to be enough time, or enough volunteers, to get the job done the way it should be."

I started to reply, but Liz didn't give me the chance. "Most people don't even know that October is Domestic Violence Awareness Month as well as Breast Cancer Awareness Month. All you see are pink ribbons everywhere, from October 1 to Halloween. I'm not saying that breast cancer isn't an important issue, but so is domestic violence."

"I can see how much you care about this," I said. "You're very passionate about it."

"You would be, too, if you'd seen first-hand how domestic violence can destroy a family."

I could see that Liz was verging on tears, and tried desperately to think of something to calm her down.

That's when I heard The Voice.

"Carol Elizabeth Kerr. Is that you?"

I immediately snapped to attention. Practically saluted, as a matter of fact.

And turned to face my high school English teacher, Sister Rose.

Chapter 18

Your opinion matters. I'm just not sure to whom.

This was turning into a helluva day. I mean, a heck of a day. No swearing in front of Sister. In high school, I believed that she could read minds. I wasn't about to test that theory now that I was an adult.

Liz immediately scurried away and began folding sweaters.

"Sister Rose," I said. "It is me. But my name is Carol Andrews now."

"The correct sentence structure is, 'It is I,' dear," Sister said without missing a beat. "You never were an English superstar, as I recall."

Ouch. That hurt. Even if it was true.

I stuck out my hand in a gesture of friendship. She ignored it. I stuck my hand in my jacket pocket. Suddenly, I was 16 years old again and being kept after class to be reprimanded for one of a hundred possible transgressions. Like a school uniform skirt that was too short. (I hated our uniforms so much, I avoided wearing navy blue until I was 30!) Or saddle shoes that weren't properly polished. Or a homework assignment that was late. Or whispering in class.

That last one happened pretty often.

Jeez, Carol, grow up already. And why the hell – I mean, heck – didn't Nancy tell me Sister Rose was connected to this shop? No doubt she was blinded by her Coach bag purchase. Some pal.

"It's so nice to see you again, Sister," I said with a sweet smile. "You look wonderful."

And she did, damn it. I mean, darn it. Her softly curled white hair framed a remarkably unlined face, and her clothes were just as stylish as mine. Actually, more stylish than mine. Of course, she probably got first pick of the thrift shop donations.

"It's good to see you, too, Carol. I always enjoy seeing my former students." Then she reached out and gave my shoulder a little squeeze.

Awkward silence.

So, what should I say now? Gotta go? It's been grand? Let's get together for coffee sometime and talk about old times? By the way, my husband Jim and I were selling our antique home, but I found our buyer dead last night so the deal's off and we may donate the house to Sally's Place for a show house?

Not hardly.

"Since Mount Saint Francis closed several years ago, the sisters' lives have been so different," Sister Rose finally said. "I thought I'd be teaching forever. But now, here I am…" she gestured around the shop… "the director of a program for victims of domestic violence. And running a thrift shop."

She gave me a meaningful look, the kind that used to turn my knees to jelly. "I don't believe I've seen you in here before, Carol. We can always use more volunteers. And donations."

And just like that, I heard myself promising to come in one morning a week to help out in the shop. Then I got the heck out of there. I didn't even try on that Lilly Pulitzer dress.

You really are an idiot, I told myself. How could you let someone you haven't seen in over forty years still intimidate you like that? And on top of that, now you've committed yourself to seeing her once a week at Sally's Closet. No matter how great the bargains are there, it's not going to be worth putting yourself through torture to snap them up.

Then, I had a great idea. If Jim and I (big "if" coming here) donated our house for a fundraiser, maybe Sister Rose would let me off the hook. I mean, how many sacrifices was I supposed to make for this program? And I could say that I was too busy planning the event to volunteer at the thrift shop.

Brilliant, Carol. One of your best schemes yet. Now all I had to do was calm Jim down once he found out the house sale was off. And convince him to go along with the show house. I definitely needed Nancy's help to pull all this off. And she needed mine, too.

Time to talk to My Beloved.

But first, I decided to take a quick drive past my house. Maybe the police activity was over and the yellow crime tape was gone. That'd be fabulous.

I was cruising down Fairport Turnpike, the main street in our town, just about to turn into the historic district, when I noticed several trucks bearing what looked like T.V. satellite dishes parked at the corner.

Hmm. I wondered what all the excitement was about, and braked to take a quick look.

Unfortunately, the excitement was centered in front of my house, where Phyllis and Bill Stevens were being interviewed by a gaggle of reporters, pushing and shoving and thrusting microphones into their faces. It was a mob scene, and it looked like Phyllis and Bill were having a swell time becoming instant celebrities.

Good grief! I floored my car and got out of there before they saw me. My Beloved was going to have a fit when he heard about this.

Then again, wasn't he the one who always used to tell me that there's no such thing as bad publicity? The key was to get your name out in the public eye – and be sure it was spelled right. I wondered if the same rule applied to real estate listings.

I just hoped we didn't make the front page of the *National Enquirer.*

At least I didn't have to face an emotional discussion with Jim by myself. By the time I got back to our temporary hovel – I mean, apartment – Jenny and Nancy were there too.

Lucy and Ethel greeted me joyously, of course. Thank God for dogs. They're always in a good mood.

The three humans had a variety of expressions on their faces – Jenny looked like she was on the verge of tears, Nancy had a bright smile pasted on her face that I knew was phony, and My Beloved, well, My Beloved had that tell-tale nervous eye tic thing going that was never a good sign.

"About time you showed up, Carol," he said. "We've been waiting for you so we can make some decisions."

Rats. I was in trouble already.

"Nancy has given us the bad news that it looks like the house deal is off. We've got to come up with a new plan to sell, and quickly."

Nancy started to speak, but Jenny interrupted her. "Before we talk about the house, I have something to tell all of you. It's pretty personal, but I wanted you to hear it from me first. We don't have many secrets."

She turned and looked me squarely in my baby blues.

"Remember this morning, when you were grilling me about Jack's death and you wanted to know if Mark could find out any information about the police investigation?"

I nodded my head. "But you reminded me that he couldn't, because you and he are, well…I think the expression you used was just that …you and he *are.*"

"Well, guess what?" Jenny said, her voice quavering. "He and I *aren't* now. We had a huge fight and broke up this afternoon. So now he'll probably be assigned to this case, and you can pump him for information all you want. You shouldn't, of course. It's probably against the law. But I'm sure you'll try anyway."

Wow. Coming from Jenny, that really stung. Even if it was true.

Nancy jumped up and said, "I shouldn't be here now. This is family talk."

“No, stay,” said Jenny. “I want you to hear this, too. The reason we had a fight is because Mark made a crack about our family.”

Her tears were gone now. Replaced by anger.

“He reminded me that there’ve been only two suspicious deaths around here within the past year. And said it was very interesting that my parents were involved in both of them. He called you two ‘a personal local crime wave.’ When he said it, he laughed, like he was making a joke. What a jerk.

“I didn’t think it was funny. And I told him so. One thing led to another, and that’s that.”

“I’m sure Mark didn’t mean it the way it sounded,” I said, wondering at the same time if he did. Or if, like a lot of men I know, he just said something stupid without thinking first.

“Maybe not,” said Jenny. “I admit that sometimes I overreact, too. It’s an inherited trait.” She looked pointedly at me.

Moi? Overreact? Well, yes. Sometimes. OK. Often.

“Anyway, this will give us a little cooling off period. Maybe it’s not a permanent break-up. We’ll see how it works out. At least this time I have my own place, so nobody has to move out. I guess I have learned some life lessons.”

“Speaking of places to live,” Nancy said, “we need to talk about a battle plan.”

“Before we get into that, how are you doing, Carol?” My Beloved asked. “I know last night was a nightmare for you, and this morning, being cross-examined by that idiot detective, wasn’t any picnic, either. Are you up to talking about the house sale?”

What Jim was really saying, of course, was that he was sorry he snapped at me when I got back to the apartment, and that he didn’t mean to jump down my throat the minute I walked in the door.

I gave him a peck on the cheek. I wanted him to know I appreciated his support and all was forgiven. This time.

"I'm doing better now, thanks," I said. "And on the way back here, I drove by our house again. I couldn't believe what was going on. There were T.V. trucks all over the place, and Phyllis and Bill Stevens were being interviewed by a bunch of reporters. It looked like a media circus. I got out of there as fast as I could."

"Carol, I'm sure you're exaggerating," said My Beloved. "How many reporters were really there? I doubt it was a media circus. I mean, after all, poor Jack Cartwright died, but people die every day. Why would reporters care?"

This from my husband, the public relations expert.

"I think I can answer that," said Jenny. "Before Mark and I had our big fight this afternoon, I checked out a few Internet sites to see if there was anything posted about Jack's death. That's what started our argument."

She looked at her father. "You're not going to like this, Dad. That interview you did with the college reporter is on YouTube. And parts of it have been picked up by some national media sites."

Jim stiffened. "What? That little twit put me on YouTube? Without my permission? I'll sue the pants off him."

"It's in the public domain, Dad," Jenny said. "You were interviewed for a news show. You didn't have to sign a waiver or anything."

Nancy interrupted and asked, "Let's try to stick to the point here, OK? What was said in the interview? Anything we can use to help sell the house now?"

"Not exactly," said Jenny. "The tag line was 'Death House.' People are dying to live there."

Chapter 19

Q: Does your husband help you around the house?
A: He's very handy with a corkscrew, especially on weekends.

This called for drastic measures. I needed to lighten the mood. Fortunately, I had a handy solution in our tiny refrigerator.

Anticipating a festive night of celebration with My Beloved after the house closing, I had purchased two bottles of expensive champagne. One of them was chilling here at the rental, and I had left the other in our home refrigerator with a note welcoming the Cartwrights to their new home.

I guess they wouldn't be drinking that one.

Anyway, between my discovering the dead body of our buyer, being interrogated by Detective Paul, Jenny and Mark breaking up, Jim's YouTube appearance, the house deal falling through, and let's not forget my re-connecting with Sister Rose, it had been a day I'd just as soon forget. I didn't know about anybody else, but I sure needed a glass of the bubbly to pick up my spirits.

Plus, I remembered hearing some New Age guru on television talk about the power of positive thinking. Visualize what you want, and it will happen. Throw in a glass of champagne and everything would look better.

I started humming "The sun'll come out tomorrow," and everyone looked at me like I was nuts.

I ignored them and started rummaging through a cardboard box until I found 4 plastic glasses. Not the Waterford crystal flutes I would have preferred, but at this point, who cared?

"This is to toast a new beginning for all of us," I announced. "Just wait a minute. I've got a surprise."

"God, I hope you haven't discovered another dead body," My Beloved quipped.

"Nope. Much better than that. Ta da!"

I turned and held up the champagne.

Jenny started to laugh. Then she started to cry. Then she started to laugh again and grabbed for the champagne bottle.

"I'll open it, Mom. It always explodes when you try."

"And while you're doing that," Nancy said, "let's talk about our next real estate move. No pun intended." She looked at me. "Have you had a chance...?"

I shook my head and telegraphed, "It'll be a better idea coming from you."

Best friend that she is, Nancy immediately got the message and switched gears into professional Realtor mode. Isn't it amazing how women always know what other women are thinking, while men flail around clueless?

But I digress.

"All right," Nancy said. "I think it's clear that we have to do some creative marketing to dilute the negative spin the media's putting on the house sale. Are we all agreed?"

Not giving anyone a chance to respond, Nancy plunged ahead.

"Jim, you're the marketing expert here. Do you have any ideas?"

I looked at Nancy in shock. What the heck was she doing? Didn't she already have a plan?

My Beloved took a sip of the champagne and looked thoughtful. "Good question, Nancy," he said. "It has to be something pretty spectacular to offset YouTube. Who knew I'd become an Internet star at my age?" He allowed himself a small smile.

I relaxed a little. Jim was starting to mellow. Must be the champagne.

"If this was a campaign you were drafting for a client," Nancy went on, "what advice would you give them?"

She paused, then added, "Wouldn't you suggest that the best way to counter negative publicity is through positive publicity? I know I've heard you say that often."

Jim nodded his head and started to speak, but Nancy didn't give him a chance. "You and I both know that the YouTube clip will fade into oblivion once some celebrity gets arrested for drunken driving or checks into rehab. We need to take advantage of the publicity while we have it. Isn't the phrase you public relations professionals use, 'put a positive spin' on it?"

Jim nodded again. "That's exactly it, Nancy."

"But how to do it?" she asked, furrowing her brow slightly so as not to add any wrinkles.

"Of course, the chief consumer in every family is the woman," said Jim, shooting me a look. I sipped my champagne and smiled at him.

Jenny chimed in, "So we have to come up with a marketing strategy to appeal to women," she said.

"Exactly," said Nancy. "We need a fresh approach. Something so the house won't look like a tired old listing."

"With a dead buyer," I added.

Jim and Nancy frowned at me. Oops. Shut up, Carol, and let Nancy handle this.

And handle it, she did. Brilliantly. First, she talked about the popularity of home and garden television shows these days. "Women love to peek at other people's homes and get decorating ideas," she said. "I know Carol and I do."

Then she gave Jim a roadmap of issues that women care about – breast cancer, hunger and homelessness, abused children, and, finally domestic violence.

"You're talking about cause marketing," Jim said. "If we could find a marketing strategy for the house that hit on one of these issues, I think we'd hit a home run." Poor guy. He fell right into the trap Nancy had so cleverly set for him.

"You're right, Jim," she beamed at him. "That's a brilliant idea. And something's just occurred to me. But before I tell you about it, I need to make a quick call to the office. I'll do it outside."

I counted to 60. Then, Nancy was back, with a big smile on her face. "You're going to love this idea. My office wants to use your home as the show house to benefit Sally's Place, the domestic violence program in Fairport. It's the perfect project to counter all this negative publicity. You'll come out looking like heroes, and you'll get the house decorated for free. I bet that people will be fighting to buy it.

"Plus, you could get a tax write-off, and my office will pay for your rental and any storage fees while the show house is going on. It's going to be great, you'll see."

She threw her arms around Jim and gave him a smooch on the cheek. "Jim, you're the best public relations person I ever met. And you just may have saved my job."

Well, what could the poor guy do after that but say yes?

It's wonderful what a little champagne can do.

"Are you sure you're OK with this show house idea?" I asked Jim as I served out a portion of the fish and chips we'd ordered from Seafood Sandy's for our dinner. I hadn't been able to find enough pots and pans to cook a meal myself – well, I didn't really look too hard. And after the trauma of the past 24 hours, I didn't feel like cooking, anyway. Tomorrow,

I promised myself, I'd get organized, unpack a few boxes, and do some food shopping.

We were alone now, except for Lucy and Ethel, of course. Nancy had done a super sales job about the event, but there were a few other hot button issues Jim and I still had to discuss. Like carrying two mortgages at the same time, for example.

My super fiscal conservative husband was bound to have a fit about that once the reality of our situation sunk in. But even after 30-plus years of marriage, My Beloved can still surprise me. In a good way.

"Now, Carol," Jim said, "I know you're really worried about our finances. I have to admit, once I found out that you were all right after the horrible ordeal you'd been through, that was my next thought. How are we going to manage this?"

He paused, took a sip of his no-longer-bubbly champagne, and grimaced. "This is warm now. Time to switch to water."

I started to get up to pour him a glass from the tap, but he waved me back to my seat. "Don't worry about that now, Carol. Let's not get sidetracked."

Jim cleared a place on the table and rolled out a yellow chart which had all sorts of diagrams and numbers on it.

"I've been thinking about this all afternoon, and I've come up with what I think is a reasonable financial plan to get us through the next few months until the house finally sells. Of course, we're going to have to cut back on lots of extras, but I think we can do it. Nancy's show house idea is a godsend, but we can't kid ourselves into thinking it's going to make the house sell right away. It may not. So here's what we're going to do."

My eyes started to glaze over as Jim droned on about his Andrews Family Financial Rescue Plan. Where was a government bail-out when I needed it? I guess that only applied to big automakers and major financial institutions.

I snapped to attention, though, when I heard Jim say, "If we have to use the home equity line of credit on the Old Fairport Turnpike house to tide us over for a while, we will. But I'd rather not dip into it unless we absolutely have to. So you'll have to try harder to get freelance jobs. We'll need the extra income."

I started to give him a smart ass answer, then bit my tongue. Figuratively, of course. Because he was right, darn it. It was high time I started carrying some of the financial burden he'd assumed all these years. Jim's New York City public relations job had provided a pretty cushy income for the Andrews family for more than 30 years, sent two kids to college with no student loans, and kept Lucy and Ethel in designer dog food – and me in designer duds – for a long time.

I assumed Jim was referring to my writing and editing career, as opposed to my detective career – when I literally saved him from being accused of murder. Now was probably not a good time to bring that up.

Later, after I had cleaned up the kitchen and walked the dogs, I sat in the dark and thought about my options. That's when I came up with my brilliant idea, I would write a story about domestic violence in Fairport. And I knew just where to start.

I would go back to Sally's Closet and interview Sister Rose.

Chapter 20

Rules of the House:
1. The woman is always right.
2. If the woman is wrong, refer to Rule Number 1.

I woke up to the sound of someone knocking on the door. Huh? What time was it? Where was I? I stretched and was surprised to find I'd fallen asleep in a living room chair. Wow. My neck and back were protesting big time.

And what was this note on top of my chest? I squinted to read it without my glasses.

"Hi Carol. I didn't want to wake you. You were snoring so peacefully. I've gone to the paper to work on this week's column. Back later. Love, J."

Me? Snore? No way.

"Down, girls," I said to Lucy and Ethel, delighted to find the procurer of their kibble awake and available to serve them breakfast.

The knocking had stopped, then started again. More persistent this time. The dogs started to bark.

"I hope whoever it is can take the shock of seeing me in my current state," I said. "Not everyone is as forgiving as you girls are.

"All right, I'm coming," I yelled. "Give me a second to get myself together."

Then I realized I had no idea who was out there. It could be Detective Paul, here to ruin another day. Or a newspaper reporter. Or – even worse – someone from a television station.

I tried to peek out the front window without being seen, but to no avail.

"Who is it?" I asked. "And what do you want?"

"It's Mark Anderson, Mrs. Andrews. I really need to talk to you."

My former-almost-son-in-law. I wondered if he was here in an official capacity, or as a family friend. Well, if he had any thoughts about cross-examining me, I figured just looking at me in my current state would scare him speechless. And I had a few choice words to share with him. His comment about the Andrews family's connection to the local dead body count was way out of line.

But when I opened the door, my maternal instincts immediately kicked in.

Mark looked like – with apologies to Sister Rose – hell. Sure, he was dressed in a sport jacket and tie, but they were both rumpled. His hair was barely combed, and he hadn't shaved. I know that in some circles that's considered a hip look, but not for a member of the police force. Except on television, of course.

It was hard to decide who looked worse, him or me.

I gave him a hug. "Come on in, Mark. Even though I'm not sure I'm glad to see you."

Lucy and Ethel were, though. They danced around his legs, begging for attention, and for any treats Mark might have in his pocket.

"I'd offer you a cup of coffee, but I haven't unpacked the coffee pot yet," I said. "Besides, I'm not really sure how I feel about you right now. Jenny told us what happened between you two. And why."

I suppose that was reckless of me. I shouldn't have told him that Jenny still confided in her parents about some of the intimate details of her life. But what the heck. Mark, of all people, knew what a close family we were.

"Can I sit down for a minute and explain?" Mark asked. "Or try to?"

I nodded my head and pointed to the one kitchen chair that didn't have a box piled on top of it. I told myself to keep my mouth shut and let

Mark talk. Especially since Mark was a detective, and there was a chance that I might need him if the "house problem" got any worse.

"It was stupid of me to say what I did about you and Mr. Andrews, Mrs. Andrews."

"Jim and Carol," I corrected him.

Mark flashed a grateful smile. "Thanks. I appreciate that.

"Anyway, it was just an off-hand remark about you two. I thought it was funny. It never dawned on me that Jenny would take it the wrong way. And get so upset that she'd break off our relationship."

Men. Sometimes they just don't get how sensitive we women can be about people we care about. For instance, it's perfectly all right for me to criticize My Beloved should I happen to notice that the waist band on his pants has gotten tighter. But nobody else is allowed to do that.

"Mark," I said, "after all, it sounded to Jenny like you were blaming us for the two suspicious deaths." And to me, too.

"In my own defense, Carol, you have to admit that what I said was true. You and Jim were involved in Davis Rhodes's death last year, and now you've found a dead body in your house. But that doesn't mean I believe you were responsible for Jack Cartwright's death. It's just an unfortunate coincidence."

"It was an awful experience for me," I said, "and on top of that, I had to deal with that horrible Paul Wheeler, cross-examining me like he was starring on *Law and Order Fairport.*

"Of course, it would be different if I knew that you'd be involved in this case. Like you were the last time. I think we made a pretty good team."

In fact, you might not have solved the case if it hadn't been for my help. Or been recruited by the Fairport police force and promoted to detective.

I didn't really say that, of course.

"That might not be possible," Mark said slowly. "After all, Jenny and I are a couple now."

I gave him a hard look. "That's the point, Mark. You're not a couple any more." Thanks to your big mouth.

"Of course, I hope that this death will be ruled a tragic accident, and there won't be any further police investigation. But if that doesn't happen, God forbid, couldn't you keep your ears open at the station? That's not asking a lot, is it? Especially since you know that Jim and I aren't responsible."

I paused, then played my trump card. "I know Jenny would be grateful, too. In fact, that's a sure way to get her back."

"That went pretty well," I said to Lucy and Ethel. "I feel better knowing that Mark's on our side."

They each gave me a reproachful stare.

"All right, Mark didn't exactly promise anything. But with getting Jenny back as his incentive, I think he'll try pretty hard to find out what's going on."

I sighed. "I just hope he shares what he finds out with us." Particularly me. Especially since I had already proven my impressive sleuthing ability last year.

I sat down on the chair where I'd spent the night and thought about my options for the day.

The chaos around me was overwhelming. And I needed to talk to Sister Rose about my article.

I had to prioritize.

"I hate to admit this," I said to Lucy and Ethel, "but it looks like we'll be stuck living here for a while. We can't go back to our old house, and our new one won't be ready for another two months." Assuming we could afford to move into it. So far, we had given the builder several deposits, but the final payment was yet to be made. The money for that was supposed to come from our house sale. Still another thing to worry about.

"I have to unpack some things and try to make this apartment look like home. And then I'll take a quick shower and go food shopping. Jim deserves a home-cooked meal for a change, instead of take-out. And I promise I'll buy dog biscuits, just in case you were worried you were going to starve to death."

Lucy, the food diva of the pair, immediately assumed a begging position.

"You have to wait until we've unpacked at least one box," I said to her. "Then we'll take a break and have a snack."

I decided to start with a box marked "Kitchen Supplies. Open This First." It was in Jim's handwriting, so I figured he must have packed it. I wasn't sure what he thought of as critical to a kitchen, but what the heck.

Hmm. A corkscrew. A can opener. A screwdriver. A hammer and nails. Plastic garbage bags. Candles. This certainly was an eclectic box.

Underneath all of this were two carefully wrapped dinner plates, two coffee mugs, two juice glasses, and a few knives, forks and spoons.

Well, now we were getting someplace. At least these items were food-related. But dirty. Very dirty. My Beloved had wrapped them in old newspapers he must have taken from a stack we had in the garage. Some of those papers had been there for years, since Jim never wanted to recycle anything that mentioned one of his p.r. clients.

I couldn't help myself. As I started unwrapping the china, I took a quick peek at the newspapers, too. I was right. Some of them were at least 20 years old. I had a great time looking at *The New York Times.* Boy, fashions sure had changed over the years. And many of the stores with the splashy ads had gone out of business years ago.

This is why you have so much trouble accomplishing things, I told myself. You're too easily distracted and you don't get anything done. Focus. Keep unpacking.

There were a few more old newspapers wadded up in the corners of the box. I guessed My Beloved had stuck these in as an afterthought, so the contents of the box didn't shift in transit.

Oh, what the heck. I decided to check those out too, before I moved on to the next box. These were from our local paper. April 1988. This was the spring that Jim had been assigned to a client in Rome. The whole family had moved to Italy for six months. What a glorious time that had been. Of course, I had put on seven pounds, eating all that delicious food. Which I'd never been successful in taking off.

Ah, well.

I settled my back against the chair and started to scan the headlines. It took a few minutes for my brain to register what I was looking at.

Ohmygod. It was a story about Mary Alice's husband. And his tragic death in a car accident. Brian was killed instantly, when his car went down an embankment and exploded. The driver of the other car was a teenaged boy driving on a learner's permit, who escaped without a scratch.

My eyes filled with tears. How could I have forgotten that, while we were living it up in Rome, one of my best friends had her life turned upside down? What a selfish person I was.

I forced myself to read the rest of the newspaper account, which apparently was a follow-up to a piece about the actual accident. The article was accompanied by a photo of Brian, and a photo of the driver of the other car.

It was Jack Cartwright, our very-dead-almost-home-buyer.

Chapter 21

This is my spirit, honey. My body left a long time ago.

My friends may tell you that I never stop talking. But let me tell you, looking at that yellowed newspaper clip left me speechless.

Then, my brain kicked in. First of all, when you reach a certain age – not that I'm anywhere near that yet – I'm told that everyone you meet looks like someone you already know. A grade school classmate, for instance. Or someone you worked with one summer at the beach. Truth to tell, I've been known to go up to someone I'm sure went to high school with me at Mount Saint Francis Academy and say, "Gosh, I haven't seen you in ages. You look terrific. We sat next to each other in French class. How've you been?" And then be totally embarrassed when the woman (it was an all-girls' school, in case you didn't know that) looked at me and said, "Who are you? I think you've confused me with someone else."

So, it was completely possible that this was not my Jack Cartwright.

During my very brief experience with Pilates, the instructor always said, "Inhale to prepare." I inhaled. Then exhaled slowly. Once more. Twice more. There, that was a little better. Maybe if my life ever calmed down, I'd go back to that class again.

This called for a closer examination with my bifocals. I plopped myself back into the chair and closed my eyes. Inhale to prepare. OK, I was ready to take another look at that damned news story.

"Local Doctor Killed in Car Crash," read the headline. I shuddered. How awful to find this after all these years.

I forced myself to read the brief story.

"Doctor Brian Costello, noted local pediatrician and staff physician at Fairport Memorial Hospital, was killed instantly in an auto accident yesterday afternoon. The other vehicle in the crash was driven by seventeen-year-old John Cartwright of Milltown. Speed and slick road conditions, as well as the inexperience of the other driver, were thought to be factors in the crash. Local police are investigating. Doctor Costello leaves his wife, Mary Alice, and two sons. Funeral arrangements are pending."

There was no doubt about it. The driver of the car who caused Brian's death was my Jack Cartwright.

I sat there, motionless, while a million thoughts swirled through my brain. I remembered Mary Alice's passion and grief when she talked about Brian's accident at our neighborhood Bunco party a few months ago. At least twelve people heard her say that, if she ever laid eyes on the driver of the other car, she'd kill him.

But she didn't really mean that, I told myself. She was upset. More than upset. She was almost out of control. In fact, although I'd known Mary Alice most of my life, I'd never seen her like that before.

There was no way Mary Alice could have known that the buyer for our house was the same person who was responsible for Brian's death.

Was there?

Maybe she recognized Jack at the open house. Then she waited for a chance to finally get her revenge.

This was beginning to sound like a trashy soap opera.

But Mary Alice had been at our house the night I found Jack dead. She admitted that to the police. Maybe I don't remember agreeing to meet her and hide something in the house because we'd never had that conversation. What if she just made it up to give herself a reason to be there? Who knew better than my best friends how unreliable my memory could be?

"This is ridiculous," I said to the dogs. "I'm just going to call her up and ask her. Or, better yet, ask her to meet me and go for a long walk. That way, I can see her reaction when I show her the newspaper story.

"Oh, rats."

I suddenly realized this was a bad idea. If Mary Alice was innocent – correction, because Mary Alice was innocent – confronting her with the old article might only make things worse. She'd definitely panic. She might even run away.

I couldn't give the article to Mark, because he would have to give it to Paul Wheeler. Who would be obliged to question Mary Alice.

I couldn't talk to Nancy about this. She can't keep a secret no matter how hard she tries. In fact, the harder she tries, the more likely she is to let something slip.

My Beloved would tell me my imagination was working overtime. Which it certainly could be.

I could call my friend Claire in Florida and ask her what to do, but she's married to a lawyer, so she'd probably tell me to talk to the police and clear the matter up once and for all.

In the past, I've unburdened myself to Deanna, my favorite hairdresser and miracle worker. Talking to her always made me feel better. But Mary Alice was a client of hers, too. I didn't want to plant any suspicions in Deanna's mind about Mary Alice. That wouldn't be fair at all, to either of them.

I couldn't place Jenny in the awkward position of being my confidante this time. Besides, she might also tell me to talk to Mark. Even if she wasn't talking to him herself.

Then, I had another terrible thought. What if the police found out Jack's identity and added revenging Brian's death to the ridiculous accusation that I wanted to stop the house sale?

A cold nose nudged my hand, and I looked down to find Lucy looking up at me. *You can talk to us,* she seemed to say.

I scooped her up in my arms and gave her a squeeze. Oof, she was getting a little heavy. Time to switch to light dog food.

"You and Ethel are great at support," I assured her.

"But unfortunately, this time I need some advice. And that's not your specialty."

I'd always depended on talking difficult situations out with my family or friends. They help me gain the clarity that I usually lack.

But I couldn't tell anyone about finding the old newspaper. In fact, if I was smart, I'd burn the damn thing and be done with it.

I'd never felt so alone in my whole life.

Lucy and I sat in that chair for a long time, with Ethel dozing at my feet. In fact, I think I dozed off for a few minutes, too. There's nothing like the comfort of holding a warm furry body on your lap to produce a feeling of relaxation.

Until Lucy started to squirm. *Enough of this. I need to go out.*

I finally figured out what to do about the newspaper article, thanks to the dogs. I'm not going to confess to you what I did. Let's just say that, with a contribution from both of them, the article was completely destroyed and I didn't feel the least bit guilty putting it into the trash barrel.

And, like the great Scarlet O'Hara once said under dissimilar but equally stressful circumstances, I resolved to think about it tomorrow.

Or, maybe not.

My two canine co-conspirators and I spent the rest of the morning unpacking more boxes. Well, I unpacked. They snoozed.

By noontime, the tiny apartment had begun to take on some semblance of home. Having my own dishes, cutlery, linens, and other kitchen accessories put away in the limited cupboard space was so great. I do like things to be orderly. (Sometimes I achieve order by throwing things into a closet and closing the door. I bet I'm not the only person who does that.) A few family photographs added to the cozy feeling.

I was feeling pretty positive about what I'd accomplished. Until I found a photo of Claire, Nancy, Mary Alice and me that was taken at Mary Alice's retirement shower the previous year. Mary Alice looked so happy, sitting on a chair we had decorated as a throne. She was wearing a tiara, a feather boa, and a tee-shirt that read, "Hello, New Life! The Best Is Yet To Come."

Just looking at that picture made me want to cry. Again.

"There is absolutely, positively, no way that our Mary Alice could be involved in Jack Cartwright's death," I announced to the girls. They both wagged their tails in complete agreement. "I don't care about that newspaper article. She didn't recognize Jack. Period. And if anybody dares to say otherwise, I swear that I'll do whatever it takes to prove them wrong.

"Just like I did for Jim last year."

I tossed each of the dogs a Milk Bone, made sure their water bowls were full – I know their priorities – and told them to sit tight for a couple of hours because I needed retail therapy big-time. Even if I had to get it at the grocery store.

Chapter 22

I understand the basic concepts of cooking and cleaning.
Just not how they apply to me.

I'm going to be completely honest here. I hate food shopping. Probably because, now that My Beloved was retired and had more spare time on his hands, one of the joys of his existence was to "help" unload the groceries from their reusable, environmentally friendly bags, check each item against the cashier's tape, and question everything I had purchased. "Why did you buy this brand of dishwasher detergent, Carol? Don't you know that store brand is always cheaper? We're on a fixed income now, you know. " Etc. etc.

Jeez. I've been doing the family shopping for more than 30 years and we weren't bankrupt yet.

This time, I was only going to pick up the bare necessities – eggs, milk, bread, maybe a package of chicken, some veggies. The tiny refrigerator in the apartment didn't hold much. And dog biscuits. I hoped Lucy and Ethel wouldn't notice if they got a generic brand for a change. And forgive me if they did.

Concentrating on getting the most items for the least amount of money is a game I've been playing with myself ever since Jim retired. I usually lose, to hear My Beloved tell it, but I keep on trying. It's kind of like going to one of the casinos Connecticut is famous for and playing the slots.

I was concentrating extra hard today on bargain shopping because I didn't want any stray thoughts of dead house buyers, failed real estate transactions, or possible arrests of best friends for murder to creep into my mind. So I didn't even see another grocery cart coming down the canned food aisle until I careened into it.

"I'm so sorry," I stammered. "My mind was on something else and I wasn't watching where I was going."

"You always had your mind on other things, Carol. That's one thing about you that hasn't changed," said the driver of the other shopping cart.

Good grief. It was Sister Rose.

"What's wrong, Carol? You were never at a loss for words. Didn't you think nuns ate?"

This was too much. I was in no mood for the good sister's peculiar brand of sarcasm today. And, besides, if Jim and I decided to – graciously – allow our antique home to be used as a fundraising venue for Sally's Place, Sister Rose had better straighten up and start being nicer to me.

Of course, I needed her cooperation, too, for my potentially Pulitzer-Prize-winning article on domestic violence, but I chose not to focus on that. Right now, I had other matters to clear up with my former English teacher.

"You know, Sister," I said, "I never understood why you always went out of your way to criticize me when I was in high school. And now that I'm an adult, even though we haven't seen each other in years, you're still doing it. I never had the nerve to speak up for myself when I was a teenager, but you can't give me in-school suspension any more. I think you owe me an explanation. And an apology."

We stood there, shopping cart to shopping cart, while other shoppers maneuvered around us. I was shaking, either from anger or fear. Would I be punished in hell for calling a nun out?

Sister Rose finally broke the silence.

"You're right, Carol. There are some things I need to say to you. But not here. How about if we finish our shopping and meet for a cup of coffee? You could come to my office at Sally's Place. It's more private there."

"I'm all for having a cup of coffee," I said. But not on your turf. I'm not that crazy. "I usually have a quick shot of caffeine around this time of day. But I have another idea. Why don't we meet at The Paperback Café, instead? Do you know where that is?"

Sister Rose nodded. "I'll see you there in half an hour."

I called after her, "Don't be late." Of course, I didn't say it very loud. I just wanted to have the last word with her. For once in my life.

The Café was quiet when I got there. Of course, Sister Rose had gotten there ahead of me, and was already sipping a cup of steaming coffee.

Rats. I really wanted to get there first. I know, that's childish.

I hoped our little coffee klatch wouldn't take too long. I had perishable groceries in my car. But I was curious about what Sister Rose had to say to me.

Once I had my own cup of half decaf/half regular coffee, I settled myself in the booth opposite her. So far, she hadn't even acknowledged my presence. I realized I could luck out. If she didn't talk at all, I'd be back at the apartment in no time.

"Carol," she finally said, "what I'm going to tell you isn't an apology. It's more of an explanation. You can take it any way you want to."

Sister Rose took a deep breath. Then she asked, "How old do you think I am?"

Huh? Now this was really weird. The next thing, we'd be promising to send each other birthday cards.

I took a good look at her. I mean, I *looked* at her. When I was in high school, I always assumed all our teachers were old. Really old. At least, well, forty. Fifty, even. But if Sister Rose had been forty then, that'd make her – I did some quick math, not my strong suit – close to eighty today.

The woman sitting opposite me was nowhere near that age. In fact, she looked remarkably like someone…someone my age. And never mind exactly what that age is.

"I'm only four years older than you, Carol," Sister Rose said. "Surprised?"

Surprised? I was in shock.

"Wait a minute," I said. "That means when I was in high school…"

"I was still only four years older than you."

She spread her hands wide in front of her. "Don't you see, Carol? I was a young girl, too, just like all of you. Mount Saint Francis was my very first teaching assignment. I was scared to death. But determined to be the very best English teacher I could possibly be. And I wanted everyone to respect me, so I forced all my students to toe the line. There was no fooling around in my class.

"I admit I overdid it in the discipline area. I did tone it down as I got more used to teaching. But your class was my first one. I didn't want any of you to suspect how young I was. And how insecure."

Wow. This was pretty amazing. I couldn't wait to tell Nancy about this.

"OK," I said slowly. "I get the fact that you were young and scared back then. But that doesn't excuse the fact that you're still coming down on me just like you used to do in high school."

I wasn't letting her off the hook that easily.

"Old habits die hard, Carol," said Sister Rose. "A little nun humor there."

Humph.

"I always wanted the best for you. But you aggravated me so much. You had tremendous potential and I felt I needed to push you hard to force you to live up to it. I guess seeing you again pushed me back into that same mode. Every now and then, at Sally's Place, I tend to do the same thing when I see a young woman about to make a huge life mistake. The difference there is, when I start to get like that, the women don't let me get away with it."

"Maybe you're losing your touch," I said.

Oops. My bad.

"Sorry, Sister. I still have a smart mouth."

To my amazement, Sister Rose laughed out loud. I don't think I'd ever heard her laugh before. And then I started to laugh. We made quite a picture, two middle-aged women laughing like teenagers.

"One other thing I want to get straight with you, Carol," my coffee companion said. "Please, just call me Rose. Not Sister Rose. Especially if you're at Sally's Place or the thrift shop. We try to downplay the religious connection. It intimidates some of the clients. My life now is all about helping women and children who are going through the toughest time in their lives. Some of the stories I've heard make me want to cry."

I nodded encouragingly. This could be the start of my domestic violence article.

"Not that I can share any of them with you or anyone else, Carol. I sometimes feel the burden of confidentiality is more than I can bear. But the Good Lord always keeps me going."

OK. Forget the article for now. But maybe, if I met Sister Rose at Sally's Place, she'd be more willing to talk. If only to give me some background information on the magnitude of the problem.

"I don't think I can call you 'Rose,' Sister. I bet Nancy and Claire and Mary Alice would say the same thing. You remember all of them, right?"

"Mary Alice Mahoney. Now, she was a lovely girl. Very quiet and studious."

"You mean, not at all like me?" I asked.

Sister Rose laughed. "You don't think I'm going to respond to that, do you, Carol?"

I shook my head.

"Mary Alice married Brian Costello while he was in medical school, and they had two sons. Then, Brian died tragically, in a car accident."

Should I go any further? Was Sister Rose the one person I could talk to who would absolutely keep my confidence about Mary Alice and Jack

Cartwright? That was a pretty outrageous idea. I hadn't seen the woman in years. And I certainly never thought we'd be trading secrets.

But apparently, because of her role as Director of Sally's Place, she was the keeper of many women's secrets. And took that commitment very seriously.

Hmm. Hadn't she just told me something about herself that was pretty personal.

I looked at my watch. The Paperback Café would be closing in about 20 minutes. In fact, the servers were already refilling the salt and pepper shakers and setting up for tomorrow's breakfast.

What the hell. I mean, what the heck.

I went for it.

"Sister." I paused. "I mean, Rose. I'd like to share something with you, too. In fact, you may be the only one I can tell. It's about Mary Alice. And my husband Jim and me. Oh, I forgot, you don't even know I'm married. Well, he's a great guy, and I have two terrific kids...."

Sister Rose looked at me like I was stupid. It was a familiar look.

"Carol, maybe some other time you can fill me in on your own life. But now, what do you want to tell me about Mary Alice?"

She took my hands and squeezed them. Much too tightly. Ouch.

"I could tell that you had something bothering you. That's why I decided to tell you my secret. So you'd feel comfortable sharing with me."

"You surprise me," I said. "But then, you usually did. How did you figure out I had something on my mind?"

"Years of working with families in crisis have taught me to read faces fairly well," Sister Rose said. "And I believe there are no accidents in life. Everything that happens is all part of The Plan. How else do you explain our paths crossing after all these years?"

I could have answered, "Because I like to shop for bargains," but this time, I didn't shoot my mouth off.

"Mary Alice may be in serious trouble," I said. "And I found out something today that could make it even worse for her."

I poured out the whole sad tale, as succinctly as I could, starting with the house sale, finding Jack, Mary Alice's presence at the house that night, and, finally, the old newspaper article. By the time I was finished, I was on the verge of tears. No surprise, right?

"What should I do, Sister? Should I talk to Mary Alice? Maybe try to find out what happened to Jack on my own? You don't think I should go to the police, do you?"

"I'm glad you talked to me about this, Carol. But you must understand that everything you've said about Mary Alice's involvement is purely speculation on your part. And you don't even know that a crime was committed. You're jumping to conclusions. Something I seem to remember you did quite a lot when you were younger." Sister Rose smiled to take the sting out of her words.

"Please know that you can trust me to keep this completely confidential. And you can talk to me any time you feel the need for a sounding board. I hope that, after all these years, you and I can become friends.

"I'm sure Mary Alice is innocent of any wrong-doing. But do not, I repeat, do not, start investigating Jack's death on your own. You'll only stir up trouble. Let the police do their job, and hopefully the whole thing will blow over. Mary Alice may never know who Jack really was. That may be for the best."

I knew she was right, of course. I should mind my own business.

But I also knew that if the police suspected Mary Alice of a crime, there was no way I wouldn't get involved.

Sister Rose and I parted in front of The Paperback Café. She actually gave me a quick peck on the cheek. Boy, talk about surprising me.

I was halfway back to the apartment before it dawned on me that we hadn't even talked about the show house.

Chapter 23

My idea of housework is to sweep the room with a glance.

When I pulled into the parking lot at the apartment, I was glad to see that Jim's car was already there. I couldn't wait to tell him about having coffee with Sister Rose. He'd never believe it.

It was amazing how much calmer I felt about everything now. Maybe the good sister would be an "unexpected friend," like Maria Lesco. Stranger things have happened. (Not that I ever make snap judgments about people.)

I also felt better because I'd made a real effort to make our tiny apartment into a cozy retreat. Not a honeymoon cottage – we were way beyond that. But maybe my life would be easier with only three rooms to take care of. I was going to make the best of the situation, no matter what, and I'd start by cooking a nice dinner for Jim on our minuscule stove.

My good mood evaporated as soon as I opened the door. I had left a neat apartment. What I was returning to was slightly less than chaos. Newspapers strewn all over the floor. Dishes and glasses on the counter and in the sink. The tiny kitchen table littered with files. The television turned to CNN, blaring loudly. (I guess the Jim had ordered a cable hookup after all.)

And My Beloved in the only good living room chair. Sound asleep. And snoring.

Jeez, I'd only been gone two hours. Hurricanes had nothing on Jim. He could create chaos all on his own. Probably from overdosing on The Weather Channel.

Should I be ashamed to admit that all previous worries immediately vanished from my mind, to be replaced by rage at the scene before me?

Heck, no. I don't think any wife in America would have reacted differently. I was livid.

I slammed the grocery bags down on the floor. Luckily, there were no eggs in either of them. Jim didn't even stir.

Clicking off CNN did the trick. Jim came to and rubbed his eyes.

"Hi Carol. I guess I must have dozed off. I was researching next week's column."

I resisted saying that the column must be pretty boring if it put him to sleep. Instead, I made an heroic effort to choose my words carefully.

"I did some food shopping after I unpacked more boxes," I said, picking up one of my reusable grocery bags (I am environmentally sensitive) and putting it on top of Jim's pile of papers. "I'll bet you were surprised when you came back and saw how nice the apartment looked." Before you messed it all up.

"Huh?" said My Beloved, glancing around the room. "Oh, yes, it does look better. I guess I should say, it did look better, until I spread all my work things around. Sorry, honey." He gave me a peck on the cheek. "You know my 'filing system.' I'd planned to have everything put away before you saw it."

Well, that was a little better. Jim did notice my efforts. Maybe men can be trained after all.

I was proud of myself for not lashing out at him the way I sometimes do. Poor guy. This mess had to be tough on him, too.

I grabbed a bag and squeezed my way around the table into the tiny kitchen area. And promptly banged my hip on an open cabinet drawer.

Ouch!

"Jim," I yelled, "for heaven's sake, will you please make an effort to close doors and drawers! It drives me crazy."

I rubbed my well-padded hip to ease the pain I was feeling. "This time, I really hurt myself. And if we're going to be living in such tight quarters for a while, you have to remember. I don't think that's asking too much."

"You do some things that drive me crazy, too, Carol," My Beloved shot back in his defense.

Moi? I had irritating habits? That couldn't be possible.

"Oh, yeah?" I said. "Like what?"

"You interrupt me when I'm talking. And.."

"What do you mean?" I said. "I never interrupt you."

Jim waved his index finger at me in triumph. "You see? You see? You just did it! You don't even know you do it. You do it all the time. I bet you interrupt me much more than I leave doors or drawers open."

Jeez. He had me there.

We hadn't gotten on each other's nerves (much) in our big antique house. But living in small quarters for an indefinite period of time might require some adjustments.

After all, nobody's perfect. Even me.

Jim clipped leashes onto Lucy and Ethel and announced he was taking them for a walk. I could tell he was still annoyed with me. And I was equally annoyed with him.

Clearly someone (that would be me) had to come up with a solution that would be workable and satisfactory to both of us. As I unpacked the groceries and squeezed them into the miniscule cabinet space (carefully closing the doors), I thought about how, when Mike and Jenny were little, I used to be able to get them to do things they didn't want to do by making a game out of it. Like picking up their clothes. Cleaning their rooms. Taking out the garbage.

That's when I came up with a great idea. I could hardly wait for Jim to come back from his walk so I could spring it on him.

"I admit that I'm not perfect," I said to My Beloved when he finally made an appearance. I handed him a glass of his favorite merlot as a peace offering, and he settled into a living room chair.

"We're both stubborn, too. And we like to have things done our own way.

"So here's my idea." I plopped myself down beside him and gave him a little smooch.

"You know what a Honey-Do List is, right? A long list of chores to accomplish around the house, like clean out the attic, mow the lawn, or wash the windows."

Jim nodded. "I used to dread weekends, wondering what new jobs you'd come up with for me to do. That's one advantage to being in this apartment, I guess. No more lists."

"Don't be too sure about that," I replied. "My idea is to have a Honey-Don't List. As in, 'Honey, when you do that, you drive me absolutely crazy, so don't do it!' We'll make a list of the things about each other that get on our nerves. We'll cut our list into individual strips and put them into two jars, one for each of us. Every morning, we'll draw a strip from the other's jar, and that person will have to refrain from that behavior for the entire day.

"We could even have a prize at the end of each week for the person who makes the most effort – like going out to dinner. Or picking which movie to see. What do you think?"

The more I thought about my idea, the better I liked it. In fact, I was surprised no other wife had come up with it before.

My list about Jim's faults would be much longer than his list about mine, naturally. Oh, well. I'm sure if he racked his brain he could come up with a few. I'm not perfect, I know that. But pretty close. Most of the time.

"I think you're nuts, Carol," said My Beloved. "But I'm willing to give it a try. I even know the number one item I'm putting on your list."

"I know, too. I shouldn't interrupt you when you're talking."

"Wrong, Carol," Jim said.

"Don't find any more dead bodies."

Humph.

Over another delicious takeout meal from Seafood Sandy's – my desire to cook had evaporated – I brought Jim up to date on most of what had happened that day.

I was pleased to see that he was taking copious notes as I was talking. That meant he was listening to me, for once.

"So then Sister Rose and I met for coffee at The Paperback Café," I said. "She really is very nice. We had quite a chat." I omitted telling Jim exactly what the chat was about. I didn't want to speculate on Mary Alice with him.

"Jim, what are you writing?" I finally asked. "I don't think I've said anything that memorable."

"Making more notes for my Honey-Don't List," My Beloved said. "Do you know how long it takes you to get to the point of a story?"

Oh, boy. Maybe this wasn't such a good idea after all.

Then Jim started to laugh. "I'm just teasing you, Carol."

"Well, I don't think you're very funny," I said, my feelings only slightly mollified. "What did you do for the rest of the day?"

Jim took a healthy swig of wine to fortify himself. "As a matter of fact, I have some news for you. And you're not going to like it. I was waiting for the right moment. But there really isn't one, so here goes. And please don't interrupt me."

I clamped my lips shut. Get on with it, already. Nothing My Beloved said could be worse than worrying that one of my best friends was responsible for someone's death.

"I took a ride out to Eden's Grove this afternoon to check on the progress of our new house," Jim continued. "I expected to see some workmen laying the subflooring by now.

"But there was nobody there.

"I went to the sales office to complain. After all, we'd given them a deposit a while ago. At the rate they're going, we'd be lucky to move into the house by Christmas."

"Good for you, Jim. What did you find out?"

"They have some new salesman in the office now named Skip Campbell. I didn't see anyone there I recognized, so I had to deal with him. At first, he was pretty evasive when I demanded some action. He wouldn't give me a straight answer as to why the work had stopped, or when it was going to start up again. I wouldn't let him get away with it.

"Then good old Skip told me that the Eden's Grove Homeowners Association had an emergency meeting about us last night. With all the notoriety about our old house, and the buyer dying under mysterious circumstances, they don't want us to move in.

"Eden's Grove is voiding the contract and giving us back our deposit. And there's not a damn thing we can do about it."

My fantasy of two master bedroom suites vanished.

Poof. All gone.

And I thought the day couldn't get any worse.

Chapter 24

When life gets you down, just put on your big girl undies and deal with it.

I woke up the next morning after a restless night. I remembered the terrible dream I'd had about Adam and Eve chasing Jim and me out of the Garden of Eden with axes and hatchets in their hands. "And don't ever come back," they screamed at us. "You're not good enough to live here with us." It's funny how I can never remember the happy dreams. But the bad ones – those are seared into my brain.

Jim was still sound asleep beside me, with the dogs curled up on either side. (The rule we had about no dogs on our bed had been quickly erased once we moved into these temporary digs.) I eased myself out of bed and headed off to take a quick shower. I tried to be as quiet as possible, so as not to wake my sleeping prince.

He looked so peaceful lying there, poor baby. I knew this ordeal was as hard on him as it was on me. We just reacted to stress in different ways. I needn't have worried. Neither canines nor Jim stirred.

I used the cascading water to do my favorite meditation, and washed all the bad things, including Adam and Eve, down the drain. So there!

I needed to focus on positive things today. Like starting to research my story on domestic violence. That entailed another talk with my new best buddy Sister Rose, but that wasn't the way I wanted my day to start.

To paraphrase the Bard of Avon, "How many problems doth stress me today?"

In addition to the kaput house deal and Mark and Jenny breaking up and becoming reaquainted with my former nemesis and new buddy Sister Rose, I had a new one to add to the list. Jim and I would drive each other crazy if we were stuck in our tiny apartment for an indefinite period of time, despite the Honey-Don't List.

The person I needed to talk to first was Nancy. She had to find us permanent new digs before Jim and I ended up in divorce court. Even if two master suites weren't included.

Sigh.

I know my best friends' schedules like I know my own. Maybe better, since mine tends to be erratic.

Nancy's idea of a great start to the day was to spend an hour huffing and puffing and generally causing herself great bodily pain at a nearby women's gym, Battle of the Bulge. She called it exercise. I called it torture. Nancy was not going to slide into the senior part of her life without a fight.

Recently, she almost talked me into going with her for a consult about some procedure called a "Liquid Facelift." Fortunately, when I realized this was a lot more involved than switching moisturizer brands, I came to my senses and backed out.

Oh, well, to each her own.

"I love it when I'm right," I said to myself as I pulled into a parking space next to Nancy's snappy red convertible. "Especially when it happens so infrequently."

A young woman in sweats, gym bag in hand, eyed me as I got out of my car. I guess she'd never heard anyone talk to herself before. Wait'll she got to be my age. She'd find out.

The young woman just stood there, not moving.

Good grief. It was my darling daughter.

"Jenny. My gosh. I'm surprised to see you here," I said as I wrapped her in a big hug.

"Not as surprised as I am to see you here, Mom. Have you finally decided to start exercising? It'll do you so much good."

"As if!" I said, laughing. "I'm here because I have to talk to Nancy. I know this is where she always starts her day."

"You'll be surprised who else starts her day working out," said Jenny, eyeing my baggy sweatshirt and jeans with a critical eye. "I'll bet those pants have an elastic waist. If you exercised properly, you wouldn't have to wear things like that."

"I like these pants," I said defensively. "They're comfortable."

Jenny laughed and held the gym door open for me. My ears were immediately assaulted by pulsating music coming from an interior room.

"I'm going to get changed for my yoga class," said Jenny. "Sit here and wait for Nancy." She thrust a multi-colored brochure into my hands. "You might as well read this while you wait. Maybe it'll give you a nudge in the right direction."

Hmm. I put on my bifocals and quickly scanned the sheet. Apparently the loud music was coming from a class called "Mature Women's Aerobics." I wondered if the gym also offered one for "Immature Women."

The door opened and about 30 women spilled out of the room, towels around their necks, water bottles in their hands. I had no trouble spotting Nancy. She was the only one who looked fresh as the proverbial daisy, while the rest were, well, sweaty.

She waved when she saw me and mouthed, "Going to take a quick shower. Wait here for me."

Good grief. Was that my hairdresser Deanna in the crowd? Now, that was a surprise. I thought the only thing she ever exercised was a comb and brush. I shrunk down in my chair so she wouldn't notice me and scold me for trimming my bangs again.

Too late. She saw me, all right. And made a scissor-like motion across her brow, followed by shaking her right index finger at me.

"I'll come see you later this week," I yelled.

"You better. Your bangs are all uneven." Then she disappeared into the locker room.

The last two stragglers came into view, deep in conversation.

"I can't believe what you've been through, dear," said my neighbor Phyllis Stevens.

"It's an absolute nightmare," said Sara Miller. "I will always believe that neglected old wreck of a house was responsible for poor Jack's death. Our family has been completely shattered by the shock."

My family isn't doing too well, either, I wanted to respond. But, coward that I am, instead I shrank down in my chair and prayed they wouldn't notice me. I didn't want a confrontation.

They walked right by me into the locker room, Phyllis's arm around Sara's shoulder.

Good grief.

"I think you're overreacting again," Nancy said. "Nobody's accusing you of a crime, for heaven's sake."

"Oh, yeah?" I shot back. "Sara told Phyllis that the reason Jack died was because we hadn't taken proper care of our house. That sounded like an accusation to me."

We sat in silence for a few minutes. I had suggested getting take-out coffee and driving to Fairport Beach. Looking at Long Island Sound and hearing the soothing sounds of waves as they rippled onto the sand never failed to calm me.

Except this time.

"Listen, sweetie," Nancy finally said, "I know you're still very upset about this situation, and you have a perfect right to be. It's terrible, I agree. But I've told you, and please believe that I know what I'm talking about, that your house was – is – in excellent condition. If there had been anything wrong, the inspection would have shown it. And it didn't. Because there isn't. Sara is just grasping at straws, trying to find someone or something to blame for Jack's death. And, unfortunately, you and the house are the logical culprits. We'll do the show house, people will flock to see it, you'll get a full-price cash offer, sell the house, and move to your dream house at Eden's Grove. With two master bedroom suites."

"Well, Nance, I've got news for you." Tears pricked my eyes. "Jim and I are not moving to Eden's Grove because the damned homeowners' association has decided they don't want us there. Because of the notoriety about our old house. We may be in that small box of an apartment until we're carried out feet first."

Nancy, Realtor extraordinaire, immediately swung into professional gear. Just as I hoped she would.

"Listen, Carol, this may be a blessing in disguise. I'll find you and Jim the perfect property. Forget those snobs at Eden's Grove." Her eyes narrowed. "You are getting your deposit back, aren't you?"

"In full," I said. "But I feel like Jim and I are damaged goods. Second-class citizens. Do you know what I mean?"

"Believe it or not, I do," Nancy replied. "On a whole other level. I've been spending some time volunteering at Sally's Place, and some of the stories I've heard from the women there are just unbelievable. Too many of them feel like they caused the abusive behavior, rather than being the victim of it." She shook her head. "It's tragic. That's one reason why I feel so strongly about doing this show house, to help them and all the other families who will benefit from the program in the future."

"Nancy, you didn't tell me you were volunteering there. When did you start?"

"Believe it or not, I don't tell you everything, Carol." She gave my hand a squeeze. "Just almost everything. And, of course, there was the Sister Rose factor. I knew you'd freak when you found out she was involved."

I had to laugh. "Well, my friend, I did freak when I walked into their thrift shop and saw her for the first time in umpteen years. I haven't had a chance to talk to you about that, with everything else going on.

"Was that your plan? Not to warn me in advance? Just suggest, every so casually, that I drop in to Sally's Closet and check out the bargains?"

Nancy took another sip of her coffee before she answered me.

"I admit, I took the coward's way out. She scared me to death in high school, too, though not nearly as much as she did you. I figured you'd never go for the show house idea if you found out in advance she'd be involved, no matter how desperate you and Jim are to sell your house.

"Forgive me, please."

Well, what could I say? Of course, Nancy was absolutely right.

"As a matter of fact, once the initial shock of reconnecting with her has worn off, I'm finding out that Sister Rose isn't such a bad egg after all," I said. "I saw her again yesterday in the supermarket, and we ended up having coffee together, believe it or not. And had quite a nice conversation. I don't know which one of us was the more surprised about that."

Talking about my coffee date brought back the ugly suspicions I'd been harboring about Mary Alice. I wondered if I could trust Nancy to keep her mouth shut if I probed a little about Jack Cartwright.

What the heck. I'd be subtle.

"I'm getting excited about the show house," I said, "although I still can't get beyond the shock of finding Jack. I realized last night that, even though he was buying our house, Jim and I didn't know very much about him. Except for the fact that he was married to Sara Miller's daughter Alyssa.

"Was he from Fairfield County originally?"

Nancy looked at me hard. "I know what you're getting at, Carol. You figured out who Jack was, right?"

Huh?

"You knew who Jack was and didn't say anything to me?" I couldn't believe this.

"I didn't recognize him," Nancy responded.

"Mary Alice did."

Chapter 25

Dust bunnies make ideal pets.

I couldn't believe what I was hearing.

"Do you mean to tell me," I said, "that Mary Alice knew who Jack was all along? And you did, too? And neither one of you said a single word to Jim or me about it?"

I was shaking with rage.

"How could you do this? Why did you, for God's sake?"

"Take it easy, Carol," Nancy said. "And let me explain what happened. Believe me, please, that we kept the truth about Jack from you and Jim with the best of intentions. In fact…"

She stopped herself.

"In fact, what?" I prompted her. "What?"

"Well, I guess I'm the one who's really to blame about this. Mary Alice wanted you to know. But I was a selfish bitch. I was afraid that if you knew who Jack was, you'd call off the house sale. And I needed the commission. You know how hard the real estate market is these days."

She turned her face away from me and whimpered, "I'm sorry, Carol. I'm truly sorry.

"And I guess the Good Lord had the last laugh on me, because the house deal is off, anyway."

I can be a little slow on the uptake sometimes. I admit that.

Sometimes I only hear half of what's been said and immediately react, before I hear the whole story. I admit that.

And I do tend to speak before I think about what I'm saying. I admit that, too.

This time, I exercised as much self-control as I could and willed my mouth to stay shut. I wanted to take Nancy and shake her. I don't think I've ever been as angry with her before in our forty-plus year friendship. Even the time that she started dating Richie Russo during freshman year of high school, though she knew I had a major crush on him and used to pray each night before I went to bed that he'd call and ask me out.

I wanted to be sure I understood exactly what Nancy had told me.

"Let's go over this again," I said, using my most adult voice. "You're admitting that both you and Mary Alice knew Jack Cartwright was the person driving the car that caused Brian's death. Mary Alice recognized him first, then told you. When, pray tell, did this happen?"

"It was at the St. Patrick's Day Open House," Nancy said. "Mary Alice had volunteered to help greet people, so I'd be free to show prospective buyers around the house and do what I was supposed to do – sell your house. She didn't tell me right away about Jack, because I guess she wasn't sure. It had been so many years since she'd seen him. And he went by 'Johnny' back then, not Jack.

"By the time she was positive 'Jack' and 'Johnny' were the same person, you and the Cartwrights had already signed the preliminary papers to sell them your house.

"You know Mary Alice," Nancy went on.

Well, I thought I did.

"She knew how much you and Jim wanted to sell up and move to Eden's Grove. And she figured, probably correctly, that if you found out who Jack was, you might cancel the deal out of loyalty to her. Well, I guess I have to take the blame for that suggestion. But she agreed with me. We decided not to tell you. "

"I don't see how you planned to keep all of this a secret, not just from Jim and me, but from everybody else. Fairport is a pretty small town. Word was bound to leak out.

"And how could Mary Alice bear the thought that she could see the man who ruined her life shopping at the CVS on any given day? She was bound to run into him sometime."

"Mary Alice had a solution for that. She was going to contact him and suggest they meet. So she could put the past behind her, once and for all.

"They planned to meet at your house the night before the closing."

Ouch. Could this get any worse?

"Nancy," I said with extreme patience, "what you're saying is that Mary Alice had both motive, and opportunity to put Jack out of her life once and for all. Don't you get it?"

"I'm not stupid, Carol," Nancy snapped back at me. "Of course I know what this could look like to someone who doesn't know Mary Alice. But you and I know she doesn't have a mean bone in her body. She's a nurse, for crying out loud. She's trained to save people, not hurt them. Or worse."

"Why didn't Mary Alice tell me herself?" I asked. "It's been a few days since Jack died, and she knows that the house deal is definitely off. She even admitted to the police that she was at my house that night. She had some nutty story about waiting for me to come so we could hide something of mine there. So there'd always be a part of me in the house. I don't remember that conversation at all. I wonder if she made the whole thing up, so that if someone had seen her there late at night, she'd have an explanation. Even though it was a lame one.

"This makes absolutely no sense to me."

Nancy held out her cell phone to me.

"There's only one way to find out. Call her and tell her we're coming over."

She cranked the engine. "You talk, and I'll drive."

The phone rang and rang at Mary Alice's. She didn't answer.

"Maybe she's not home," I said to Nancy as we sped up Beach Road toward Mary Alice's condo.

"She's home," Nancy said. "I talked to her this morning, before I left for the gym." She pressed her foot down on the accelerator and I held onto my seat belt for dear life. "Nancy, slow down. All we need now is a speeding ticket!"

"You're right, Carol," Nancy said, easing her foot back off the pedal just a little. "I'm just anxious to see Mary Alice. I don't know about you, but I'll feel a little better when the three of us talk this out and figure out a plan."

"A plan?" I asked. "What kind of a plan?"

"A plan to keep Mary Alice out of jail if it turns out Jack was murdered."

"You look like hell," said Nancy, never one to mince words. I had to agree with her assessment. Mary Alice's eyes were red and puffy, and she had the kind of dark circles below them that indicated sleep had not visited her for quite a while.

"I feel like hell, too," she said. "Or like I'm in the middle of it.

"How are you doing, Carol?"

Nancy cut to the chase. "She knows, Mary Alice. I told her that you recognized Jack Cartwright."

Mary Alice started to cry. I think that, in all the years I've known her, I'd never seen her cry before.

Wordlessly, I put my arms around her and held her. That seemed to make the situation even worse.

"This is like going through Brian's death all over again. It's all my fault," Mary Alice said, sobbing into my shoulder.

"Sweetie, how could this be your fault?" Nancy asked, leading a still weeping Mary Alice to the living room sofa.

"I should have told Carol and Jim who Jack was. Even if it meant they called off the house sale." She glared at Nancy. "Come to think of it, not telling them was your idea, not mine. I never should have listened to you."

Nancy, for once, looked truly penitent. "I've already told Carol that I gave you bad advice. You're right. It really is my fault. But now, what are we going to do?"

"You know what the ironic thing is?" Mary Alice asked. "I chickened out and never contacted Jack. When I thought about it some more, I realized it was a very bad idea. I figured I'd just take my chances. If I ran into him anywhere around Fairport, I could just walk the other way."

She shuddered. "When I think of Jack lying there inside, dying, I feel so terrible. I would have helped him, if only I'd known he was there. I wonder if anyone will believe that.

"Oh, God, what a mess this is."

I had had enough of Mary Alice's tears and Nancy's guilt. I know that sounds harsh, particularly due to my overindulgence in the same behaviors myself.

Well, tough.

What I wanted now were answers. Because I had plenty of questions.

"OK, kids. Let's get everything out in the open. No more secrets. Mary Alice, did you and I really agree to meet at my house the night before the closing, or did you just say that to the police in case somebody saw you there? You know my memory isn't very dependable these days."

Mary Alice looked hurt. "Why don't you remember? You loved the idea of hiding a trinket in the house before the closing, and asked me to come with you. You didn't want Jim to know because he'd think we were crazy."

"I still don't remember," I said. "I've had a few other things on my mind, you know. But why in the world did you tell the police about it?" I asked. "Didn't you realize being at our house that night could make you look guilty?"

"Guilty? Of what? I had no idea Jack was inside your house."

Huh? Just a second ago Mary Alice was blaming herself for Jack's death.

"Anyway," Mary Alice continued, "besides the three of us, who's going to know about my connection to Jack? And I know you guys won't say anything."

"Of course we won't, sweetie," Nancy said, patting her hand.

I looked at the two of them. What a pair. I wondered if they both lived in Fantasyland instead of Fairport.

"I hate to burst your bubble," I said, "but this is bound to come out. I'm betting that Jack's family knew, for one. That includes Sara Miller, whom I saw getting very cozy with that blabbermouth Phyllis Stevens at the gym this morning. If Sara said something to Phyllis, it'll be all over town in a heartbeat.

"And as long as we're sharing secrets, I found out about your connection to Jack on my own, Mary Alice. I just didn't know how to talk to you about it."

I proceeded to share my unpacking story with Nancy and Mary Alice. And my discovery of the incriminating newspaper article. When I got to the part about Lucy and Ethel's "disposal" of the article, I must have painted quite a vivid picture, because all three of us howled with laughter for a good five minutes.

"I guess we all needed that," Nancy said. "There's nothing like a good laugh to clear out the brain and put things into proper perspective.

"Now, we have some other things to figure out. Like the preview party for the show house. Remember, we talked about that, Carol?"

What? I'd forgotten something else?

"Nance, I have no clue what you're talking about. What's a preview party? And shouldn't we be coming up with a plan to help Mary Alice?"

"I don't know yet if I need help," said Mary Alice. "And to tell you the truth, I'm sick of thinking and worrying about Jack. Just talking to you both has been so therapeutic. No more secrets. No more guilt. We're on the same wave length again, and that's all that matters.

"Now, to echo Carol, what exactly is a preview party?"

"Before the designers come into a show house and do their thing," Nancy explained, "the sponsoring organization holds a fancy black tie, invitation-only party so guests can see the empty house. The date's already been set for this coming Saturday night."

"What?" I shrieked. "Jim and I are giving a black tie party this weekend? How the heck do you expect us to pull it off with such short notice? Are you nuts? Jim's going to pitch a fit when he hears about this."

"Easy, Carol. You and Jim don't have to do a thing but dress up and show up. No cooking, no cleaning, no decorating. All the arrangements have already been made."

Now I was really confused.

"Don't frown at me that way, sweetie," Nancy said to me. "At our age, frowning can cause permanent wrinkles."

Trust Nancy to know something like that. In her quest to retain her trim figure and unlined face, she was inclined to try every new product that came on the market. A one-woman consumption machine.

"All right, already. I won't frown. But I'm still confused."

"Me too," said Mary Alice. "Although talking about a party sure beats talking about...well, you know. And I guess that if the preview party is going ahead, that must mean that the police have OK'd using the house, right? Maybe the investigation is over, and I can breathe a sigh of relief."

"All I know is, my boss called the chief of police and put a little pressure on," Nancy said. "The next thing I knew, we had the green light to hold the event and start the renovations for the show house. Superior Interiors will be doing the whole house, which is perfect because Marcia Fischer already knows the property.

"It may seem to be happening super-fast," said Nancy, turning to me, "but remember that your house is a last-minute venue substitute. The first home owners backed out after all the preliminary arrangements had been made. Invitations for the preview party had already gone out. We're using Maria's Trattoria to cater the party, of course."

"That makes me feel a little better," I said. "So Jim and I don't have to do anything but show up? You're sure? You're not going to spring something else on us at the last minute, are you?

"And who are these guests anyway? Will we know any of them?"

"There are about one hundred people coming so far," Nancy said. "As a matter of fact, when word got out that we were using your house instead of the other one on Roseville Road, the phones at the real estate office and Sally's Place started ringing off the hook. More people want to come. We may have to turn people away.

"Oh, by the way, you should know we're charging one hundred and fifty dollars a person to tour your empty house. It all goes to support Sally's Place."

"Wow," I said.

"Wow is right," said Nancy, warming to her subject even more. "This could be the biggest event to hit Fairport in years. The national media attention alone will be tremendous. We'll sell your house for sure after this is over."

"National media attention?" I repeated. "I'm not sure how Jim will react to that. He was pretty upset to find himself a media star, even though it was only for a short time. If it happens again, he'll freak out for sure."

"He won't freak out when all the house offers come pouring in," Nancy said. "He'll be absolutely, positively, overjoyed.

"Now, to the important stuff.

"What are we all going to wear?"

Chapter 26

I highly recommend the 30-day diet. I'm on it, and so far I've lost 15 days.

To my surprise, Jim didn't freak out about the preview party. The possible media exposure didn't bother him either.

What he did complain about, loudly, was having to wear a tux.

"Good lord, Carol, a black tie event in our empty house? Why does it have to be so formal? I never heard of anything so ridiculous. I don't even know where my tux is. Probably packed away in some box in the storage unit."

What this translated to, of course, was, "I don't think my old tux will fit me, and I don't want to try it on and find out."

Mindful of my number one crime on Jim's Honey-Don't List, "Thou shalt not interrupt thy personal beloved under any circumstances (even though he's carrying on like a lunatic)," I let Jim rant and rave for a few minutes without a response. I knew he'd eventually calm down. And do things my way.

"We're the host and hostess of this event," I finally said in my most reasonable tone of voice. Technically not true, since the preview party was a benefit for Sally's Place. Hmm. Did that mean Sister Rose was going to show up in a snazzy, sequined off-the-shoulder dress and greet people at our door?

Perish the thought.

"I hope we don't have to pay to get into our own house," Jim said.

"Of course we don't have to pay, silly," I replied, and made a mental note to confirm that with Nancy.

"Maria's Trattoria is doing the catering, so you know the food will be good," I continued. When in doubt, pull out the food card. It works on Jim every time.

"I'm not shelling out money for a new tux," Jim repeated. "But I do have some good news for you on the financial front."

He reached in his pocket, pulled out an envelope, and waved it in my face. "I got back our entire deposit from Eden's Grove. We're well rid of that place and all the snobs who live there."

I snatched the envelope from his hand.

"This is going right back into the bank," I said. "But I'm taking out a little money to buy you that tux. And no arguments.

"You have to look your best for the preview party, especially if some of our almost-neighbors from Eden's Grove show up. We've gotta show them what they're missing.

"And I have to lose ten pounds before Saturday night."

I wasn't totally serious, of course. Nobody can lose weight that fast. So what if I was no longer a size 6? I mean, size 8. Oh, well. Might as well tell the truth. I'm now what I call a size 10 ½ on a good day, 10 ¾ on a bad day if I hold my breath. Time and gravity march on.

I rationalized that I needed a new dress for Saturday night's bash. Jim also needed a new tuxedo. And I had to get cracking on research for my article on domestic violence.

What better place to combine all these tasks than Sally's Closet? If I got really lucky, I wouldn't have to go anywhere else.

Shopping is my form of therapy. Nancy gets her high from exercising. I get mine from scoring a major bargain. In fact, I get positively giddy when I anticipate what I might find.

So I was in extra good spirits when I pushed open the door of the thrift shop, even though the Lilly Pulitzer dress I'd coveted during my last visit was no longer in the window. "You snooze, you lose," I told myself. The next time I saw something here that I really wanted, I was going to snap it up, whether it fit or not. Heck, Jenny could always wear it if my bargain purchase was too small for me.

Sister Rose wasn't in her place at the cashier's desk. I confess that, surprisingly enough, I was disappointed not to see her. After our exchange of girlish secrets, I knew she was someone I could trust. And like. After my shopping binge, I decided I'd try to see her at her official office, Sally's Place.

Two young women, deep in conversation, came through the swinging doors at the back of the thrift shop, dressed in the customary lavender aprons. They were pushing a cart piled high with new donations.

Bonanza! A chance to score bargains before anyone else could get to them.

When they saw me, conversation immediately ceased. Hmm.

"Hi, Carol." It was my neighbor Liz.

I gave her a bright smile, and turned toward the other young woman.

She was the most adorable little thing I'd ever seen, with the face of an angel framed by a halo of dark hair. Tiny in stature, probably not even five feet tall. She looked like a stiff wind would blow her right over, that's how thin she was.

"I don't think we've ever met, Mrs. Andrews," she said. "I'm Alyssa Cartwright, Jack's wife."

"I guess I should say, I'm Jack's widow."

Her eyes filled up. "That's going to take some getting used to."

Jeez. What could I say? No etiquette book I'd read ever covered a situation like this.

"Mrs. Andrews, in spite of what my mother may have told you, I want you to know that I don't hold you and your husband responsible for Jack's death," Alyssa said. "It must have been a terrible accident. The family may never know the cause, but it could have happened anywhere."

She wiped away some runaway tears from her face. "Jack and I were both looking forward to moving into your beautiful house and raising our children there. Excuse me. I have to go in the back and mark some more clothes now."

There was an awkward silence. Liz and I just stood there, looking at each other.

Finally, I recovered my wits enough to say, "I feel terrible. I never realized I'd see Jack's widow here. She took me by such surprise, I couldn't even express my condolences.

"I feel terrible," I repeated.

"There was no way for you to know that Alyssa volunteers here once a week," Liz said. "We didn't expect her in today, but she said that it was important for her to keep as normal a schedule as possible, especially for the children's sake.

"I guess you're here to buy something to wear to Jack's memorial service on Saturday."

"The memorial is Saturday? I didn't know. That's the same day as the preview party for the show house." There are obviously many things you don't know, I chided myself.

"I don't think the two events will be at the same time, Carol," said Liz.

"I didn't expect they would be," I shot back. I wanted to add that I wasn't that stupid. I didn't, of course.

"Does that mean the police have completed their investigation into the accident?" I asked, emphasizing the word "accident." If that was true, it sounded like good news for Mary Alice.

"I have no idea," Liz replied. "All I know is what Alyssa told me when she came in this morning. I'm sure the family just wants to get the whole ordeal over with."

"I can see why," I said. Me too.

"I have to confess, Liz, that what I really came in for this morning was to see if I could find a fancy dress for the show house preview party. And maybe a tuxedo for my husband. I thought it was a good idea to buy something here, because all the money raised from the thrift shop goes to support Sally's Place, just like the show house proceeds will.

"You know that our home was chosen to be the show house for the Sally's Place fundraiser, right?"

Liz's face brightened. "Sister Rose was just talking about that. She was praising you to high heavens, saying how generous it was of you and your husband to allow your home to be used."

Huh? Sister was singing my praises?

"I hear that tickets are already sold out for this weekend's preview party," Liz said as she rummaged through the dress racks searching for the perfect dress for me to wear. "I shouldn't have waited to buy tickets. It's too late now."

She looked pointedly at me, and I got the message loud and clear.

"I'm sure we can squeeze in two more people," I said with the confidence of someone who has no clue what she's talking about. "Leave it to me."

I realized it was time for me to beat a hasty retreat, in case Alyssa came back. The encounter with her had shaken me up, and I was sure it'd been just as upsetting for her.

"I'd like to see Sister Rose today," I said to Liz. "But I'm not sure where her office is. And whether I need an appointment."

"Her office is next door to our shop," Liz said. "If you go outside and stand in front of our building, look to your immediate right. There's a red brick two-story building with a discreet sign that says 'Sally's Place.' She likes to pop back and forth between her office and the thrift shop and keep an eye on all of us. When I first started volunteering here, it used to creep me out that she'd suddenly show up with no warning. I never even heard her coming."

That brought back a high school memory of Nancy and me (Claire and Mary Alice were the goody-goodies in those days and never were involved in these hijinks) sneaking out of school to have a quick cigarette. Sister Rose always found us, no matter where we were hiding. We never figured out how she did it. Her sudden, soundless appearances made all of us finally quit the smoking habit. Which, in hindsight of course, was a good thing.

"Do you want to talk to her about the show house?"

"I'm doing an investigative story on domestic violence in Fairport," I said, and watched Liz's eye widen. "I thought Sister would be a good person to start with."

"For that, you won't need an appointment," said Liz. "Sister's been on a personal crusade to bring attention to this issue for years.

"Wouldn't it be something if you turn out to be the one who makes that happen?"

Yes, indeedy, that certainly would be something.

Chapter 27

It's great to have a friend to grow old with. You go first.

I rang the doorbell, then tried the door for Sally's Place. It was locked up tight. Hmm. I wondered if it was closed for the day.

"You doofus," I told myself. "This is a program for domestic violence victims. Of course the door would be locked, for safety reasons."

I started to knock but the door flew open before my knuckles made contact and revealed, not Sister Rose, but Marcia Fischer from Superior Interiors.

"I was on the phone when you rang the bell," she said. "Sorry to keep you waiting outside. Sister'll have my head if she hears about that. I'm supposed to keep an eagle eye on the front door through the closed circuit television monitor, but sometimes I have to take a phone call."

She peered at me through her designer eyeglasses.

"Don't I know you? Of course, you're Carol Andrews. You and your husband are letting us stage your beautiful home for our show house. Are you here to talk to Sister about the event?"

I resisted reminding her that when she was in the house before it went on the market, she'd found thousands of things to criticize about it. And made me so mad I wanted to slug her.

Sidestepping the question, I said, "Sally's Place seems like a wonderful program, and Jim and I are happy to help in any way we can.

"Is Sister Rose in? I'd just like a few minutes of her time."

"For you, of course she's in," said Marcia. "And I know she'll be glad to see you."

I was amazed at the change my inadvertent foray into philanthropy had made in Marcia's attitude. I guess people like Bill and Melinda Gates were used to this kind of treatment, but it was new to me.

Marcia led me down a silent hallway to an office at the rear of the building. For a brief moment, before she knocked and opened the door, I had a kneejerk flashback that I had been called to the principal's office to be disciplined. Again.

But that feeling passed.

Sister's back was to us as we walked into the room. She was hard at work on the computer and didn't look our way.

Marcia cleared her throat. "I'm sorry to disturb you," she said, "but Carol Andrews is here to see you."

Sister whirled around in her chair, her face wreathed in a big smile. I was afraid she was going to hug me. But she didn't. Thank God. I was still adjusting to our new relationship. Maybe she was, too.

"It's so good to see you, Carol," she said. "I don't think you've ever been to our office before. Are you here to talk about the preview party? Or the show house? I never got a chance the last time we spoke to thank you for your wonderful generosity.

"Please, sit in this chair," Sister went on, gesturing me toward an oversized wing chair. "It's the most comfortable one in the office. Would you like some coffee? Tea? Perhaps Marcia could...."

But Marcia had made a discreet exit.

"I don't need anything to drink," I said. Then, remembering my manners, I added, "Thank you. And I'm not here about the show house.

"I want to talk to you about domestic violence."

Sister's expression instantly changed from upbeat to serious. "What is it you need to know, Carol?" she asked me in a gentle tone I'd never heard from her before. "How can I help you?"

"Thank you, Sister," I said, unsure of exactly where to begin.

Oh, Carol, for heaven's sake grow up and get on with it already.

"You may not know that I've done quite a bit of freelance writing over the past several years. Since our home is being used as the fundraiser for Sally's Place, I thought that the event would make a great backdrop for a feature story on domestic violence in Fairport. I'd like to write an in-depth piece, and sell it to our daily paper, perhaps even go national with it. You know the angle, 'Idyllic Suburbs Mask Dirty Secret.' "

I stopped myself. "I sound like exploitation journalism. But do you know what I mean?"

"As I told you when we had coffee, Carol, I'm the keeper of many secrets," Sister Rose said. "Many of them break my heart."

"That's exactly what I want to know, Sister," I said. "I know you can't reveal names. But perhaps you can share some stories? Or at least tell me how Sally's Place started? Was there really someone named Sally?"

Sister Rose looked thoughtful. Then she apparently came to a decision.

"I've been working to raise the public's consciousness about this for years," she said. "Perhaps this is one way to do it. We can work together. But you must promise me that I will have final approval of the story you write, and no names or any other references to clients will be used that could in any way identify them."

I raised my hand.

"I solemnly promise," I said, crossing my heart.

"I hope you're not being facetious, Carol. This is serious business."

"Honestly, Sister, I know I have a smart-alecky mouth at times, but I'm not kidding around now. I really want to help."

Sister seemed satisfied.

I took out a small notebook and a pen. Waited. And tried not to fidget in my chair.

"All right, Carol," Sister Rose finally said. "I'll tell you how the program started. Domestic violence has been a problem for years. I know for a fact that, years ago, when someone reported a domestic assault and the police were called to investigate, they frequently looked the other way and just gave the abuser a warning. The old boy network at its worst.

"Of course, one of the many problems about domestic abuse, even today, is that the victim often feels it's her fault. She's done something to provoke the violent behavior. Or she's ashamed of being abused. So she's reluctant to press charges against her abuser. Or, she's afraid of retaliation against herself. Maybe even against her children.

"I say 'she,' but we sometimes see men who have been victims of domestic abuse as well. That's even more complicated, as men are embarrassed to admit that the abuse is going on. But it does happen.

"You have to understand that domestic abuse isn't always physical. Sometimes it's emotional, like constant criticism, isolating the victim from family and friends, sexual abuse."

I opened my eyes wide at that one.

"What did you think, Carol? That because I'm a nun, I'd never heard of sex?"

Sister laughed, then her expression immediately became serious again.

"Several years ago, a woman in town came up with the idea of starting a local program to help victims of domestic abuse. She got together with some others and together they brainstormed the idea, raised some seed money to open a shelter, then came to us and presented the idea. The timing for us was perfect, as Mount Saint Francis had just closed down due to low enrollment, and the sisters were looking for a worthwhile project to spearhead.

"The name 'Sally's Place' was chosen to represent all women. There is no 'Sally.' Or, rather, everyone whom we serve here is 'Sally.' "

"This woman who had the original idea," I asked, "is she still in town? Do you think she'd talk to me? Was she a victim of domestic violence herself?"

Sister frowned at me, then said in the icy tone I remembered so well from high school, "Apparently you weren't listening to me, Carol. This is all confidential information. The original donor has chosen to remain anonymous. And as for whether she was a victim herself, well, there's no way I can speculate on that. Nor would I tell you if I knew."

Oops.

"Sorry, Sister. I completely understand. I just want to write the best story I can, to bring attention to domestic violence in Fairport. I think most people believe that abuse is much more common in low-income families."

"That is absolutely not true," Sister said. "In fact, you'd be shocked at how many women from our so-called 'respectable' families have turned to Sally's Place for help."

"I respect your insistence on confidentiality. But it's going to be very difficult for me to write a story with any substance to it without getting more personal information. You do want me to write an accurate story, don't you?"

Sister stood up like she'd been shot out of a canon. Clearly, our little chat was over. I had blown the conversation big time. She took my arm and steered me toward her office door.

"I have to give this some thought, Carol. I see your point, and I want you to be able to write the very best story you can. But my primary responsibility is to the clients we serve."

I started to reiterate that I knew that, but I found myself on the other side of the office door, which Sister then shut in my face. My cheeks flamed red, and not from a hot flash, either. I had been disciplined like a ten-year-old.

Unfortunately, Marcia Fischer was still at the reception desk and witnessed my humiliation. Great. Just what I needed to add to my woes.

"Sister get to you a little, Carol?" Marcia asked me, a slight smirk on her face. "She can be a real piece of work sometimes. Believe me, I know. Some days I leave here after she's chewed me out over some trivial thing, and decide I'm not coming back to volunteer ever again. But, of course, a week goes by, I forget how angry I was at her, and come back to do my usual stint.

"If you don't mind my asking, what'd you get in trouble for? She can't be too mad at you, after all. She needs your house to raise money for the program."

I laughed. "You're right, Marcia. Sister Rose does need me, and my house. I want to write a story on domestic violence in Fairport. I'm hoping to time the local story with the opening of the show house, to bring it even more publicity." I'd just thought of that idea, but it sounded like one of my best.

"She was giving me background information on how Sally's Place started. I started to ask questions about the woman who'd come up with the original concept, and Sister clammed up. Said she couldn't reveal her name. Or anything about her.

"And when I asked her about the possibility of interviewing some clients the program has served, she got really angry. Said I had to respect the confidentiality of the clients. No interviews. Period. It's going to be difficult to write a story that will grab readers without some sort of personal information." Much less sell it to the media.

"I may be able to help you, Carol," Marcia said. "I know someone who was in an abusive relationship when she was in high school, but managed to escape from it. She wasn't a client of Sally's Place, though. Does that matter?"

"Marcia, that's wonderful," I said, immediately putting my foot in my mouth. "I don't mean it's wonderful about someone being in an abusive relationship. That's terrible. But do you think she'd talk to me? I promise to keep her confidence. It doesn't matter if she wasn't a client of Sally's Place."

"You're already talking to her," Marcia said.

I blinked at her. Say what?

"I'm the person."

Wow. Talk about being hit by a bolt of lightning. In all my wildest imaginings about domestic violence, I never dreamed it could happen to someone I actually knew.

I know. Stupid.

"Marcia, I don't know what to say." I laughed nervously. "If you knew me better, you'd realize that doesn't happen to me very often.

"If you're willing to share your story with me, I promise to respect your privacy. And I'll let you read my finished piece before I submit it. You can trust me."

"We can't talk here," Marcia said. She looked at her watch. "It's time for my afternoon break. Let's go into one of the private conference rooms. Nobody will bother us there. But just in case…" she fished around in her desk drawer and found a sign which read, "Confidential Session in Progress. Do Not Disturb."

"Let's do this now, before I change my mind."

"I'm going to set some ground rules about this interview," Marcia said. "I'm going to tell the story, my way. If there are questions I don't want to answer, I won't. And you have to be satisfied with that. And I get to see what you write before it's shown to anybody else. Do we have a deal?"

"Deal," I said.

I held my breath and waited for her to start talking.

"The relationship started years ago, when I was a freshman in high school. I started dating a guy who was in his junior year. He was one of the stars of the football team, and all the girls had crushes on him. I couldn't believe it when he asked me out the first time. It was like a dream come true for me.

"At first, we used to hang out with some of my friends, but then he decided they were too immature. I was blown away by his attention. He told me he loved me and he couldn't live without me."

I was writing furiously, trying to take neat notes so that I could read them later. But, so far, it all seemed pretty innocent.

"He started to control all my activities. He'd pick me up and drive me to school, and then pick me up and drive me home. My parents thought it was sweet, that he doted on me that way. Even my brother thought he was cool.

"But I was feeling more and more boxed in. He wouldn't let me see my friends, except in class. He wanted to be alone with me all the time. He tried to talk me into running away and getting married, even though I was only fifteen. When I tried to break it off, he threatened to kill himself."

Marcia paused, and her voice trembled. "I remember the first time he hit me."

"Marcia, you can stop now if this is too hard," I said.

"No, I want to keep going. Maybe my story will stop someone else from making the same mistakes I did."

She cleared her throat. "I'm all right now. Anyway, the first time he hit me, he accused me of lying to him about where I'd been and who I'd been with. I wasn't waiting for him after school, like usual. I'd gone to study for a chemistry exam at the library with two girlfriends. Can you imagine anyone becoming violent over something so innocent?

"Anyway, he said he felt terrible about hitting me, and promised he'd never do it again. I believed him. In some way, I felt I was responsible. Like I had done something bad, and deserved to be punished. I was so ashamed. And I couldn't tell anybody.

"Then one night, I did something really terrible. I didn't mean to do it." Marcia clamped her lips shut and shook her head at the memory. "I can't tell you what it was. But he took the blame. He said he was doing it to protect me. But, of course, what he was really doing was finding another way to control me.

"Then, he went away. You don't need to know those details. Let's just say his family packed up and moved away. I don't know where they went.

"I can't tell you how relieved I was when he was out of my life. But I've always been afraid that he'd come back and try to hurt me again."

She started to sob.

I didn't know what to do. My maternal impulse was to touch her hand, hug her, do something physical to comfort her. I settled for taking a packet of tissues out of my purse and putting it within her line of vision.

As she reached out to take one, I said, "Marcia, I am so sorry for what you went through. I know that's small comfort to you. It was so brave of you to share your story with me. I guess I never realized that domestic abuse could start when the victim is still in her teens. I'm so lucky that it hasn't happened to my daughter."

Marcia blew her nose, then wiped her eyes. "Sorry for breaking down like that in front of you, Carol. After all, we barely know each other. But I haven't told anyone that story, except in therapy sessions. And believe me, I had a lot of those over the years.

"And as far as your saying it hasn't happened to your daughter, what makes you so sure about that? Maybe she's been in an abusive relationship and you don't know about it. After all, my family never picked up on the signs."

The encounter with Marcia Fischer rocked me to my core. All the way back to the apartment, I kept wondering if she was right about my daughter.

Last year, quite unexpectedly, Jenny had broken up with her live-in boyfriend, Jeff, left California, and shown up at our door. She complained that he didn't want her to finish her graduate degree, and insisted she stay home and take care of him, instead. She told Jim and me that she couldn't take his trying to manage her life, so she packed up and came home to Fairport. I wasn't sure if they'd had any contact since then. I knew she decided not to go back and pack up more of her things. She said she wanted to start fresh in Connecticut.

Was there more to the story that she hadn't told us?

No matter what, I decided I couldn't ask her about it. But I made up my mind, there and then, to write the best damn story I possibly could to shed some light on domestic violence. In all its ugly forms.

Chapter 28

Lead me not into temptation. I can find the way all by myself.

As excited as I was about the show house preview party, that's how much I was dreading the memorial service for Jack Cartwright.

"You don't have to attend," said My Beloved. "In fact, you probably shouldn't go. The family may be upset to see you there." He gave me a look which translated to, "I think you're nuts to go."

I had to admit, he had a good point. But my mother, and the good sisters, all said that paying your last respects to any deceased with whom you had even the remotest connection was a must. It may sound ghoulish, but that's the way I was raised.

I was determined to go to the memorial. Even if I went alone. I'd sit in the last pew in the church, I decided. Nobody would even know I was there.

When Jenny heard about my plan, she pitched a fit, just like Jim had. Like father, like daughter, at least in this case.

"Mom," she said, "don't you remember that phone call you made to the family, when Sara Miller threatened to sue you and Daddy for negligence? She practically accused you of causing Jack's death."

Heavy sigh. From Jenny, not me.

"But if you insist on going, you're not going alone. I'll go with you."

I didn't admit that I was hoping she'd say that. But I was. I guess some of my "funeral guilt" had passed on to the next generation.

"I've never been to this church before," I said to Jenny. It was Saturday morning and we were circling the blocks near the Fairport Community Church, trying to find a parking place. "I guess we should have gotten here earlier. I never dreamed there'd be so many people."

"Some folks just can't resist a good funeral. Or a chance to see some drama. Even pick up a little gossip," Jenny said.

"I hope you're not referring to me," I said as I finally spotted a parking spot five blocks away from the church and made it my own.

"No, Mom. I'm not. But you have to admit that we really didn't have to attend the service."

"On the contrary, I think we did. At least, I did," I said as we walked briskly toward the church. "It's my way of showing respect to the family, and also showing that I have nothing to hide. We'd better hurry. It looks like they're about to close the doors."

An usher gave us each a program whose cover showed a beautiful picture of all four Cartwrights. Jack was holding the little girl in his arms, and Alyssa had her arms wrapped around her son. Big smiles on all the faces.

Heartbreaking.

We squeezed into the very last pew in the church. The place was packed, mostly with young people. (Meaning under age forty.)

I spotted a few of the neighbors. Phyllis and Bill were sitting in a prominent place, along with Liz. I was surprised to see Marcia Fischer sitting a few rows up from us with Leon, her brother and business partner in Superior Interiors. Leon had his arm around Marcia's shoulder, and she seemed to be wiping her eyes with a handkerchief. Curious.

For a quick second, I wondered how they knew Jack Cartwright. Then I realized the Cartwrights had probably consulted the design store about decorating their new home. Which now they'd never move into. But it was still nice of Marcia and Leon to come and show their respects.

"There's no casket," I whispered to Jenny.

"It's a memorial service. Usually there is no casket," Jenny replied. "It's more a celebration of a person's life than a funeral."

I craned my neck and saw a table in front of the altar which was filled with photographs. The altar was decorated with a simple arrangement of blue hydrangeas.

The whole congregation rose to its feet as the family walked down the aisle. Alyssa looked dazed, and was clinging to her father's arm. Sara Miller was ramrod straight, and held both her grandchildren's hands.

I couldn't bear to look at them. The reality of the situation hit me, and I knew, belatedly, that Jim and Jenny were right. I had no business being at this memorial service. I felt like a voyeur.

But it was too late to sneak out without calling attention to myself. Jenny, sensing my discomfort, gave my hand a little squeeze. "Hang tight, Mom," she whispered.

Reverend Donaldson, the minister, led the congregation in singing "A Mighty Fortress Is Our God." Then, after a few readings from scripture, he gave a brief eulogy for Jack. It was obvious from the impersonal nature of the eulogy that he didn't know the Cartwright family that well.

Another hymn – this time, "Joyful, Joyful We Adore Thee." Then Reverend Donaldson asked if any members of the congregation wanted to share a remembrance of the deceased.

A young man, probably in his early twenties, rose to his feet and walked slowly to the pulpit. His voice cracked as he introduced himself.

"Good morning. My name is Luke Saunders, and I'm here today to mourn the passing of my friend and mentor, Jack Cartwright. It's no exaggeration to say that Jack Cartwright saved my life. I was a pretty wild kid about eight years ago, when Jack and I first met. I'd been in and out of juvy homes a few times for drugs. Both using and selling."

Luke cleared his throat, then continued.

"I met Jack at the program for at-risk kids he started in Massachusetts. I didn't want to go to it, but my probation officer told me it was either attend the program or serve more time in a juvy home.

He allowed himself a small smile. "Of course, I chose the program.

"Jack worked with me, one-on-one, for months. He treated me like a son. He told me how he'd made some pretty stupid mistakes when he was younger, and he didn't want to see me, or any other kid, do the same thing. Thanks to him, I went back to school and got my G.E.D. I'm now working in a garage, paying my own way, and going to college at night.

"Jack Cartwright did that for me. And for lots of other kids, too. He was a stand-up guy, and I'll miss him every day of my life."

Wiping tears from his eyes, Luke went to the family pew and gave Alyssa a wordless hug, then took his place in the row behind her.

Wow. "I had no idea," I whispered to Jenny. "He must have been quite a guy."

The next person to speak was one of Jack's fraternity brothers. He, too, extolled Jack's virtues. I had never heard anyone spoken about in such glowing terms, living or deceased.

Two more young men, former neighbors of the Cartwrights, also spoke about Jack. How he coached the local Little League team, what a wonderful husband and father he was, etc. etc.

Finally, the tributes were over. I heard muffled sobbing from the front of the church in the direction of the family pew.

Then Reverend Donaldson introduced the youth choir director from the Cartwrights' former church in Massachusetts, who led a chorus of angelic-looking children in a beautiful rendition of "Amazing Grace." From his brief remarks at the end of the hymn, I gathered that Jack was also the volunteer assistant director for the children's choir.

Uncharitably, I wondered if Jack had any time to hold down a job and provide for his family with all his other activities. Then, I slapped myself. Figuratively speaking. The poor guy was dead, after all.

Jenny poked me and we all rose as the family filed out of the church.

"Do you want to go to the collation, Mom?" Jenny asked me.

"Collation? What's that? I haven't heard that term before."

"That's when the people who've attended the memorial service meet the family and express their condolences. The church ladies usually serve tea, finger sandwiches, and desserts."

No way was I pressing my luck. So far Sara Miller hadn't noticed my presence, and I wanted to keep it that way.

"We'd better skip that," I said. "I think we've done our duty."

"Let's go out the side door," Jenny suggested. "Everyone else is headed the other way."

We made our way through the throng of people with several muttered "Excuse me's" and eventually found ourselves outside, at the back end of the church, near the meditation garden.

One other person had left the memorial service the same way. She looked just as surprised to see us as we were to see her.

It was Mary Alice.

I shook my head just a tiny bit as we hugged and said our hellos, and hoped Mary Alice got what I was hinting at – that Jenny had no idea about her connection to Jack. After all, it wasn't my place to share that information with anyone, even my daughter.

"It was so nice of you to come to support me," I babbled. "Jim didn't think I had any business being here, but I felt it was something I had to do. If I'd known you were coming too, we could have all sat together."

Jeez. Was this making any sense? Even I thought I sounded pretty stupid.

Mary Alice, smart cookie that she is, picked up on my words immediately. "I figured you'd want to be here out of some misplaced sense of responsibility. Me, too. I'll always wonder if I could have saved Jack that night. If I'd just looked in the window and seen him lying there."

"It's very interesting to hear you say that, Mrs. Costello," said a male voice from behind us.

I turned around and …good grief. It was Detective Paul.

"You mentioned a misplaced sense of responsibility. I wonder if you meant to say, a sense of guilt.

"The medical examiner has determined that Jack Cartwright's death was not an accident. Somebody smacked him on the head and left him there to die.

"I hope neither of you ladies," Paul said, glaring at Mary Alice and me, "have any travel plans in the near future. We're definitely going to want to talk to you both again."

"Don't look at me that way, *Mother*," Jenny said to me, peering at me over her Maria's Trattoria menu.

Mary Alice had developed a major migraine after our confrontation with Detective Paul and begged off having lunch with us. No wonder. Talking to Paul was liable to give anybody a pain in the head, neck, and various other body parts. He certainly was a cop who enjoyed lording it over people any time he got the chance. And when you coupled that with my fear that he'd discover the connection Mary Alice had with Jack Cartwright, well, there wasn't enough Advil in the world to relieve that stress unless I wanted to risk a massive overdose.

I ignored my daughter's comment and concentrated on the menu.

"I'm going to have the fruit salad with baby greens and gorgonzola cheese," I said. "No point in having a heavy lunch when we'll be eating at the preview party tonight. Maria's doing the catering, you know."

"Don't try and change the subject," Jenny said. "I know what you're plotting. And I'm not comfortable doing it."

I opened my baby blues as wide as I could and feigned an innocent expression.

"It makes me nervous when you call me Mother," I said. "Like I'm in trouble or something. What happened to good old Mom?"

"You were very quiet on the way over here from the church," Jenny said, "and I could tell the wheels in your head were turning. I know exactly what you were thinking. And I'm not comfortable with what you're going to ask me to do."

She sighed. "But I'll probably do it anyway. Go ahead, spring it on me. I'm ready."

"Honestly, Jenny, I don't know what you're talking about," I protested. "What do you think I'm going to ask you to do?"

"Call Mark and see if he'll tell me anything about the police investigation into Jack Cartwright's death. Without putting him into a conflict of interest situation. And don't deny you didn't think of it. I know you too well."

Actually, I hadn't gotten that far in my plotting and planning process. But it was a good idea. A very good idea.

"And I'll bet you also e-mailed Mike and asked him to start an Internet search on Jack Cartwright, just like he did last year when Daddy was in trouble."

"You may not believe me," I said, handing my menu to the waitress after placing my order, "but I hadn't thought that far ahead."

"You're slipping, Mom. Just so you know, I already e-mailed Mike and asked him to check out background info on Jack. I got an automatic out-of-the-office response, saying that Mike was temporarily away from Cosmo's and would be back in touch soon. Any idea what that's about?"

Thank God, I was back to being Mom again.

"No clue," I said. "I haven't heard from him. But I'm sure he's fine. At least, I hope he is. He's been known to maintain radio silence for a few weeks, and then get back in contact. I refuse to worry about that."

Liar, I thought. You will worry about it. Just not right this instant. Too many other things preceded Mike on my current worry list.

I frowned, remembering my recent conversation with Mark. "As far as Mark is concerned, when he stopped in to see me…"

"Whoa. Wait a minute," Jenny interrupted. "When did you see him? You didn't tell me that."

"There's been a lot going on," I said in my own defense. "I intended to tell you. Mark stopped by the apartment a few days ago to apologize for what he said about Jim and me. And also to ask for help in getting you back."

Jenny's eyes took on a dreamy look. "He really asked you for help? What did you tell him?"

"I suggested to him that the best way he could win you over would be to get me off Detective Paul's suspect list. He said that since it wasn't his case, he wasn't sure how much he could do.

"Maybe you should follow up with him, Jenny. What do you think? If you want to call him, it's a perfect excuse. Especially now that it looks like Jack was, well, you know." I couldn't bring myself to use the word murdered.

"I don't need an excuse to call him, Mom," Jenny said.

"As a matter of fact, we've already made up. I couldn't stay mad at him for long."

Jenny grinned. "Mark's so easy to be with. Even our fights are fun. He's so different from Jeff. What a control freak he was."

My maternal antenna immediately went up. Take it easy. Don't push her.

"Did I tell you that I've decided to write a piece on domestic abuse in Fairport?" I asked. "It seemed like a natural, since the show house is benefitting Sally's Place. I'm hoping the local paper will run it as part of the show house publicity.

"I interviewed Sister Rose about the problem, and some of the things she told me came as a huge surprise. And I talked to one victim, who'd suffered abuse from her boyfriend when she was only a teenager. I guess I'm pretty naïve. I never realized it could happen to someone so young."

I paused and took a sip of water. The question I wanted to ask required very delicate phrasing, something that's definitely not my specialty.

I decided to risk it.

"I don't mean to be nosy, sweetie, but, well, you've mentioned several times that Jeff was kind of a control freak. Did he...well...did he ever...?"

"I see where you're going with this, Mom. And the answer is no. He was a jerk, and always thought he knew more about everything than I did, including what I should do with my life. But I wouldn't call it domestic abuse."

I sat back in my chair. Phew. I would hate to think I was as stupid as Marcia Fischer's parents.

"Sorry if you think I've overstepped my parental boundaries, Jenny. I guess after some of the things I've heard from Sister Rose, I see domestic abuse possibilities everywhere.

"Now, tell me, what's up with you and Mark? That is, if you want to tell me."

Jenny laughed. "Talking about Mark and me isn't off limits for you, Mom. As long as I get to stop the conversation whenever I think you're getting too nosy. Deal?"

I nodded my head. A little info is better than none, right?

"We're not completely 'back together' yet, but we're going to the show house preview party as a couple tonight. It'll be our first official date since our fight."

"I'm glad you two are working things out," I said. "And if you can find out any information about the Cartwright case at the same time, that'd be great. I didn't care for Paul's suggestion to Mary Alice and me about not having any travel plans in the near future. We've both been above board and completely honest with answers to all the questions he's asked us." Thank God he hadn't asked Mary Alice more pointed questions. So far.

"I hope Paul won't be at the preview party tonight."

"The police weren't on the official guest list," Jenny said. "Why should they be? This is a party, not a trial. Don't worry about Paul showing up. The only reason Mark will be there is because he's my date. I heard the event's a sell-out."

"Yeah," I said. "Everyone wants to get a peek at the scene of the crime. Now that it's officially a crime."

The server had just given us our lunch, and it looked delicious. My fork was about halfway between the plate and my mouth when a young man approached us and said, "Excuse me. Aren't you Carol Andrews?"

I squinted at him. "Do I know you?"

"I'm Rich Reynolds from Channel Seventeen. The police have just made a statement calling the death of Jack Cartwright a homicide.

"I'm wondering if you have any comment about that? Since you discovered the body. In your house."

Good grief.

Chapter 29

When life gives you lemons, turn it into lemonade and mix it with vodka.

"Who the hell are all these people and why are they parked in front of our house?" Jim groused as our car crawled up Old Fairport Turnpike. "I can't even get into my own driveway. If you hadn't dithered so long about what to wear, we would have been early."

"Until the show house is over, it isn't our house," I reminded him for the umpteenth time. "And if things had gone the way they were supposed to, it'd be the Cartwrights' house now."

I decided to ignore his dig about my taking so long to get dressed, because he was right, darn it. I had limited wardrobe choices since most of my "good clothes" were in storage. I finally settled for wearing the same black suit I'd worn to the memorial service, but I jazzed it up with some sparkly jewelry I was lucky enough to come across in one of my suitcases. And everybody in the New York metropolitan area knows that black is THE official party color, no matter what season it is.

"Stop being so grumpy. At least you don't have to wear a tux, because I didn't have time to find you one. It's a good thing you saved your navy suit from going into storage. You look very nice."

Jim tightened his lips, which I chose to interpret as a smile.

"And we got our deposit money back from Eden's Grove, so we're not destitute any more. Homeless, yes. Destitute, no."

I was determined to look on the bright side, despite everything. And My Beloved wasn't making it easy.

"Oh, look. Phyllis and Bill are waving at us. It looks like they want us to park in their driveway," I said.

Jim slammed on the brakes, almost causing the car behind us to smash into our rear bumper. "I wish you'd noticed that before, Carol. You could have caused an accident."

Jeez. This was going to be a rotten night if My Beloved continued in his present, miserable mood.

Fortunately, when he got out of our car and headed toward our (former) neighbors, he had a smile on his face.

"Isn't this thrilling?" Phyllis said, giving us both a hug. "Bill and I decided to wait till you two arrived before going over to the party. The police didn't remove the yellow scene of the crime tape until late yesterday afternoon. I wonder if they're going to allow guests to go into the living room, where you found Jack Cartwright's body."

Good grief. I shot Phyllis a look to see if she was serious. Unfortunately, she was. In fact, she was positively quivering with excitement.

"It's going to be quite a night," I said. "Just look at the line of people waiting to get into our house."

I spotted Nancy in our driveway, talking to what appeared to be a reporter for the local television station. She caught sight of us and motioned us around the side of the house to our kitchen door.

"Follow me," I said. "Nancy wants us to go in the kitchen way, probably to avoid the crush at the front door. And the press."

Phyllis looked disappointed, probably hoping to get another five minutes of fame through an interview with the local paparazzi. "Bill and I will go in the front way, Carol. We don't mind standing in line for a few minutes. You and Jim go ahead."

Humph.

The inside of our house was chaos. There were people everywhere. It was a good thing all our furniture was in storage. "We never had this many bodies packed into the house before," I said to Jim as we fought our way to one of the bars, which was set up in what had been our family room. "I hope the fire marshal doesn't shut the party down because there are too many people in the house."

"At least all the bodies are alive," said My Beloved. He squinted at the couple who had just pushed their way in front of us in their haste to get to the booze. "Excuse me. I hope we weren't in your way."

The couple ignored him.

"Who are all these people anyway?"

"I guess they're supporters of Sally's Place," I said. "At this rate, the program is going to make a bundle on the show house."

"Just goes to show you that crime sometimes pays," said My Beloved.

I shot him a look. "Not funny, Jim. Especially since Detective Paul made it clear this afternoon that he still wants to talk to Mary Alice." And me. I didn't add that, though.

"Look, there's Jenny. She's talking to Mary Alice, and someone I don't recognize. For a second I thought it was Claire, but the hair color's wrong. And she's about twenty-five pounds thinner. It's probably just wishful thinking on my part."

Jenny waved us over. "Isn't this something? There sure are more people here tonight than there were at my Sweet Sixteen party." She gave us both a kiss.

"Where's Mark?" I asked, always the nosy mother. Jenny pointed toward the line at another bar. Which used to be my kitchen counter a short time ago. From the length of the line, it looked like Mark would be waiting a while.

"Mary Alice," I said, "you look fabulous in that navy dress. Very dramatic. Is it new?"

"I just got it. And you'll never guess where,"

"I bet you got it at Sally's Closet," I said with a laugh. "It's my new favorite boutique, too. Gotta support the cause."

"Aren't you going to welcome me home?" asked the third member of the group, a stunning redhead. She threw her arms around me and gave me a big hug.

Good grief. It was Claire.

"My God," I said. "I can't believe it's you. You look fabulous. What happened to you in Florida?"

I clapped my hands over my mouth, realizing how that came out. "I don't mean to imply that you ever looked bad, Claire. But now, you look like..."

"A hottie," said My Beloved, giving Claire a smooch on her cheek. "Larry better keep an eye on you."

The lawyer-in-question was working his way through the crowd toward us, holding two drinks aloft. When Larry reached our small group, he handed off a white wine spritzer to Claire and gave me a peck on the cheek.

"Nice of you and Jim to throw this big shindig to welcome us back," he said. "How do you like my new trophy wife? Isn't she something?"

I had so many questions I hardly knew where to start.

"When did you get back? Why didn't you let us know you were coming?

"With everything going on up here, we decided to cut our Florida stay short and head home," said Larry.

"Nancy's been keeping us in the loop about your house sale," Claire said, "and the buyer's death. And your finding him. It must have been so terrible for you, Carol.

"But this," Claire said, waving her hand around the family room, "shows that every cloud has a silver lining, right? You're going to get top dollar for your house this time, move to one that's easier to maintain, and you're helping a great cause at the same time.

"I couldn't believe it when Nancy told me you had re-connected with Sister Rose," Claire went on. "You certainly weren't good buddies when we were in high school."

"Believe it or not, we're getting along well," I said. "Of course, it helps that Jim and I have loaned out our house to be used as the major fundraiser for Sally's Place. I may be Sister Rose's new best friend.

"But enough changing the subject," I said, looking Claire straight in the eye. "At the risk of repeating myself, what the heck happened to you in Florida?"

"Waist Watchers," replied Claire.

"Waist Watchers?" echoed Jenny. "I've heard of Weight Watchers. But I've never heard of Waist Watchers. What is it? Some kind of new diet thingy?"

"It's much more than that," said Claire. "It's a whole new way to embrace, and live, your life. Diet and exercise are important components, of course. But so are yoga and meditation, Pilates, guided imagery, journaling, and, gosh, so many other things. It's just phenomenal."

Jeez, it sounded like a lot of work to me. And, well, weird. Not the kind of thing that would ever appeal to someone as staid as Claire.

Claire has always been able to read me pretty well.

"I know it sounds kind of New Age," she said. "But it isn't. Waist Watchers is such a joyous experience when you really get into it, like I have. And I made some terrific new friends through the program. I just hope I can keep my motivation going now that I'm home."

"And I hope that you won't replace your old friends with your new ones," said Nancy, sidling into our little group. "If you need motivation to exercise, I'll be glad to take you to the new gym I'm going to. You'll just love it."

"Say Carol," said My Beloved, eyeing my middle, "maybe you should join this trend, too. Your waist could use a little watching."

I ignored him. Something I've had lots of practice doing over the years. But just wait until I got him back to the apartment. Then I'd let him have it, the big jerk.

"I will if you will, dear," I said sweetly. Jenny raised her eyebrows. She'd witnessed her parents' sniping before, and knew sometimes it wasn't pretty.

I gave Jim a kiss on the cheek. To show him I'd forgiven him for his tactless remark. But, of course, I wouldn't forget it too soon.

Like never.

"Where's Bob tonight?" I asked Nancy. Sightings of my very best friend's husband had been few and far between in the past few months. Not that that was a problem for us. We females generally preferred to get together *sans* spouses as often as we could.

"Oh, you know," Nancy answered vaguely. "Since his company merged with Tyson Financial, he's traveling all over the place. I tell him that if he doesn't come home more often, I'm going to put our house on the market and move. It'd serve him right." For a millisecond, her eyes took on a hard look, and I realized that she wasn't kidding.

"What does Sister Rose look like now?" asked Claire, stepping in to change the subject.

"You can check her out right now," Nancy said. "That's her standing by the fireplace with the microphone in her hand."

Claire gaped. "That's her? She looks better than I do."

"There's a story there," I assured her. "I'll tell you later."

Sister Rose was trying to quiet the guests, but it wasn't working. Then, suddenly, she put her fingers to her lips and let out an ear-piercing whistle. The kind that brings New York City cabbies screeching to a halt. Jeez. It almost punctured my ear drum.

The crowd quieted down immediately. I mean, who wanted to hear that sound again?

"Thank you, everyone, for coming tonight to this wonderful preview party for the show house to benefit Sally's Place," Sister said. She then went on to highlight all the wonderful things Sally's Place did for victims of domestic violence.

It was a great speech, but I have to admit, I kind of zoned out. The excitement of being in my own home again, plus the crowd of guests at the party and the stress of the last few days, must have ganged up on me. I thought I was going to faint.

Then I heard Sister say, "We owe this wonderful night, and the upcoming show house, to my good friends Carol and Jim Andrews. Let's bring them up here and give them a big thank you for all they're doing to help Sally's Place and the victims of domestic violence we serve."

Huh? Jim pushed me forward to join Sister Rose by the fireplace. I felt like I was sleepwalking. Nothing seemed real.

Then I turned, and saw Mark coming toward our group, along with Detective Paul. My first thought was, "I'm glad Mark finally got back with Jenny's drink." My second thought was, "Why is Paul here? He wasn't on the guest list."

The pair stopped in front of Mary Alice. Paul whispered something in her ear, and Mary Alice turned toward the sliding glass doors and lurched forward toward them. The two men took her by the arm and guided her out of the room. Mary Alice was struggling in their grasp. Larry, propelled by Claire, followed them. They both looked upset.

I heard Mark say, "Mrs. Costello, all we want to do is ask a few more questions. There's no need to be afraid."

Then I heard Detective Paul say, "You have the right to remain silent."

Chapter 30

You know you're getting older when it takes you longer to pack your medicine than your makeup.

"Here, drink this," said My Beloved, handing me a cup of steaming black coffee. "It'll wake you up. And maybe even help you feel better."

I gingerly opened one eye, then the other. Lucy, who was lying at my feet, stirred, gave me a dirty look, then settled back down. I took the coffee, drank deeply, then gave the cup back to Jim. "Thanks for this, but it's going to take more than caffeine to make me feel better after last night's debacle."

I sank back into the lumpy pillow and closed my eyes. "I don't think I've ever used the word 'debacle' in a sentence before. Sister Rose would be proud of me for broadening my vocabulary at this late stage of life."

I opened my eyes again and looked at My Beloved. "Do me a big favor and tell me that last night didn't happen. Mary Alice is snug in her bed, or hard at work at the hospital. Lie to me if you have to."

Jim carefully placed the coffee on the relic that served as our bedside table. "I wish I could, Carol. But it happened, all right. Just like you remember it. I was on the phone early this morning with Larry. He said that the police finally let Mary Alice go home last night after questioning her for several hours about her connection with Jack Cartwright. The only evidence they have against her is circumstantial, but it still doesn't look good for her. Apparently several people heard her say that if she ever met the person who was responsible for Brian's death, she'd kill him.

That's pretty damaging. And she's already admitted being at our house the night before the closing, when Jack Cartwright died."

I sat up in bed like I'd been poked with a cattle prod. "That's just ridiculous, Jim. I was one of the people who heard Mary Alice say that at our last Bunco party. She was very upset at the time. But she wouldn't ever do such a horrible thing. She's a nurse, for God's sake. Her whole life has been devoted to helping people, not harming them."

"You know that," Jim said. "And I know that. Because we both know Mary Alice very well. But you have to admit, it doesn't sound good."

I sank back on the pillow again. Even lying on lumps was preferable to the way this conversation was going.

"One more thing, Carol," said My Beloved.

I reached for the coffee and took a healthy swallow. Something in Jim's tone told me I needed the extra fortification.

"Yes, Jim," I said. "What?"

"I have one very important item to add to your Honey-Don't List. Not just for today. For the future, too. And you better not argue with me about it.

"Do not interfere in the police investigation into Jack Cartwright's death. No matter how much you want to help Mary Alice. Under. Any. Circumstances. Understand?"

"I understand, Jim," I said meekly. "I won't."

Which was, of course, an easy promise for me to make. Because I'd already decided to investigate Jack's death on my own.

Jim left the apartment shortly after his ultimatum, undoubtedly headed toward the newspaper so he could work on another column without interference from me.

I scrambled for the phone. Time to make calls and assemble my team of very private (as in, "If our beloveds knew what we were up to, we'd be in big trouble, so mum's the word") investigators: Claire, Nancy, Jenny,

Deanna, and Maria Lesko. We arranged to meet at Maria's Trattoria at 10:00 this morning, before the restaurant opened for business, so we could talk privately and come up with a plan.

I deliberately left Sister Rose out of the group. I figured I could always call on her if I needed to. And she might not approve of some of the methods we might have to use to get Mary Alice out of the fix she found herself in. Nuns tend to frown at things like little white lies, right?

Nancy had already positioned herself at the head of the table by the time I'd arrived. For a minute – OK, two minutes – that annoyed me, because it was, after all, my investigative team. Ah, well. In the interests of harmony, I let that pass.

Maria had thoughtfully provided coffee and a plate of freshly baked muffins to jump start our brain cells. Nothing like the combination of caffeine and sugar to get the mind going.

As usual, everybody was talking at the same time. At first, we all had to vent about how terrible it was that Mary Alice had been dragged (Nancy's word – she always tends to overdramatize) out of the preview party by Mark and Paul.

Jenny immediately took offense at that, and pointed out that Mark was not on duty last night. According to her, Paul had enlisted his help on the spur of the moment. We all peppered her with questions about whether Mark would now been assigned to the case he'd inadvertently become involved in.

Jenny threw up her hands in frustration. "I tell you, I don't know."

I let it go. If Jenny and Mark were together again, their private life was (mostly) none of my business. Though I suspected she knew more than she was saying.

"OK, everybody," I said. "It's time for us to get organized. I bet if we put our collective heads together, we can come up with a sure-fire plan to clear Mary Alice of any possible police suspicion."

My baby blues honed in on Claire.

"Before we get serious, I have to say I can't get used to you as a redhead."

"Well, you better get used to it," my hitherto meek, mild and white-haired friend retorted. "I plan to stay this way for a long, long time."

"I think you look terrific," Deanna said, "and I'll do everything I can to keep your hair as red as you want."

Claire beamed at Deanna, and I thought, "Of course you will. Think of all the money you'll make at the hair salon giving Claire touchups." Then, I mentally slapped myself. Deanna was a good friend, and never charged me for trimming my bangs between haircuts.

"I think you're gorgeous, too, Claire," I said. "But I always thought you were."

I cleared my throat. "Anyway, since Larry has committed himself to representing Mary Alice, can you find out from him what defense strategy he's planning, should it come to that?" God forbid.

Claire looked hesitant. "I don't know about that, Carol. One of the reasons Larry and I have been married so long is that I don't stick my nose into his legal cases."

"Then maybe it's time you did," I snapped back. "After all, this is Mary Alice we're talking about. One of our dearest friends in the world. You want to help her, don't you?"

Claire nodded her head. "All right, I'll see what I can do."

"Good," I said. "Now, Nancy, remember last year when Jim was in so much trouble? You and your Realtors' network were terrific getting information on that phony retirement coach, Davis Rhodes. Do you think you can use the network again to find out some background stuff about Jack Cartwright?"

Usually Nancy jumps at opportunities like this without hesitation, but this time she didn't look as gung ho as I expected.

"I don't know what I can find out this time, Carol," she said. "The reason I was helpful before was that both Davis Rhodes and his ex-wife had rented property in Fairport. The only Fairport property the Cartwrights were involved with was your house."

I was getting exasperated. We weren't getting anywhere.

"Look, Nancy," I said with as much patience as I could dredge up, "so many mystery stories have the detective investigating a murder by first finding out everything he can about the victim. That usually leads to the motive for the crime, and then to the guilty party. I think we have to start by finding out everything we can about Jack before he and his family moved to Fairport."

"OK, Carol," Nancy said. "I'll poke around and see what I can do. Maybe Dream Homes Realty has a partner agency in the town he came from. Wherever that was."

"I think I can help you there," said Maria. "The Trattoria catered the 'welcome to the neighborhood party' that the Millers gave for their daughter and her family. I couldn't help but overhear Jack talking about his college days in Boston. That's apparently where he met Alyssa. When they got married a few years ago, he and Alyssa moved to Cape Cod. That's where they started their family. I don't think he mentioned what town, though."

"That's great information," said Nancy. "How many towns can there be on Cape Cod? I'm sure I can find out where they used to live."

I started to get excited. It looked like we were finally starting to roll.

"Now, Deanna," I said. "Yes, sir," she snapped back at me, giving me a salute. "Reporting for duty, sir."

"Very funny," I said. Then I realized I better be extra nice to her. I didn't want to come off as too high-handed and have her turn my hair green.

"Deanna," I said, "you're in a special position because of the hair salon. By any chance, is Sara Miller or any member of her family a customers of yours?"

Deanna beamed at me. "I just knew you were going to ask me that, Carol."

Then, her face fell. Well, not actually fell. But you know what I mean.

"As a matter of fact, Sara's not a customer. Neither is her daughter. But I do volunteer at Sally's Place, doing hair for the clients for free. If I pick up any information I think would be helpful, of course I'll tell you. That goes for the salon, too. You never know who's going to walk in and need a touchup."

"Ditto," said Maria. "You never know who's going to come into the restaurant, either. It's amazing what people will talk about in a public place. They have no idea how many others overhear their most private conversations. Or maybe they just don't care. I'll alert all the servers to keep their ears open and their mouths shut."

"Well, I guess that's all of us," I said. "We each have a job to do. Let's get back together at the end of the week and report in. But if anyone finds out something important, share it right away, OK?"

"What about you, Mom?" asked Jenny. "What's your job?"

"Don't worry about me. I have plenty of leads to track down."

And I knew exactly how I was going to start, by e-mailing my wandering son, the Internet super sleuth, and having him research Jack Cartwright. His e-mail wouldn't dare give me that automatic "Out of office on a special project" response.

"Maria, all right if we meet here?" I asked.

"Works for me," said Maria. "Friday morning, eight-thirty?"

"Let's get to work, everybody," I said, and dismissed the troops.

When I arrived back at the apartment, I was greeted by two very grumpy English cocker spaniels. They were right to be grumpy. In my haste to get to Maria's to rally my sleuthing team, I had completely forgotten to give Lucy and Ethel their breakfast. Which they let me know in no uncertain terms.

Let me tell you, if you think hell hath no fury like a woman scorned, you've never met two English cockers who've skipped a meal. It's not a pretty sight.

Fortunately, they were easy to placate. A quick bowl of kibble for two, a brisk walk around the neighborhood, and all was forgiven. They soon settled back into a post-breakfast nap.

"OK, girls," I said. "We're going to get online now and contact Mike. We need his Internet research skills."

No comment. Just a lot of heavy breathing. The kind that happens when someone is in a heavy sleep, not the other kind.

"And we've got to get this done before Jim comes home. You know that he won't approve of my meddling...I mean, helping clear Mary Alice."

We were lucky our computer was hooked up, but, alas, no high-speed Internet service here. Jim didn't want to invest the money – big surprise. It was good old "dinosaur dial-up" for us. As he'd pointed out, we were only going to be in these temporary digs for a short time. Which, under the current circumstances, was now an indefinite time.

We were also sharing a single computer. With agreed-upon hours as to when it was available to each of us without interfering with the other. But since Jim was out of the house, even though it was his "time of day," I logged on without feeling guilty that I was encroaching on My Beloved.

I fired off an e-mail to Mike, giving him the bare facts about what was going on here in Fairport. I didn't want to alarm him, but I did want to get his attention and make him respond to me, the woman who endured 19 hours of horrific labor to bring him into the world.

I pressed "Send" and decided not to sit at the computer and wait for his response. After all, a watched computer never boils. Or maybe that was a pot.

Anyway, there was always another box to unpack, and I still had to go over the notes I took at Sally's Place and put them in some semblance of order for my story on domestic violence.

Bing!

I smiled. I knew my son would respond right away to his dear mother.

Wait a minute. What was this? I couldn't believe my eyes. It was the same automatic 'out-of-office' response. The little twit. What was going on with him?

I was determined to track my son down and get a real response out of him. Plus, I needed him to research Jack Cartwright. Hmm. I needed another plan.

I'd heard Jenny say that it's possible to write to someone via Facebook, and I knew Mike had a Facebook account. Of course, I didn't. In fact, I didn't have a clue about how all this social networking stuff worked, but I figured trying it was worth a shot.

Twenty frustrating minutes later – I'd always heard setting up these accounts was easy but it sure was a big learning curve for me – I finally succeeded.

Apparently the next step after setting up an account was to find friends. I didn't want to find friends. I wanted to find my son.

I typed in his name, and was rewarded with the prompt that not only could I request we be "friends," but I could send him a message along with the "friend request."

Yippee. I'd track my son down yet.

I composed a similar message to my previous one and sent it off. I hoped Mike was as addicted to Facebook as I'd heard other twenty-somethings were.

Then I forced myself to log off and transpose my chicken-scratch notes from Sister Rose and Marcia Fischer onto the computer. Reading Marcia's story again made me want to cry. I couldn't believe what she had been through as a teenager. Talking to Sister Rose had opened my eyes to the magnitude of domestic violence, but Marcia put a real face onto it.

Maybe my article would help save another young woman from going through what Marcia had. I made up my mind that I was going to finish the story and get it published, no matter what. Maybe My Beloved could help.

I sighed. In what exact order was I proposing to save the world? Clear Mary Alice? Eradicate domestic violence in Fairport? Find a new place to live? Track down my wandering son?

I saved the beginning of my article and logged onto the Internet again. Time to see if Mike had responded to my Facebook message. And, to my great relief, he had.

Sort of.

He'd confirmed me as a "friend." That was good. And there was also a personal message.

"Dear friends and family, especially my mother. I know you're wondering what's up with me. Sorry to say, I CAN'T TELL YOU. But I can tell you I am well – wonderful even. The best I've ever been. And I'll be back in touch and explain everything soon. For the indefinite future, I must maintain 'radio silence.' Thanks for your understanding."

Understanding is not my strong suit.

What the heck was Mike up to?

I picked up the apartment phone to call Jim. I needed a man's perspective on this. I heard beeping, indicating a call had come in when I was on Internet dinosaur dial-up. I heard Nancy's voice, screeching in a tone that always meant trouble.

"Carol, I don't know where you are. But when you get my message, get over to your house right away. Jim is here ordering everyone around and driving the contractors crazy. You gotta get him out of here pronto, or there won't be any show house." Then she slammed the phone down.

Good grief.

I curbed the impulse to curse out loud. I don't like to use bad language in front of Lucy and Ethel.

Instead, I forced myself to take deep calming breaths. One breath. Two breaths. Three breaths. By the time I got up to ten, I had a plan. And, if I do say so myself, it was one of my best.

This morning Jim had added something to my Honey-Don't List – Thou shalt not interfere with the police investigation into Jack Cartwright's death. Now it was my turn to add to his: Thou shalt not interfere in the design of the show house.

I sat down at the kitchen table and wrote Jim's new Honey-Don't mantra on a sheet of paper again and again. Then I cut the paper into individual strips and stuffed them into the Honey-Don't Jar, grabbed my car keys, and told the girls to be good.

After all, turn-about was fair play, wasn't it?

Heh, heh heh.

Chapter 31

Smile often. It confuses people.

I didn't panic when I rolled to a stop in front of our house and found no cars or workmen's trucks there. Maybe they were all taking a late lunch, I told myself. Or having a design planning meeting at Superior Interiors.

"Hello? Hello?," I called, walking around the side of my house. "Anybody here?"

Then I spied My Beloved sitting on the back porch steps. Alone. Looking like he'd lost his last friend. Or, possibly, mine.

Put on a happy face, I told myself. He didn't need to know that Nancy called me in a panic and ordered me to get him out of there.

"Hi, honey," I said, sitting down beside him and putting the Honey-Don't Jar in plain sight. "Where is everybody? What are you doing outside all by yourself?"

"That...that decorator person, Marcia what's-her-name, had the nerve to tell me to leave my own house. She practically threw me out. All I was doing was making a few simple suggestions about the way they were doing the show house. It is our house, after all. I have a right to an opinion, especially since we want to put it back on the market once the show house is over. I couldn't believe it.

"And when I refused to leave, she had two of the workmen shove me out the kitchen door. And then she locked it. I tried to get back in, but my key wouldn't work. She must have changed the lock. What a witch."

"Jim," I said, "for heaven's sake, calm down. And don't talk about Marcia that way. You don't know her at all. She's just doing her job. And, we've been over this before. For the next few months, this isn't our house. I repeat, this isn't our house."

I shook the Honey-Don't Jar in his face. "Remember how, this morning, you added something new to my Honey-Don't list? Well, now it's my turn. Pick one. Any one."

Jim reached in and pulled out a slip of paper. Read it carefully. Shook his head. Pulled out another one. Then another. Then another.

"OK, Carol, I get it. You're right. But I was just trying to be helpful. You see that, don't you?'

"If you want to be helpful, Jim, I have a few things that you can do for me. Like go over the domestic violence article I've been working on. I interviewed Sister Rose and a domestic violence survivor, and I've done a quick first draft from my notes, but I really need more help fleshing out the story and editing it. And then, I have to get it into print. I'll even forfeit my computer time for the rest of the day if you'd take a look at it. You've had so much more experience with this than I have."

After a certain age, sex may not do the trick. But give a man a good meal, or an important (as in "Honey, you're the only one who help me") job to do, and he'll be putty in your hands. All smart wives know that secret.

Jim leaned over and gave me a peck on the cheek.

"I know what you're doing, Carol," he said. "You figure that if you divert me with your article, I'll stay away from our house."

He waved the slips of paper in my face. "But don't forget your part of the bargain. No interfering with the police."

"I already agreed to that, dear," I said. And gave him a sweet smile.

"I'm going back to the apartment to read your article," Jim said. Before he left, turned and peered in our kitchen window. Then he fired his parting salvo.

"You better be sure Marcia doesn't paint the kitchen puke green."

Over all, I was pleased at how I'd handled that situation. Of course, it was the most trivial of all the crises I was currently dealing with.

Which brought me squarely back to Mary Alice and The Big Problem. Imitating My Beloved's recent movements, I stood on tippy toes and peered in my kitchen window. Nope, there was no way Mary Alice could have seen Jack Cartwright lying on the floor from this vantage point. And I was sure she would come to my kitchen door. It was the way all of us, family and friends, came and went. The antique front door, which looked great from the street, was hard to open and a devil to close, so we never used it.

I heard a chirping sound, and for a split second I looked up at the sky to see if a bird was flying overhead.

But it wasn't a bird, it was my cell phone, which I was actually able to locate in my purse before the caller clicked off or went into voice mail. (Some of you may not know what a feat finding my cell phone was for me. If you're one of them, don't worry. I'll tell you another time.)

"Carol, for God's sake, pick up this phone," said Mary Alice. "If I have to leave you a message too, I swear I'll really lose it."

"I'm here!" I screamed back, parking myself on the back porch steps. "Don't hang up!"

"Thank God I got you," Mary Alice said. "I've been calling all over. Where's Claire? Where's Nancy? I need all of you. I've never been so humiliated in my life as I was last night at your house."

She started to cry. "And I'm so scared. The police think I've been hiding the fact that I knew Jack Cartwright."

She stopped talking for a minute and I distinctly heard her inhale something.

"Mary Alice, are you smoking again?" I yelled. "For heaven's sake, it took you years to quit. Please don't start that filthy habit again."

She coughed into the phone. "I just had one. And it tastes terrible. I found an old pack of cigarettes in my dresser."

She coughed again. "Larry said last night that any evidence against me is circumstantial. That's why the police questioned me and then let me come home. But I feel like a criminal. The way I was escorted out of your house in front of all those people.

"Oh God, I'm so scared. I don't think I've ever been so scared before. You've got to help me. I didn't do anything to hurt Jack. Really, I didn't. You believe me, don't you?"

"Well, of course I believe you, sweetie," I said. "As a matter of fact, Nancy and Claire and Deanna and Maria and I all had a meeting this morning at the Trattoria. We have a brilliant plan that's sure to get you out of this mess." OK, I know that was stretching the truth, but I was trying to cheer Mary Alice up, so I can be excused for that white lie, right?

"Everyone has a job to do, and we'll keep at it until the real perp is caught."

Mary Alice laughed. "I can't believe you used the word 'perp', Carol. You've been reading too many mysteries again.

"I should have known I could count on all of you to come through for me. What can I do?"

"Keep your chin up and think positive thoughts," I said. "I'll be back in touch with you soon with news. We'll get through this together."

And you might start a novena or two, just to be on the safe side.

I didn't really say that. Of course.

As surprising as this may sound, for the next few days My Beloved was more helpful to me than my personal posse of girlfriends. He did a good edit of my article – very thoughtful, helpful, and non-critical. He did have some changes to suggest. But he presented his suggestions as just that – suggestions.

"This is a strong article, Carol," Jim said as he went over it still again. "It really opened my eyes to the domestic violence issue. Say," he said, flipping his glasses up to ride on his receding hairline, "do you think that Jenny was in an abusive relationship in California? I know Jeff was a control freak, but it never occurred to me that it could be abuse."

"I thought of the same thing," I said. "No matter what happened out there, let's just be grateful that she's back in Fairport and seems to be involved with a terrific guy. I guess parents never know, unless the child chooses to share it. And even then, I know we're not getting the whole story.

"Speaking of which," I said, "you may be interested to know that our son is maintaining radio silence for the next few weeks. I even tried to reach him using Facebook and got a cryptic e-mail back which said he'd be in touch when he was ready to be and meanwhile don't worry. Hah! As if a son can tell his mother not to worry."

"Since when did you join Facebook?" My Beloved asked. Trust him to zero in on the least important piece of my conversation.

"I'm trying to live in the twenty-first century," I replied. "And what do you think about Mike?"

"You've always worried too much about him," Jim said. "Especially since he moved to Miami. You know the old saying, 'Boys will be boys'."

Isn't it fascinating how a father's take on a son is so different than the one he has on a daughter?

"You need to leave him alone and let him live his life. What were you bugging him about, anyway?"

"I was not bugging him, dear," I said. "I wanted his help doing some Internet sleuthing about Jack Cartwright. You remember how helpful Mike was finding out information about your retirement coach last year. If it wasn't for him, you might be making license plates in the local lock-up for the indefinite future."

Jim looked me squarely in my baby blues. "I thought we agreed that you were not going to interfere with the police investigation. You promised me."

"I'm not interfering," I said in my defense. "But Mary Alice, who is one of my oldest and dearest friends, called and begged me for help. So I just decided to do a little investigating on my own. How could I refuse her? In fact, since she was a bridesmaid in our wedding, maybe you should pitch in and help her, too, instead of criticizing me for doing it."

"Knowing you, you've already involved Nancy and Claire," Jim said.

"I didn't involve them. They want to help Mary Alice. And so do Deanna and Jenny and Maria Lesco."

Jim took a full minute to process this information, then said, "All right, Carol. How about if I take on the job you wanted Mike to handle? I'll do some Internet searches on Jack and see what I can come up with.

"But you have to promise me that anything we find out goes right to the police. Whether it's helpful to Mary Alice or not."

"Of course, Jim," I said. Over my – excuse the phrase – dead body.

Chapter 32

Dear God: My prayer this year is for a thin body and a fat bank balance. Please don't mix these up like you did last year. Amen.

No matter how many tragedies life throws at you, the mundane domestic chores still have to be handled. The next morning, when I reached into my large black suitcase to see what clean clothes I had left, I realized I was down to my very last pair of undies.

Yikes! Crisis! I couldn't ignore this. The laundry had to be done.

I had a brief flashback to my house, with my matching washer and dryer tucked side by side in the basement like best buddies. And Jim marching down the basement stairs, laundry basket held high, ready to throw in a load. Or two. My hero.

When Jim initially took over the laundry chores, I resented it. I felt like he was encroaching on my female territory. Nobody did the laundry better than I did. But once he got the hang of separating colors – huge learning curve there – and started hanging up clothes right from the dryer to avoid needless ironing, I encouraged him in his new-found hobby. Took it for granted, even.

But today, according to the note he'd left propped up by the computer, he was off to the newspaper and wasn't sure when he'd be back. I wondered if he'd taken my article with him. Well, I'd find out about that later.

Meanwhile, I had to load up the car with dirty clothes, towels, sheets (might as well strip the bed while I was at it), detergent, fabric softener, bleach, spray spot remover, dryer sheets – good grief. And then find a convenient Laundromat. What a way to spend the day.

I fed and walked Lucy and Ethel, and told them not to expect me back before dark. I handed them the remote control for the television (only kidding) and was on my way.

Jeez. What a hot place. I'm talking temperature here, so don't get the wrong idea. I couldn't believe how many people were at Sissy's Suds in the middle of the morning. I had to fight to commandeer the three washers I needed for all my stuff, and even then, I was packing the machines so tightly that I prayed they didn't overflow.

Then I found an empty chair next to an overflowing ashtray (probably why the chair was empty) and settled myself in to read the year-old magazines scattered around the sticky table. And this was a place where I was supposed to get my clothes clean?

I was zeroing in on an article about the Angelina Jolie/Brad Pitt/Jennifer Anniston "love triangle" – "Brad and Jen Caught in Secret Tryst; Angie Livid!" – when I heard a familiar voice on the other side of the high bank of dryers.

It was my neighbor, Liz.

"Alyssa's handling the whole situation so bravely," she said. "But I think part of her is relieved she won't have to put up with Jack any more. From what I've heard, he wasn't the easiest person in the world to live with."

Huh? Now this was very interesting. In fact, it was the first time I'd ever heard anyone say anything negative about Jack. Let's hear it for public Laundromats.

I strained to hear more, but didn't want to give my presence away.

"Have you seen her?" asked the other person, whose voice I didn't recognize.

"Not since the memorial service," Liz admitted. "But we've talked on the phone a few times. I wanted her to know that she can count on me to be there for her, if she needs to cry, or talk, or just plain vent. It's so hard for her to keep up a positive front. She doesn't want anyone to know how awful her life with Jack really was.

"I promised I'd keep her secret."

I wanted to shout, "Then why are you talking to someone about the Cartwrights' private business, Liz?"

But I didn't, of course. Instead, I inched as close as I could to the dryers, hoping to hear more.

Then Liz's companion said, "I think these quilts are finally dry. Let's get out of here and grab some coffee."

Rats. Just when things were getting interesting.

The Laundromat door closed behind them, leaving me with lots to think about. I finally had something that might clear Mary Alice. Or, at the very least, a place to start looking for answers to some very interesting questions.

I broke every speed limit in Fairport to get back to the apartment and my computer. I couldn't wait to send out an a.p.e. (all-points-e-mail) to my posse of sleuths.

Of course, when I burst in the door, struggling to carry two baskets full of clean laundry, I found My Beloved trolling away at the computer, checking his stock prices. Argh. But according to our agreed-upon schedule, it was his computer time.

"You look like you're about to explode, Carol," said Jim. I assumed he was referring to my excited expression and not making a nasty crack about any possible weight gain. (We had been eating a lot of take-out food lately. Not good for the waistline.)

"Jim, you won't believe what I just overheard at the Laundromat," I said. "I'll tell you if you take this laundry from me. These baskets are very heavy."

My Beloved, chivalry personified, countered with another suggestion. "Just put the baskets down by the desk, Carol. No need to struggle."

I almost let him have it, but then remembered his heart problem a few months ago, and followed his suggestion. Without comment. Points for me, right?

"Jim, you have to hear this. When I was at the Laundromat today, I overheard a conversation between Liz Stone and someone else. I couldn't see who the other person was, but that part doesn't matter."

Jim opened his mouth to speak, but I headed him off.

"Liz said that Alyssa Cartwright wouldn't be mourning Jack's death, because he was far from an ideal husband. Liz said that Alyssa's life with Jack was 'awful.' That was the exact word she used.

"Isn't that something? We need to check that out. I need to send out an e-mail to the troops and tell them."

Jim looked at me in that "you must be crazy" way that I've seen all too often over the course of our marriage. Sometimes I ignore that look. But not now.

"What are you checking out, exactly, Carol? Some offhand conversation you overheard in a Laundromat? Who knows what Liz meant by that comment. Or if she even knew what she was talking about.

"Instead of sending out an e-mail to the 'troops,' as you call them, maybe you should check out your source first."

I hated to admit it, but he was right. Again.

"And while you're checking things out, Carol," Jim continued, "it might be a good idea to check out a few things in your domestic abuse story, too. I showed it to Ted, the paper's managing editor, just to get a preliminary reaction, and he thought the description you gave of a typical abuser wasn't credible. It needs more fleshing out."

"Wasn't credible?" I sputtered. "Why, that's outrageous. I quoted Sister Rose word for word, and she's been in the front lines of this problem for years."

"I'm just repeating what he said," Jim replied. "Talk to her again. Try to get a few more specifics. And while you're checking your facts, I'll go online and check a few old newspaper sources on Cape Cod. Maybe I'll find out a few things about Jack Cartwright to back up what you overheard from Liz.

"Deal, Carol?"

Whattaguy.

"Deal, Jim."

In no time at all, I hustled myself over to Sally's Place. First, though, I placed a quick call to be sure Sister was there. Surprisingly, she answered the phone herself.

"Hello, Sister Rose," I said in my most polite voice. "It's Carol Andrews." I started to inquire about her schedule today, but she cut me off.

"I think I recognize your voice by now," Sister said. "Of course, having caller i.d. on our phone does help. I was hoping you'd call. Can you stop by today? We need to talk about what happened at the preview party. And the sooner, the better."

"I'll be there within the hour," I said. "And I'll bring coffee and snacks from The Paperback Café."

"Perfect," Sister said. "I'll be waiting for you."

You'll be pleased to know that I resisted the siren song of the thrift shop, hardly giving the attractive window display, with all its new merchandise, a third glance. No shopping for me today. I was a woman on a mission.

Well, maybe if the talk with Sister Rose went well, I'd reward myself with just a quick walk through the shop. After all, the proceeds went to such a worthy cause.

Balancing the two coffees and the paper sack of goodies, I rang the bell and announced myself though the intercom.

"Come in, Carol," said Sister Rose. "I've been waiting for you."

"There was a time when if you told me you were waiting for me, it paralyzed me," I said. "I hope those days are over."

Sister gave me a thin smile and waved me into an office chair. Opening a cup of coffee, she took a quick sip, then got down to business.

"Tell me what's happening on with Mary Alice," she demanded. "Did the police release her after that disgusting display at the preview party? The very idea," Sister huffed, "taking one of my students out of a public place like she was a common criminal."

"She's home," I said. "But very scared. Mary Alice is terrified that since the police have made the connection between her and Jack Cartwright, they think she has a perfect motive for wanting Jack dead. Plus, she already admitted to the police that she was at my house the night Jack died."

I sighed. "It's a real mess. But Nancy, Claire, and a few other folks I'm not sure you know, are working with me to try and clear her. We may not be professional sleuths but," I paused for just a minute. "Not to brag, but we do have a little experience in solving crimes. And I just found out something very damaging about the Cartwrights' marriage that could affect the case."

Sister Rose gave me the cold stare that struck fear into students for decades.

"Carol, dear," she said, "you do realize that this is a human life we're talking about. This is not a game. You sound like you're playing 'Clue,' for heaven's sake. Who are you? Miss Marple?"

Whoa. That was harsh. I sat up very straight in my chair and glared at her.

"I assure you, Sister Rose, that I'm very aware of the fact that this is not a game. This is one of my best friends we're talking about here. I hope that, if you have any information that could help her, you would share it with us.

"In fact," I matched her frozen look with one of my own that's been known to elicit confessions of wrong-doing from my children in a single second, "I would expect you to do so."

Sister Rose nodded her head slightly. "Your point is well taken. I'm glad we understand each other." She pursed her lips. "I don't mean to be so hard-nosed, Carol. I'm just as worried about Mary Alice as you are. And I'm afraid I'm taking it out on you.

"Now, you said you have more questions about the article you're writing on domestic violence," Sister Rose said, indicating our discussion about Mary Alice's troubles was over. "How can I help you?"

I whipped open my little notebook and rummaged in my purse for a pen. Too late. Sister Rose handed me one. That broke the ice between us.

"I'm not going to remind you of all the times you came to class unprepared, Carol," said Sister with just a hint of a smile.

Humph.

"I've been asked to expand on the profile of a typical abuser," I said. "For instance, if a young boy witnesses domestic abuse in his family, would that be a major factor if that boy becomes an abuser himself when he grows up? Is my question making any sense?"

"It makes perfect sense," Sister replied. "But unfortunately, things are never as black and white as that. Each abuse case, and each abuser, is different. Some children who witness abuse between their parents make choices that lead them into abusive relationships as adults. Abuse is about control. One person controlling another. The patterns set in childhood can continue into the next generation. But they don't always. And there have been many articles written about the role alcohol and drugs play in an abusive relationship. Again, the answer is not black and white.

"There's a non-profit organization, the National Coalition Against Domestic Violence, which gives excellent information on domestic violence statistics. Their motto is, 'Every home a safe home.' You might want to mention their web site in your article. It's www.ncadv.org.

"I hope you really understand what I'm telling you here, Carol. Read the information on this web site very carefully. And think about what you already know. Few relationships are what they appear to be. There are always secrets."

I looked up from my scribbling. "I'm trying to write down everything you've told me, Sister."

"Find the secret, Carol, and you can save a person's life."

Chapter 33

There will be a $5 charge for whining.

I puzzled over what Sister Rose had told me all the way back to the apartment. It was a very strange conversation. I felt that we were talking on more than one level, about more than one thing. It was very frustrating.

Fortunately, My Beloved was out. I guess that sounds terrible, but sometimes I need to process things on my own, without explaining what I'm doing, why I'm doing it, and, most important, when I'll be finished so I can start dinner.

I gave the girls a quick run, a bowl of water, and some Milk Bones, which made me a goddess in their eyes.

Then I poured myself a glass of chardonnay (it was a very small plastic glass, in case you were wondering), fired up my computer, and searched for the web site Sister Rose had told me about for the National Coalition Against Domestic Violence.

Wow. What an eye-opener. It was such an organized web site, and the purple hue of all the pages made for very easy reading for...ahem...older eyes, like mine. I'd known some of these facts before, but I was especially intrigued by the national fact sheets relating to abusive relationships. The list was even broken down by state.

I continued my Internet search, and eventually found another excellent web site, www.domesticviolence.org. This one included common myths about domestic violence. There was so much to learn. I was overwhelmed by all the information I could use for my article. And saddened by all I'd discovered. The domestic violence issue was a national tragedy. And one of our country's ugliest secrets.

I put my head back in my chair and closed my eyes for a minute, to clear my head. I guess I must have dozed off, because I had the weirdest dream. In it my mother – good grief, where did she come from? – was chasing a man who had no face. When she caught him – she never was a good runner so I was quite impressed – she started hitting him and screaming, "Not my daughter. Not my daughter. You leave her alone."

That dream really spooked me. First of all, my mother and I never had, shall we say, the closest of relationships. She died when I was in my mid-twenties, and it was only later in life I finally realized that, hey, she wasn't perfect, but she loved me, and she was the best mother she knew how to be. Nobody could ask for more than that from a parent.

I tried to be a good mother to Jenny and Mike, but who knew if I succeeded? There are no fool-proof how-to books for parenting. At least, none that I've found in my local independent book store or library.

I sat there, lost in thought, going over the dream and trying to figure out what it could mean. I wasn't even sure I was remembering the whole thing. Mother couldn't possibly be warning me about Jim. No way. She adored him, and he was wonderful to her right up to the day she died.

Then I thought, maybe my mother was a symbol for all mothers, and she was warning me about how often daughters are abused by their partners. That would make sense, because I was so focused on the domestic violence article. Perhaps my subconscious was reiterating the message, in case I didn't understand the seriousness of the problem.

I massaged my forehead. Too much thinking sometimes gives me a headache, and I could feel one coming on.

I heard a car door slam, and Jim burst through the door. He looked so upset that, at first, I thought someone had died.

"Larry just called with terrible news," Jim said. "He's working at the courthouse to try to arrange bail, but....

"God, Jim, what is it? Bail? Why?"

"Mary Alice has been arrested."

"Orange is definitely not your color." I held Mary Alice's hand tight and made a feeble attempt to make her smile.

I had called Mark immediately after Jim told me about Mary Alice. Of course, at first Mark had protested that this wasn't his case, there was nothing he could do, blah blah blah. But I didn't let him off the hook that easily. So, sue me. I used a little maternal threatening. Jim was making all sorts of faces at me during this conversation, by the way. I just closed my eyes and ignored him.

And here we were once again, My Beloved and I, in the Fairport Police Station. No preliminary coffee stop this time. Once Jim announced our names to the officer on duty – I guess the perky receptionist went home at 5:00 – Mark came out and took us back to the holding cells at the rear of the building. He gestured us into a bleak room with the bare basics of furniture – think "yard sale retro."

Before we even had a chance to sit down, he led in Mary Alice.

"You have five minutes," he informed us. "And if you stay any longer, and my boss finds out, I'll be probably be fired." Then he closed the door and left us alone.

Mary Alice held onto my hand like she was on the Titanic and I had the last life preserver.

"Carol, you've known me for over forty years." She looked at My Beloved. "And you've known me for almost as long. For God's sake, you can't believe that I'm responsible for Jack Cartwright's death.

"You don't, do you?"

She looked at us, hard.

"You don't, either one of you, do you?" she repeated. "I swear, I didn't know Jack was inside your house. If I did, I would have done something to help him. No matter what our past history was. How many times do I have to say this? Jack was a human being, above all else. And, I swear, he'd be alive today. If only I'd known he was in there."

She buried her head in my shoulder and sobbed.

"This isn't getting us anywhere," Jim snapped. I stared at him, shocked by his harsh tone.

"Listen, Mary Alice," he said. "Carol and I both believe in you. Hell, I think even Mark believes in you."

His face hardened. "But all this sniveling of yours isn't helping."

Jeez, what a creep. Wait'll I got him out in the parking lot. I was going to let him have it.

Mary Alice blew her nose with a tissue I'd found in my pocket. True to form, she did check it carefully and removed a few particles of lint before she used it. Then she straightened up in her chair and said, "You're right, Jim. Crying isn't helping at all. What do you want to know?"

"Now you're talking," said My Beloved. "I want you to think back to that night. Did you see anyone, or anything, outside our house? A person walking a dog, maybe? A car? A couple pushing a baby carriage? Kids on bikes? Close your eyes and think hard."

Mary Alice squinted her eyes shut. So did I. After all, I'd been there that night, too.

"I'm sorry, Jim," she said finally. "I don't remember seeing anybody. I wish I did. I just drove in the driveway to the back of your house. Then I got out of my car, sat on the back porch steps, and waited for Carol to come. I waited for half an hour, and Carol never showed up. So I went home."

My eyes snapped open. "But I saw something, Jim," I said excitedly. "When I got to our house, I remember there was a car cruising down the street. There's not a lot of traffic out at that hour, so I paid attention to it."

Oh, rats. It was a tomato red Mini Cooper. I'd seen that car before, the day Nancy was prepping our house before it went on the market.

I knew I wasn't crazy. The car was Marcia Fischer's.

When the car passed under a street light, I'd had a quick, clear view of the driver. And there was no mistaking that vanity license plate, Styln 1. It was Marcia in the driver's seat, all right.

Both Mary Alice and Jim looked at me expectantly. It was so quiet in the room that I could hear the ticking of Jim's watch.

"The car was Marcia Fischer's, from Superior Interiors. And she was definitely driving it. I saw her face clearly. It could just be a coincidence, but I don't think so."

Jim looked at me skeptically. "Are you sure, Carol? Why didn't you tell us this before?"

"A few things have been going on since then, dear," I said. "As you may recall, right after I saw the car, I came in our house and found Jack's body. That pretty much took my mind off anything else that happened that night.

"And, besides, I don't know about you, Mary Alice," I looked at her, "but nobody ever asked me about this before."

I took a deep breath and made a giant leap in what I was sure was the right direction. Because I finally understood what Sister Rose had been trying to tell me. Jack Cartwright was an abuser. And I'd bet that he was also the one who traumatized Marcia when she was a teenager. That explained a lot of things, including why Marcia had been at Jack's memorial service. Sister Rose couldn't break Marcia's confidence, but she hoped that if she dropped enough hints, I'd eventually catch on.

This was unbearably sad. Did I have to betray a new friend to save an old one?

Before I had the chance to voice my theory, the door opened and Mark stuck his head in again. "I'm sorry, everyone, but I have to insist that you leave now. Mrs. Costello's lawyer is here and wants to see her.

"But he has good news. He's arranged for bail, so after you sign a few papers, Mrs. Costello, you're free to go home. For now."

Mary Alice started to cry. Again.

I was so excited I threw my arms around Mark and gave him a big kiss on the cheek. I guess I embarrassed him.

"Jeez, Mrs. Andrews, I mean, Carol, I didn't do anything," Mark said. "This isn't even my case. Remember? It's Paul's case."

Just call me Mom, I said to myself. Or mom-in-law. Someday. Maybe.

Jim shot me a warning look and guided Mary Alice out of the interview room. I understood that look. It meant, Don't interfere.

Naturally, I ignored it.

"Mark, I know this isn't your case. But I also know that you and Paul have worked together before, and if you give him some information he doesn't have, you could help him get to the bottom of how, and why, Jack Cartwright died."

Mark raised one eyebrow – I've always admired a person who can do that – and said, "Talk."

So I did. I was careful about what I said, though. I didn't betray Marcia's confidence. Instead, I told Mark I'd just remembered I'd seen a car on Old Fairpoint Turnpike the night before the closing. It was a red Mini Cooper and the license plate was Styln1. And I told him about the conversation I overheard in the Laundromat about Jack.

"So maybe he wasn't the great guy we heard about at his memorial service," I said. "I don't want to tell the police how to do their job," (much). "But it might be worthwhile to check with the local police in the Cartwrights' former town in Massachusetts to see if any charges had ever been filed against Jack."

Mark, bless him, went along with me. And then I let the police do their job. Without any more interference from me.

Honestly, I did.

Chapter 34

Time passes, whether you're having fun or not.

At long last, it was show house time. The opening night party had been timed to coincide with Fairport's annual Fourth of July celebration. Hey, when folks live in a town that was around during the American Revolution, the town fathers make a big deal out of it. Pancake breakfasts at the local churches, a never-ending (who knew there were all those Brownie and Cub Scout troops in town?) parade, free concerts in the town gazebo throughout the day and evening, plus fantastic fireworks on the beach.

One person who had been responsible for the transformation of our antique home into a show house would not be at the party. Marcia Fischer had been arrested and was likely to be charged in Jack Cartwright's death.

It turned out that the police had searched the old auto accident records and discovered that Marcia was in the car the night Brian Costello died, so they already knew there was a connection between Marcia and Jack. That made me feel less guilty about pointing the police in Marcia's direction.

But not much.

The good news was that Mary Alice was finally in the clear. Thank God.

I poked my head into what used to be my kitchen. Gone was the country look I'd slaved for years to achieve, replaced by sleek white cabinets, top-of-the-line stainless steel appliances (I always thought mine were top-of-the-line, but then I found out how much these replacements cost and almost fainted), and bright red – that's right, red – countertops. I thought the room now resembled the local morgue during an autopsy, but what did I know about interior design?

Maria and the gang from the Trattoria were flying around cooking wonderful things to satisfy the appetite of the hundreds of guests who were paying big bucks to come to the event, as evidenced by the many platters and trays that were packed tightly next to each other on the kitchen island.

I waved to Maria, turned to leave, and was immediately wrapped in a giant hug by, of all people, Sara Miller.

Good grief.

"Carol, I don't know how to thank you," she gushed. "We're all so relieved to finally know how Jack died, and Alyssa and the children can get on with their lives. It's just wonderful.

"I can't believe Marcia was afraid of Jack," Sara continued, pressing me for more information than I was prepared to share. "At least, that's what everybody's saying. They supposedly dated when they were in high school, and Marcia's claiming that he was abusive toward her," Sara said, emphasizing the word '*claiming*'.

"I brought a special treat to celebrate the fact that this horrible ordeal is behind us. You know how I am. I just love to cook."

She gestured toward a large cooler, placed smack in the middle of the floor where everyone from Maria's Trattoria would trip over it.

"I had some delicious beef tenderloin languishing away in the freezer just begging to be turned into the Marvelous Meatballs that were such a hit at your Bunco party, and I decided they'd be the perfect addition to this wonderful party. I knew Maria would be pleased. She loves my cooking, too. One gourmet chef admiring another."

I pulled away from her embrace, embarrassed by the attention.

"I really didn't do anything," I said. "I was sure that Mary Alice wasn't responsible for Jack's death, and one thing sort of led to another. The whole situation is very sad."

I remembered our conversation at Sally's Place, when Marcia had talked about her abuser. She seemed so frightened of him, even after all these years. I felt so guilty about pointing the police in her direction. But I felt I had no choice.

"I guess Marcia snapped when Jack came back after all those years," Sara said. "But he'd changed. He was a wonderful husband and father. Look at all the people who came to his memorial service to talk about the difference he'd made in their lives. She had nothing to fear from him."

I remembered what Sister Rose had said: abusers rarely change their pattern. Instead, they look for another person to control.

I realized that some of the pieces weren't fitting together as neatly as I wanted. What if I'd put them together wrong?

Sara hugged me again. Jeez, this was too much.

Maria had been looking daggers at us for the past few minutes. Finally she mouthed, "Get out of here and take Sara with you. There's not enough room in the kitchen as it is."

I took the hint.

"There's something I'm curious about, Sara," I asked, extricating myself again from her grasp and leading her out the side door toward the huge tent that had been erected in our back yard.

I snagged two glasses of champagne from a passing waiter and passed one to Sara.

Sara took a sip and smiled. "Tattinger's. My favorite. I see no expense has been spared for this party."

"All for a good cause," I said. "Nancy thought serving really good champagne would make the guests open their wallets wider when it came to the auction part of the evening."

I took a sip myself. Nancy was right. This was the good stuff.

"Sara," I began again, "I don't mean to pry." Much. "But I've been doing research on domestic abuse for an article I'm writing, and I can't help but wonder."

I took a deep breath. What I wanted to know was probably going to put the brakes on our rekindled friendship.

Sara nodded encouragingly. "Go ahead and ask me whatever you want." That champagne was doing a great job of relaxing her, all right.

"Did you ever see any evidence of Jack abusing Alyssa?" I asked. Sara's eyes narrowed. "I don't mean hitting her, Sara. But from everything I've been told, domestic abuse is a pattern of behavior that usually continues over a lifetime. It's all about control. So I couldn't help but wonder."

"That's a terrible thing to say," Sara said. "I already told you that Jack was a loving husband to Alyssa and a wonderful father to those two kids. Believe me, as Alyssa's mother, I'd know if something else was going on.

"A mother always knows. I'm going to see if Maria needs any help." Sara turned so quickly that some gravel from the driveway shot into my face, and marched toward the kitchen at a brisk pace.

A mother doesn't always know, I thought. I remembered Marcia Fischer's mother and how she didn't have a clue what was going on when Marcia was a teenager.

Then I thought about my own mother, and all the things I'd kept from her when I was growing up. Those memories made me smile, until I remembered that weird dream I had. "Not my daughter, not my daughter." What was my mother trying to tell me?

I was interrupted in my musings by Jenny, with Mark close behind her. I had to admit, my darling daughter was positively glowing.

"Isn't this wonderful, Mom? What a great party."

I was tempted to respond, yes, but I wish it was your rehearsal dinner. And you guys were being married tomorrow.

But I didn't. I hope you're all proud of me.

The opening night party for the show house was a huge success. Sister Rose was thrilled, especially when a preliminary tally of the night's receipts showed a gross profit of $80,000. Wow!

My Beloved and I had hardly seen each other all night, except across the crowded tent once or twice. But I did feel his disapproving eyes on me when I raised my hand to bid on a two-week vacation at a villa in Tuscany. This time, I didn't ignore his glare. I was smart enough, after all these years of marriage, to know which battles to fight, and this wasn't one of them.

In the crush of people, I lost sight of Jenny and Mark, which could have been deliberate on their part. I mean, who wanted to hang out with an oldster like me at a bash like this?

The music had everybody on the dance floor. Nancy whirled by in the arms of someone who definitely wasn't her husband, Bob. Even Claire and Larry made a valiant effort. Mary Alice was nowhere to be seen, which wasn't surprising.

I was just wondering if I'd have to hitchhike back to our apartment when I felt a tap on my shoulder. To my amazement, it was Detective Paul Wheeler. "I wanted to thank you for your tip about Marcia Fischer, Mrs. Andrews," he said. "You were right, and I was wrong."

Whoa. Quite an admission, coming from him. I started to respond, but he melted away into the crowd before I could. Of course, being so short, that was pretty easy for him to do.

Something nuzzled the back of my neck. Then My Beloved whispered in my ear, "Hey, gorgeous, wanna dance? I haven't seen you all night, and the band's playing a slow one."

I knew those dance lessons I gave Jim for Christmas a few years ago would pay off.

So we took it nice and slow around the dance floor, celebrating this wonderful night. And then we went back to our apartment and celebrated a little more.

But I'm not going to tell you about that.

An hour later, I sat in our darkened living room/dining room/kitchen, Lucy snoring in the chair beside me. Sleep wouldn't come, despite the wine I'd had and, um, the exercise.

So, naturally, I had to replay the events of the party over and over in my head, especially my talk with Sara Miller. Something just didn't fit. Like that cute pair of shoes you try on in the store, and they are soooooooo comfortable that you have to buy them, and then you get them home, try them on, and they hurt like the dickens. Has that ever happened to you? And, oh yeah, you can't find the receipt to return them.

I decided to talk things over with Lucy. She was a great listener, and shared space with me as long as she got more than I did.

"It was a great party, Lucy," I whispered. "Too bad you had to miss it."

Lucy opened one eye and looked at me reproachfully. *I wasn't invited,* she said.

"Don't feel bad, Luce. There weren't any other dogs there, either," I said and stroked her head. "And you and Ethel did go to lots of parties that Jim and I had at the house over the years, remember? You really loved Bunco parties the best, especially the leftovers. You got to sample all the neighbors' cooking. But the kitchen doesn't look the way you remember it. Believe it or not, the kitchen counters are red!"

I closed my eyes and pictured my old kitchen with its bead board cabinets, black granite countertops, and large center island. A memory, quite unbidden, flashed into my head. The Bunco party I'd hosted the night I listed the house for sale. All the neighbors packed around my island, sampling the goodies. Sara Miller, bragging about her top-secret family recipe, Great Aunt Sharon's Marvelous Meatballs. I could hear her saying, "I *never* use frozen meat. I buy it fresh every day. That's why my meals always taste so wonderful."

My eyes snapped open. But she'd brought the Marvelous Meatballs to the party tonight. And she definitely said she'd had the beef "languishing in her freezer" for a while and wanted to use it up. This was, pardon the pun, food for more thought.

"OK, Lucy, by itself this probably means nothing," I whispered. "But add to it the fact that Sara's son-in-law had a history of domestic violence. She had to know about that. No matter what she said to me tonight, I don't believe that Jack's basic personality changed when they moved to Fairport. What if Sara saw Jack abusing Alyssa? As a mother, she'd want to protect her daughter, right?"

Hmm. How did this fit in with the Marvelous Meatballs? Because, somehow, I knew it did.

"This is too much for me to figure out tonight, Lucy," I whispered. "But I still can't sleep. How about if we put the television on really low, so it doesn't disturb Jim? Whatever's on at this time of night is bound to be boring."

I channel-surfed for a few minutes and settled on Classic TV. Tonight was a real smorgasbord of shows: *Dragnet, The Ed Sullivan Show,* and *Alfred Hitchcock Presents.* I might have bags under my eyes in the morning, but at least I was going to enjoy myself.

"Alfred Hitchcock was kind of a weird guy," I told Lucy, since these shows were way before her time, "but he was a genius, too. You would have loved this one show about the woman who clocked her husband over the head with a leg of lamb."

Holy cow. Was that it? Did Sara hit Jack over the head with the beef tenderloin and then freeze the evidence?

Oh, Carol. You've really lost it this time.

What did Sara do? Bring a beef tenderloin to our house the night before the closing, and during the final walk-through with their real estate agent, say to Jack, every so sweetly, "Do you mind standing still for just a minute while I hit you on the head?" Smack him, and leave?? And what about the Realtor? Jeez, you'd think she would have noticed something like that, no matter how fixated she was on getting her commission at the closing.

No, you're crazy. You're way over the top. You're wrong.

Except. How about this? I remembered reading about the tragic death of a young woman a few years ago. She had been in a skiing accident, fell, and hit her head, really hard. Initially, except for a minor headache, she appeared fine. But she died, because the blow to the head had done terrible damage that the doctors didn't initially pick up on.

It was possible. Yes, it was certainly possible. Sara could have witnessed a violent incident between Jack and Alyssa in her kitchen, and in an effort to save her daughter, smacked Jack on the head with whatever was handy – the beef tenderloin she'd purchased at the market that day. He could have fallen, even been unconscious briefly, then come to. All apologies. It won't happen again. I was out of control. Blah blah blah.

Jack meets the Realtor, does the walk-through, and appears fine. The Realtor leaves. Jack collapses in our living room, and dies.

Yes. It was plausible. Just as plausible as Marcia Fischer. Maybe even more so.

But would Paul Wheeler believe me? Because I had absolutely no proof.

I had to get some evidence. Because Paul wouldn't pay any attention to me if I had nothing to back up my wild theory.

I looked at the lighted dial on the kitchen microwave. It read 2:12. That would be a.m., in case you were wondering. I rapidly calculated that today, Saturday, was garbage pickup day in our part of Fairport, if residents chose to pony up and pay the exorbitant fees the local trash haulers demanded. In our fair town of Fairport, garbage pickup wasn't included in our taxes. So residents either went to the dump – excuse me, the transfer station – or they paid some guys lotsa money to haul away their trash. I was betting that Sara was of the latter persuasion.

And if I found a certain cellophane wrapper from a particular piece of meat, perhaps Paul would take my new theory seriously. I wasn't sure if cellophane would show traces of human blood or hair – yuck! – but it was worth a try.

I need to tell you all something about English Cocker Spaniels. First of all, they look absolutely nothing like their American cousins who are – dare I say it? – much more common. Think Springer Spaniels, only smaller, and you've pretty much got a snapshot of the breed.

And they eat, well, everything. I mean, *everything*. I don't want to gross you out and tell you about some of the things the girls've chomped on in our yard over the years. But suffice it to say that Tucker, one of our earlier English cockers, once ate an entire loaf of whole wheat bread – including the wrapper – while I was packing our car to go to the beach. Need I say more? And I'd match their olfactory powers against a bloodhound's any day, especially where meat was involved.

So I knew that if I needed a partner in crime for the upcoming caper – which would involve going through Sara Miller's garbage can, placed at the curb, Lucy was my number one choice.

I had to act fast, because the clock was ticking and the garbage guys arrived soon after sunup – 5 a.m.

I jumped up from the chair. Lucy growled at me. She doesn't like to be disturbed when she's sleeping. Until she heard the magic words. "Come on, Lucy. Wanna go for a walk?"

She looked at me. And clearly telegraphed, *Are you crazy? Do you know what time it is? It's dark out there.*

"Lucy," I whispered desperately, "I need you to go with me. It'll be fine. I promise you. And when we get back, I'll give you a treat."

That did it. She jumped out of the chair and ran for her leash.

I clipped it on her collar and headed out the door. In my pajamas. Oh, well, no time to worry about making a fashion statement. And I was confident that my chances of running into somebody I knew were slim to none.

"Look casual," I said as we snuck out the apartment door. Lucy sent me a look that clearly said, *I'm a dog. What you see is what you get.*

Naturally, Lucy took her sweet time on our late-night walk, stopping to sniff and investigate each blade of grass and bush along the way. At least, that's how it seemed to me. And trying to get her to move once she found any interesting trash which had been placed along the curb in anticipation of the morning pickup was a challenge, no matter how much I tugged at her leash.

Oh, joy. We were finally in front of Sara's house and – bummer – no trash can. Sara preferred trash bags, and there was one large one at the end of her driveway. That meant I either had to haul it back to the apartment and go through it there, or do a quick spot check and hope what I wanted was near the top.

Better get it over with. I knelt down, opened the bag and let Lucy take a good sniff inside. I was so intent on my task that when a police officer shone a flashlight on me and demanded to know what the heck I was doing, I was, well, surprised.

Who knew going through other people's garbage at 3:00 in the morning could be interpreted as criminal behavior?

Some people just can't take a joke, and sad to say, My Beloved is often one of them. So when the Fairport police called him to say Lucy and I had been taken into the station for – Well, what exactly was the charge? Invasion of garbage? – he wasn't pleased.

Of course, Jim immediately called Jenny (who was not the least bit surprised at her mother's latest antics) and Mark, and they all hustled to the police station to spring Lucy and me. Lucy, by the way, was having a grand time, having won the heart of the arresting officer by turning on the charm and being extra loving and adorable. The fact that there were some doggy biscuits involved definitely helped.

I had not endeared myself to the officer, however, since I refused to get into the police cruiser without the bag of Sara's garbage. I thought that was a reasonable request, since I'd always intended to give it to the police as evidence. Or possible evidence.

Anyway, by the time the sun came up over the Fairport police station, and I had shared my new theory 20 or 30 times about Jack Cartwright's death with Jim, Jenny, Mark, Paul Wheeler, and the assorted police staff who were unlucky enough to be working that shift, I finally convinced them that it was worth looking inside the garbage bag for the meat wrapper.

They made me do it, of course. And I got lucky. Because Sara Miller was a complete neat freak, and the wrapper was inside another plastic bag marked, "For Show House." Jeez, who labels their garbage? Was she expecting a tax receipt for a donation?

OK, so this wasn't solid evidence that a crime had been committed. I knew that. But Mark went to bat for me – still again – and convinced Paul and the other detectives to at least examine the wrapper for traces of, well, you know.

All in all, a good night's work. If it turned out I was wrong, well, I was wrong. But I'd given the Fairport police not one but two viable suspects, and after that, it was up to them.

After all, a private citizen like me can only be expected to do so much. (Smile.)

Chapter 35

The only reason I have a kitchen is because it came with the house.

"I still can't believe she labeled her garbage," Nancy said. "How anal-retentive is that? It's like she was begging to be caught."

It turned out to be Sara Miller, of course, who was responsible for Jack's death. She admitted to the police that there had been a fight in her kitchen between Alyssa and Jack that began as words but ended with Jack becoming violent and hitting Alyssa across her face again and again. Sara walked in on the abuse and let Jack have it with the first thing she could lay her hands on, the beef tenderloin defrosting on the counter. (Turned out that Sara had exaggerated about always 'cooking fresh.' But you figured that out already, right?)

Jack came to the house walk-through, complaining of a minor headache. But nobody suspected how seriously he was hurt. The theory is that, for some unknown reason, he stayed behind after everyone else left, collapsed in our living room, and died there. Just like I'd imagined.

Larry McGee, good guy that he is, took on Sara's case pro bono and is currently negotiating for a dismissal of the charges based on Sara's right to defend her daughter. I pray it doesn't come to trial, especially for Alyssa and her children's sake. They deserve some peace in their lives.

Two months had passed since the Great Garbage Caper, and it was almost Labor Day weekend. Where did the summer go?

Of course, I ask myself this same thing every year.

My article on domestic violence had been published by our local paper, and even though it wouldn't be nominated for any awards, I was pretty proud of it. And Sister Rose was, too.

The show house was over, and Jim and I were still without permanent digs. We'd finally had another offer on our house, and I let My Beloved handle the whole transaction this time. I had such bad memories of the last deal, and one of us had to concentrate on finding a new home before we came to blows in our tiny apartment.

"You're a fine one to criticize Sara about being anal-retentive," I said to Nancy as we whipped along some country roads outside of Fairport's town limits in still another house search. "I seem to remember that someone I know and love keeps closets in her home with clothes organized by season. And a journal of when she's worn what outfit, where she's worn it, what accessories she used, and who saw her in it. Not that I'm mentioning any names, of course."

"Point taken," said Nancy.

"Now, sweetie," she said, leaning over and patting my arm, "I just know you're going to love this house. You better, because, quite frankly, trying to find you and Jim a new home is getting to be a royal pain. You've found fault with every single property I've shown you. Nothing is going to be perfect. You've got to compromise. If you don't love this one, I swear I'm giving up, and you're on your own. In fact," Nancy swerved her brand new silver gray Mercedes over to the side of the road and parked, "I have an idea. You're going to complain this one is too far out of town, but it's a gorgeous house. Put this on."

She handed me a blindfold.

I gaped at her. "What the heck are you doing?"

"Put it on, Carol, or you're going to have to walk back to town. No arguments."

Sheesh. "All right, all right." I covered my eyes and tied the blindfold on tight.

"No peeking," Nancy said, and we took off again.

After about another twenty minutes – I'm guessing here because I couldn't see my watch – we rolled to a stop.

"Sit tight. I'll come around and get you. Don't open the door."

Nancy took my arm and pulled me from the car.

"Hang on to me. There are two steps. OK, we're at the front door."

"Can I look now?" I asked. "This is ridiculous."

"Now!" Nancy said, whipping off the blindfold and pushing me into the foyer of my very own house.

Holy cow. Holy everything. I was back home. Not the show house, but my house. Only better. Newer. Wider doorways. No crooked floors. A new staircase with safer, less steep treads. And a banister that didn't wriggle.

She led me into the kitchen. Hello bead board cabinets. Hello black granite island. Goodbye red countertops. My kitchen. *My kitchen.*

"Nancy, I don't know what to say. How did you do all this? I don't understand."

"I didn't do much at all," Nancy said. "But there's a pretty wonderful guy in the family room who organized the whole transformation. Go in and say hello."

Jim came toward me, arms open wide. "Surprised, honey?" he asked.

"Surprised? I'm in shock. And what about your heart. Jim? I don't want you to risk your health taking care of this house just for me."

"I'm way ahead of you," My Beloved said with just a hint of a twinkle. "I already hired someone to do the yardwork. He also does snow plowing, so we're covered for all seasons. When we need more help, we'll hire someone. I figure we'll be helping the economy in our own small way. This is where we belong, Carol.

"But I didn't do this all by myself. Marcia Fischer was a tremendous help. She wanted to thank you for figuring out what really happened to Jack Cartwright.

"There are a few more folks here who wanted to come and say hello. Close your eyes again."

"Jim, I don't think I can take any more surprises," I said.

"Welcome home, Mom," said Jenny, throwing her arms around me and giving me a big kiss. "And you thought I couldn't keep a secret.

"Well, here's another one." She waved her hand in front of my face to show off a beautiful diamond solitaire. Mark stood behind her, beaming.

"Oh, I'm so happy," I said. "For you. For all of us. This is the best surprise anyone's ever had." I hugged them both so hard my arms felt like they were going to fall off.

"There's one more surprise, Carol. In the hall. And this one's a doozy. Wait a minute," My Beloved said. "And close your eyes one more time."

I stood there, eyes closed, tears streaming down my cheeks.

"Open your eyes, Carol."

"Surprise, Mom," said my long-lost son, giving me a gigantic bear hug. Then he stepped away to reveal the adorable girl standing behind him.

"This is Marlee.

"My wife."

I guess it was then that I fainted.

The Moving Quiz

Are you (and Your Beloved) having the Relocation Conversation? Should you stay in your current home, or strike out for someplace new?

To get the conversation started, here are some things to consider:
How do you rate the community where you now live? Include factors like public safety, property taxes (and the possibility of an increase), access to public transportation, availability of senior services, and trash/recycling collection.

Do you love your current home? Is it convenient to stores, dry cleaners, your faith community, and other things that are important to you? If you live alone, is there someone you can count on to check on you to be sure you are OK?

Does your current home have potential for a first-floor master bedroom and bath, with no stairs involved? Ditto a convenient laundry area? Are doorways wide, or could they be widened easily if necessary?

Could you close off some unused rooms and save on energy costs?

Is your mortgage paid off? Can you manage the property taxes, insurance and maintenance expenses?

Does the idea of cleaning out closets and packing up belongings overwhelm you?

Could you keep your house in "company" condition all the time? Could you tolerate showing your house to potential buyers at a moment's notice?

Are you prepared to move away from family and friends? Your doctors and dentist? (Your hairdresser?)

OK, let's say you've thought about all these questions and you've decided to move. Let's think about where to go.

Do you have a bit of wanderlust, and want a complete change in lifestyle, climate or even country?

Do you prefer to live in a city, suburb, small town, or rural area?

Which of these appeals to you the most: a golf community, beach resort, over-

55 development or a diverse, mixed-age neighborhood? None of these?

If you are a couple, do you both want to move, or is one of you doing it for the other? (Be honest with your answer. This is a big step and both partners should agree.)

How quickly do you think you'd develop friendships in a new location?

Do you have hobbies or other activities that will get you out of the house in your new community? Does your partner?

Realistically, could you have a change of heart, and want to move back home before too long?

Would you want to try a new location for a year or two, or make this a permanent move? If the former appeals to you more, perhaps you should consider renting for a while to be sure you really love your new location.

What happens if your partner dies, and you are on your own in a new town?

Everyone's answers to this quiz will be different, of course. And there are many other factors which may play into whatever decision you make about where to spend the next part of your life.

If you decide to stay in your current home, here are some resources that can help.

CAPS is a Certified Aging-In-Place Specialist program developed by the National Association of Home Builders (NAHB) in association with AARP. Check out www.nahb.com/caps.

The National Aging in Place Council's website has information on all matters relating to safety and Universal Design. Check out www.aginginplace.org.

The American Society of Interior Design (ASID) also has an aging-in-place component on its website: www.asid.org/designknowledge/aa.inplace.

Good luck!

It's time for Bunco!

Bunco is a game of dice requiring very little concentration and skill, which is fortunate because most of the time, players are talking, laughing, eating and imbibing. To learn how to play, check out www.buncorules.com. (The wearing of feather boas and tiaras is completely optional.)

Now, to the important things about a Bunco party – the food! To make things easy on the hostess, every guest should contribute an appetizer or a dessert. *The Cape Cod Times* ran a contest in December 2010 to choose a recipe for the Bunco party in this book. There were so many entries it was impossible to choose only one. So, here are the finalists. This first one I actually used in the…ahem…body of the book.

Grand Prize Winner – as seen on Pages 38, 222 and 226

Sharon's Marvelous Meatballs
a.k.a. One Bag, One Jar, One Can
Ingredients:
One jar of chili sauce
One can of jellied cranberry sauce
One bag frozen Italian meatballs – appetizer size

Combine first two ingredients and mix thoroughly to break up the cranberry sauce.

Add frozen Italian meatballs (Stop & Shop's are a good choice). Cook on the stove or in a crock pot until the meatballs are heated all the way through.

In this book, Sara Miller prefers to make her own chili and cranberry sauces from scratch, and meatballs from a prime cut of beef she grinds herself in her own kitchen. But look at the trouble that got her into!

Thanks to Sharon Thompson from Falmouth Massachusetts for this terrific recipe, which is quick and easy but doesn't look (or taste) it!

Crab and Brie Tartlets

Ingredients:
2 cans of Prince Edward Island crab meat, drained
2 medium wedges of Brie cheese, rind cut off
1/4 tsp. Beau Monde seasoning
1 Tbs. good brandy
3 packages Athens mini phyllo dough cups
Fresh or dried parsley
Paprika

In a medium sauce pan, mix first four ingredients slowly until melted. Stir well.

Spoon mixture into phyllo cups.

Place on cookie sheet and sprinkle fresh parsley and ground paprika on top.

Heat in 350° oven for 10 minutes or until hot.

Melanie Garrison, Chatham MA

Oniony Cheese "Its"

Ingredients:
1 loaf rye or pumpernickel party bread
1 wedge of Parmesan cheese, grated (or make it easy and use shredded Parmesan)
1 small-medium onion, grated
1/2 cup mayonnaise
Black pepper

Mix cheese and onion with mayonnaise until moist. Add black pepper. Stir. Spread on bread rounds and place under the broiler until they are brown and bubbly – watch carefully so they don't burn!

You can make these ahead of time, place on a cookie sheet, freeze, and broil later.

Marie Sherman, Brewster MA

Versatile Dip

Ingredients:
1 cup mayonnaise
1 cup grated Parmesan cheese
Secret ingredient (creates a contrast flavor that accents the Parmesan - but you don't really know it's there): mix 1 tablespoon sour cream with 1 teaspoon blue cheese, make into very smooth paste and add to mayo-Parmesan mix.

Combine ahead and let rest in refrigerator until ready to serve.

Options to add prior to heating or have available for individuals to "top" their cheese with:

1/4 cup thinly sliced green onion
1/2 cup drained crab meat (if adding to the cheese before heating, add single dash of Worcestershire and hot sauce for additional contrast)
1/2 can drained and chopped artichoke hearts
1/8 cup drained, chopped roasted red peppers
Chiffonade basil or parsley

Heat in microwave 30-45 seconds, stir and serve warm.

Can be spread on crackers or bread slices and baked or broiled.

Also great as dip for veggies and/or small lettuce leaf wraps.

Paulette DiAngi, www.paulettesredkitchen.com, Osterville MA

Kristian's Shrimp

Ingredients:
1/2 cup olive oil
2 Tbs. Cajun or Creole seasoning (McCormick's works well)
2 Tbs. lemon juice
2 Tbs. chopped fresh parsley (or 1 Tbs. dried)
1 Tbs. honey
1 Tbs. soy sauce
Pinch of cayenne pepper
1 lb large raw shrimp, peeled and deveined

Combine first 7 ingredients in a 9"x13" baking dish. Add shrimp and toss to coat. Refrigerate at least one hour.

Preheat oven to 450°. Bake shrimp with the marinade, uncovered, until shrimp are cooked through - about 10 minutes. Serve hot with toothpicks.

Betsy Menser, Harwich MA

The Burg's Original Sausage Bread Roll
Ingredients:
1 tube of Pillsbury crescent rolls – the full flat sheet
1 lb of bulk sausage, hot or sweet
1 red or green pepper, chopped
1/2 onion or whole (depending on how much you like onions!)
1 Tbs. olive oil (or less if you are using a small skillet)
Shredded Parmesan or Mozzarella cheese

Roll tube of crescents onto a cookie sheet.

Mix bulk sausage with peppers and onions and brown in skillet with olive oil.

After sausage mixture is cooked, drain the oil and crumble the mixture over the bread dough. Spread shredded Parmesan or Mozzarella cheese on top; roll the entire loaf and close up and bake in oven according to instructions on crescent rolls tube until golden brown. Slice warm bread and enjoy!

Mary Leone, Trenton NJ

Bunco Babes Crab Dip
Ingredients:
1 lb crab meat (remove any shell or cartridge)
8 oz cream cheese (softened)
Dash or two of Worcestershire sauce
2 tsp. horseradish
1 Tbs. sherry
Old Bay Crab Seasoning

Mix cream cheese and next 3 ingredients; gently stir in crab.
Spray a decorative ovenproof bowl with Pam and add crab mixture.
Sprinkle top of crab mixture with Old Bay.

Bake at 350° for 15-20 minutes.
Serve with crackers or a sliced baguette.

Carol Lloyd and the Bethany Beach, Delaware, Bunco Babes

Boursin en Croute

Ingredients:

1 package (5.2 oz) plus 1/2 package of a Boursin cheese with herbs, about 8 oz. total
1 lb mushrooms, sliced thick
6 slices or 1/4 lb. cooked ham, julienned
1 shallot, chopped
5 phyllo leaves

Have pan or dish of melted butter handy.

Saute mushrooms in enough butter to coat the skillet for 2-3 minutes on high flame, but don't let their juices seep out.

Butter a medium-sized ovenproof dish or pan; oblong shape is easiest.

Spread a phyllo leaf across the pan and brush with melted butter. Repeat 4 more times, (5 leaves total).

Slice Boursin cheese and put on each phyllo. Scatter chopped shallots, then mushrooms, on top and finish with a layer of the julienned ham.

Butter 3-4 phyllo leaves as before, adding each separately to the top.

Roll up edges and make a rim.

Bake at 375° for 20 minutes.

If you make it early, cover with dry towel then bake just before eating.

Carol Smilgin, Osterville MA

Parmesan Cheese Puffs

Ingredients:

1/3 cup Parmesan cheese
3/4 cup mayonnaise
1/2 cup finely chopped onion
Dash Worcestershire sauce

Directions:

Mix and spread on party rye bread. Broil at 400° until golden brown.

Nan Connell, Centerville MA

Tortilla Spirals

Ingredients:

6 oz cream cheese at room temperature
4 oz mild chevre (goat cheese)
1 clove garlic, minced
3 scallions, trimmed and minced
1 can (4 oz) chopped green chilies
6 sundried tomatoes, packed in oil, drained but reserve oil – slice tomatos into thin slivers
1/3 cup pitted black olives, minced
4 ounces Monterey Jack cheese, shredded
1 cup finely diced cooked white chicken meat (optional)
3 Tbs. minced cilantro
2 tsp. chili powder
Cayenne pepper to taste
Salt to taste
8 large (10”) flour tortillas

Beat the cream cheese and chevre together in a mixing bowl until smooth.

Beat in the remaining ingredients except the tortillas and oil from sun-dried tomatoes.

Spread 1 tortilla with a generous amount of the cheese mixture and top with a second tortilla and spread cheese mixture.

Roll up the 2 tortillas tightly like a jelly roll and wrap in plastic wrap.

Refrigerate at least 2 hours.

Preheat oven to 375°.

Cut each tortilla roll into 1/2 inch slices and place cut sides up on a non stick baking sheet.

Brush the top of each with a little oil from the sundried tomatoes (you can substitute olive oil).

Bake for 12 minutes or until tortillas are puffed and lightly browned.

Let cool a minute or two and serve.

Peggy Sullivan Crespo, Chatham MA

Ms. Chef On Deck's Mock-Crab Dip
Ingredients:
16 oz cream cheese, softened
1 cup mayonnaise (you can use light mayo but I prefer the real thing)
8 Tbs. chopped green onion
8 oz package shredded Swiss cheese

Combine all of these ingredients. Press the mixture down into a small rectangular dish or a pie plate.
Topping:
One stack of crumbled Ritz crackers
6 Tbs. melted butter
1 lb bacon, crisp-cooked and crumbled (I always drain first on paper towels.)

Mix these ingredients in a bowl. Spread the topping over the creamy mixture. This is the easy part – microwave on high for 10 minutes. If you make this earlier in the day, place aluminum foil on the top and keep the dish in the refrigerator. When ready to serve, remove the foil and microwave for 11 minutes.

Serve with pita chips, bugles, tri-colored veggie chips or anything you'd like.

Karla Carreiro, aka Ms. Chef On Deck, Chatham MA

Mini Quesadillas
Ingredients:
1 package Wonton wrappers
Filling:
2 cups grated pepper jack cheese
1/4 cup chopped black olives
3/4 cup mild salsa
1/4 cup cilantro or parsley
Topping:
Sour cream
Chopped scallions
Chopped tomatoes

Heat oven to 350°. Lightly oil mini muffin tin (24). Mix cheese, olives, salsa and cilantro in a bowl. Press one wanton wrapper in each cup. Put about 1 tablespoon of cheese mixture in each. Bake about 10 minutes or until the edges are golden.
Garnish with a small amount of sour cream, tomato, and scallions.

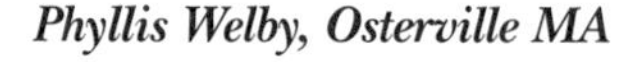
Phyllis Welby, Osterville MA

BUNCO Pizza
Ingredients:
Bacon, 4 slices, cooked
Unilever Mayonnaise (A.K.A. Hellman's), 4 tsp.
Nan, 4 pieces*
Cheese, 4 Tbs. freshly grated Parmesan or Romano
Olives and onions, 1/4 cup kalmata olives, chopped and 2 onions, peeled and sliced thin

Pre-heat oven to 450°. Heat 1 tablespoon olive oil in skillet over medium heat and cook onions until transparent, 10-15 minutes. Remove from heat and add olives.

Spread 1 teaspoon mayonnaise on each of the 4 breads. Divide onion mixture evenly on the breads. Crumble 1 slice bacon over each pizza and sprinkle with 1 tablespoon grated cheese.

Place the pizzas directly on the oven rack and bake about 3 or 4 minutes. Slice as desired.

*Nan is a flatbread available in any major supermarket (Shaw's, Stop & Shop).

Mary Lynn Kiley, Centerville MA

Desserts are also a big hit at Bunco parties. Here's a keeper recipe that's easy to make and delicious to eat.

Raspberry Mousse
Ingredients:
1 – 6 oz or 2 – 3 oz boxes raspberry Jello
2 cups hot water
1 quart vanilla ice cream, softened
2 packages defrosted frozen raspberries

Mix the hot water and Jello. When well dissolved, fold in softened ice cream until mix is smooth – no ice cream lumps! Add fruit and fold until well mixed. Pour into bowl and refrigerate for several hours or until firm.
(If using strawberries, mash them well before adding to ice cream mix.) Serve in a clear glass bowl for a very pretty presentation.

Barbara Parker, Dennis MA

Bon appétit!

To Learn More About *Moving Can Be Murder*

Please visit our website: www.babyboomermysteries.com, for a schedule of author events, book signings, general news or to send us your questions and comments. If you have tips about dealing with retirement, moving, or other stories to share, we'd love to hear them.

Attention Book Clubs: If you have made ***Moving Can Be Murder*** your book club selection and would like to have Susan Santangelo discuss the book with your group after you've finished reading it, please go to the website and send us an e-mail. Due to scheduling constraints, not all book club meeting requests can be satisfied, so please reserve your date well in advance.

About the Author

Susan Santangelo

An early member of the Baby Boomer generation, Susan Santangelo has been a feature writer, drama critic and editor for daily and weekly newspapers in the New York metropolitan area, including a stint at *Cosmopolitan* magazine. A seasoned public relations and marketing professional, she produced special events for Carnegie Hall's centennial. Susan is a member of Sisters in Crime and The Cape Cod Writers Center, and also reviews mysteries for *Suspense Magazine.* She divides her time between Cape Cod, MA and the Connecticut shoreline, and shares her life with her husband Joe and three English cocker spaniels: Tucker, Lucy, and Boomer.

A portion of the sales from ***Moving Can Be Murder*** is donated to the Breast Cancer Survival Center, a non-profit organization based in Connecticut which Susan founded in 1999 after being diagnosed with cancer herself.

Moving Can Be Murder is the second in the Baby Boomer mystery series. Susan is currently at work on her third book, ***Marriage Can Be Murder***.

You can find Susan blogging twice a month
at www.murderousmusings.blogspot.com.
Or contact her at ssantangelo@aol.com.
She'd love to hear from you.